Praise for Belle de Jour

The Further Adventures of a London Call Girl

'Full of frank humour and even more frank action'
Daily Mirror

'Her writing [is] full of refreshing comedy and eye-watering advice . . . Belle's candid humour is compulsive'
Independent

'Whether she's describing peculiar fetishes or handing out agony-aunt-style advice, it's Belle's witty, stylish writing, rather than her salacious subject matter, that really stands out. Although more Bridget Jones in a brothel than Catherine Deneuve in Chanel, this tongue-in-cheek delight will nonetheless leave a smile on your face' *Heat*

'Full of agony aunt letters and advice from her days as a call girl, Belle de Jour's diary is bold and funny. It's a book full of insightful observations written by a woman working hard to find her place in the world'
Waterstone's Books Quarterly

The Intimate Adventures of a London Call Girl

'She lists like Hornby. She talks dirty like Amis. She has the misanthropy of Larkin and examines the finer points of sexual technique as if she is adjusting the torque on a beloved but temperamental old E-type . . . [A] clever and candid new voice . . . Whoever the author is, she should give up the day job' *Independent*

Belle de Jour rose to prominence with her award-winning blog about her life as a London call girl. Her diaries, *The Intimate Adventures of a London Call Girl* and *The Further Adventures of a London Call Girl* have both been bestsellers and adapted for a hit TV series.

By Belle de Jour

The Intimate Adventures of a London Call Girl
The Further Adventures of a London Call Girl
Playing the Game

Belle de Jour

Playing
the Game

PHOENIX

A PHOENIX PAPERBACK

First published in Great Britain in 2008
by Orion Books
This paperback edition published in 2009
by Phoenix,
an imprint of Orion Books Ltd,
Orion House, 5 Upper St Martin's Lane,
London WC2H 9EA

An Hachette UK company

1 3 5 7 9 10 8 6 4 2

Copyright © Bizrealm 2008

The right of Belle de Jour to be identified as the author of
this work has been asserted by her in accordance with the
Copyright, Designs and Patents Act 1988.

A CIP catalogue record for this book
is available from the British Library.

All the characters in this book are fictitious, and any resemblance
to actual persons, living or dead, is purely coincidental.

ISBN 978-0-7538-2561-7

Typeset at The Spartan Press Ltd,
Lymington, Hants

Printed in Great Britain by Clays Ltd,
St Ives plc

The Orion Publishing Group's policy is to use papers that
are natural, renewable and recyclable products and made
from wood grown in sustainable forests. The logging and
manufacturing processes are expected to conform to the
environmental regulations of the country of origin.

www.orionbooks.co.uk

Many, many thanks to all the fantastic people who have supported my writing, including Helen Garnons-Williams, Genevieve Pegg, Michael Burton and Mil Millington. And of course, with grateful appreciation for Patrick Walsh – the most trustworthy man in London.

Dedicated to
Charlotte Ballinger, BR,
Curly B, and Robyn Wilder.

Dear Reader,

First things first, a little about me:

Hi. I'm Belle. If we haven't already met, well, hello there, and welcome. Yes, my eyes are up here, mate. If we have met, skip this part, you know all about it already.

I'm a call girl. I've been in the business of selling sex for a few years now. If you've ever seen those glossy websites with slightly out-of-focus girls throwing smouldering looks at the viewer, yes, one of those would be me. It's a neat little earner and I'm happy enough with the life but as with any job there are always compromises. In my case these are:

1 Some of my friends, and all of my family, don't know what I do;
2 Sometimes seems a bit of a waste of a good degree;
3 Makes keeping a boyfriend difficult.

I do have a boyfriend by the way, he's called, 'the Boy', who I met at university. And I do have a group of close friends whom I knew for years before I moved to London and became a call girl. They're A1, A2, and A4, all ex-boyfriends of long-standing and A3, whom I've always fancied but have never slept with. There's also N, who's my occasional fuck buddy when we're both single, my wingman when we're not and a constant source of solace when things go wrong.

If you were to pass me on the street, provided I wasn't heading for an appointment, I'd look just like any other late-twenties young professional in London. I'm good-looking but not model material; I take care with my body but am no size zero. I like a pint, good conversation with great friends and I love sex. In fact, I could be just about any girl you saw on the Tube this morning.

And this book, it takes me and my friends and continues the story, only in ways that may not have actually happened. Think of it as a parallel universe for Belle and her mates.

Apart from that? Well, you'll find out the rest as we go . . .

Love,
Belle

A few things, FAQ-style:

1 No other sex worker (or indeed anyone) speaks for me but me. I speak for no one else but me.

2 My fee is in the three-hundred-per-hour range, with deals for overnight and longer appointments. The client pays an extra thirty–fifty pounds on top for travel. About a quarter of the one-offs tip; regulars always do.

3 Most working girls I have met do not work for the same agency and are usually friends-of-friends. I only meet girls from my agency if someone hires two of us at a go. We arrive and leave in separate transportation and know nothing of each other beyond professional names. Making friends with my co-workers is not on the agenda.

4 My clients often offer wine but generally are not drinking when I arrive. I know one or two who use mild drugs; I don't partake. I have not yet run into an abusive situation. We are instructed that if this happens, we should take the money, ring the manager and leave. The client is instructed by the manager that if we find them objectionable, we leave.

You might say I'm lying or that I've been extremely lucky. You might also say that I have some skill in putting people at ease. Your call.

5 The agent – also manager or madam, if you will – takes thirty per cent of the fee. Tips and travel expenses are exempt from her commission. I only occasionally see her in person, preferring to pay in to an account – she knows I am reliable. She meets other girls at restaurants or at home. Apparently she has a boyfriend who doesn't know what she does for a living! Oh, the irony.

The agent was a call girl herself, and is a rather nice (if scatty and imperious) person, and for these reasons I trust her. She also has great legs – not that this matters but I thought it worth mentioning.

6 I get nervous if clients change the location or time of the liaison more than once. In these cases the agency provides a driver, or I ask N to do it. I tip the driver (or N) fifty quid for this. I don't know what the manager pays the drivers.

7 The manager confirms appointments with the clients by landline. I text her on my arrival and ring her when I leave. If she hasn't heard from me within fifteen minutes of the agreed end of the appointment, she rings the client, then the hotel, then her security, then the police. I know, because once I was having a rare old time and forgot to call.

8 If the manager 'plays favourites', it's not something that bothers me enough to notice. Perhaps I am the favourite?

9 Do I kiss clients? Of course. *Pretty Woman* is not real. Understood? Fiction. Julia Roberts is not really a prostitute.

Refusal to kiss is an affront similar to fake porn lesbians who won't put their tongues anywhere near pussy but are perfectly happy to pose with hands on each others' tits. Denial ain't just a river in Egypt, honey. Your tongue + girly bits in same scene = cuntlicker, so you might as well get in there. Similarly, when it comes to clients I don't hold back for the sake of imagined propriety. For goodness' sake I'm already a whore! Kissing is no more intimate than any other act – intimacy is what the mind does, not the body.

10 Today, my knickers are low-waisted, flesh-coloured lace shorts (La Perla). No bra.

Juillet

vendredi, le 01 juillet

There are two kinds of men in the world – the ones who want their sluts to look like ladies and the ones who want their sluts to look like sluts.

This one, he's definitely of the former variety. He actually requested pearl earrings. Though why he did is a complete mystery, as he's currently banging away from behind. You couldn't possibly see earrings from that angle.

'God, yes . . . you love it like this, don't you? When I take you hard like this . . .'

His short nails dig into the fabric bunched around my hips. I make encouraging noises and grind back onto him, spreading my hands over the hotel bedsheets. Maybe 'pearl earring' actually means something else, could it be some euphemism I've never heard of? If so, he'd better get round to it quickly, because with all the talk beforehand of my upbringing and educational background, the action itself has only just got under way.

'You're going to tell all your friends . . . I'm going to fuck you till you can't walk straight . . .'

Unlikely. Still, points for trying – I give a little giggle and 'ooh!' as if the very thought is making me chafe.

'That's right . . . no one's ever had you like this . . .'

Um, he did remember picking me out from the website, no? Not only have I been had like this, a hundred times at least, by hundreds of other men, he'd be doing well to be the first person who had me like this this week.

'Ahhh . . . right . . .'

Never let anyone tell you a man can fake an orgasm when he has a condom on. I feel the head of his cock swell inside me and know he's close. A few well-timed 'oh's and 'my's and he's away. I reach back and check the rolled end of the rubber is still around the base of his penis and shift myself off him. He collapses to one side, sweaty, sated. I pull my knickers back up, smooth my hair and smile. I never even had to take off the pussy-bow blouse.

samedi, le 02 juillet

Sometimes it feels as if I've been doing this job forever, but really it's only been a couple of years since I started. My preparation is down to a well-timed art: the shaving is done in under ten minutes; the plucking in under five; the last hair in place well in advance of the taxi's arrival. Makeup still needs a certain amount of time but I have the look down to a reliable result. Because I have only a handful of regular clients and there are only so many situations in which a call girl is seen in public, the capsule wardrobe is well established. This doesn't eliminate the expense entirely, of course; the last shoes I bought were a pair of Louboutins identical to a pair I'd claimed as a business expense last year. And naturally I spend something closely akin to an equatorial country's GDP every month at the chemist.

Other times, it feels all so recent. Take my boyfriend for instance – and yes, I have one who, yes, knows what I do – whether by wilful stubbornness or real forgetfulness, he still asks me what jobs I'm applying for. The answer, as he must well know by now, is none. Not for years at least. Maybe it's a coded clue to change my job. But, really, I don't consider the work to be a problem. There are no holes in my CV so gaping they can't be explained by a soft job market and a heaping helping of parental experience. Not yet, anyway.

But still, after yet another bukakke lunchtime appointment, it occurs to me that one thing that would be nice about a straight job is that I wouldn't have to worry about stinging eyes as an occupational hazard.

Something to consider.

dimanche, le 03 juillet

'Oh, mate, I had to tell you,' I said when N returned to the table with our pints – lager for him, bitter for me. 'You remember that girl from the Christmas party?'

N did. I'd bagged a hot invite that my boyfriend couldn't make it to, so took N instead. And what does he do? Only leaves with the number of the hottest girl in the room of course.

Anyway, N kept me up-to-date on their phone-related to-ing and fro-ings but between the season and suchlike, sex with the Hot-Christmas Girl never came to pass. He was up to his neck in some German lady and two or three flexible athletes, and the HCG had met a nice Irish bloke, so their hooking up amounted to a bit of talk but not much else.

'Don't keep me in suspense,' he said, raising an eyebrow. 'Out with it.'

'If you still have her number, lose it,' I announced. 'I've found her blog, and you are not going to like this . . .' and I related, to the best of my recollection, her last three entries. Turns out HCG may be fit, she may be fine – but she's an anal virgin. Who declares with some vehemence that the very idea of any minor discomfort puts her right off.

Now, I know that not all kinks involve discomfort (but a

lot of them do), and not all kinky people like anal (but a lot of them do). I also know that not all sex is kinky and that N does non-masochistic beautifully. And he's blessed with one of South London's nicer cocks. But really. If I were N I would stay well clear of someone with such arbitrarily prissy sexual demands. Intolerance of sexual experimentation definitely crosses my 'can't be doing with that' threshold. HCG has reached her advanced age, and was previously married, and has lovers stacked seven deep and has never been tempted by anal? Not even a tickle?

'Serious case of princess complex,' I declared.

Granted, I'm being a complete hypocrite in this regard. Who am I to tell someone else to back away from the prude? How many lovers have I inducted in the darker arts of sex? How many people, even years later, have commented that I was easily the best they've had? But I made a promise on getting out of the call girl business and that was, unless True Love was involved, I am so not going to be anyone's tutor again. It's one thing keeping up the kindly and interested façade when being paid but rather another to do it on a voluntary basis. I like them experienced.

'Okay, yeah, I see your point,' N said. 'But should it ever come down to it, that's a face that needs a comeshot. It would be a good one-off just for that. The fact that she wouldn't really be into it makes the thought just that little bit better.'

'Fair enough,' I said. Like so much else that goes on in men's minds, what they find appropriate wank fodder is something of a mystery to me; however, it's part of my job to know. Anticipating a client's desire is what sorts the wheat from the chaff in this biz. And while I am remarkably bad at doing so in real life, according to my exes – the ones who still talk to me, of course – I've something of a sixth sense for it in my working life.

Still, at least it's good to be settled with someone. In theory this means I don't particularly have to worry that the Boy finds being with me a turn-on; the amount of time we spend together both in and out of the bedroom would seem to confirm the fact. And he is very, very careful not to ask too many questions about my work . . . anymore.

lundi, le 04 juillet

As far as appointments go, I would rather be pissed on than give a blowjob.

There, I've said it. Whew.

Why? Well, I'm fundamentally lazy, and being pissed on is easy to do – you just sort of be there and remember to not breathe through your nose. Also, it's not remotely as bad as everyone thinks it is. It's sort of like eating (sorry, Mum) shellfish – if you dwell on the mechanics of what it is you're doing, you might be sickened momentarily otherwise, everything's tickety-boo.

Also, you can brush your teeth and have a hot shower straight after and no one would think you unromantic for doing so. (If, on the other hand, you do want to do the couply thing, be certain to wash the worst of it off before inviting him into the shower. Trust me on this.)

Honestly, I feel I shouldn't be telling you this. Now everyone will want to do it! And that being one of my extra-high-fee special services for regulars, once the word gets out, I may well find that I'm out of a job. Hmm. Maybe time to start trawling for 'real' work again . . .

But, seriously, it's not bad. Try it. You might not like it but, let's be honest, you might like it about as much as, or even slightly more than giving a lockjaw-inducing blowjob. And it buys you mega points to cash in later on the perversion of your choice, be that pony play, rope bondage, or a meal at Royal Hospital Road. Everyone's a winner!

mardi, le 05 juillet

'It's finally starting to look like your place,' the Boy said as I arranged books on the shelves.

'You think?' When A4's lease came up he decided to move closer to work, so I took over his flat. It was a self-contained granny flat above a garage. The owners were constantly threatening to knock down the house and garage to build a twenty-four-unit block of flats but, thankfully, Camden council always rejected the applications.

'All your little things we picked up on holidays, your socks scattered everywhere . . .' He picked up one limp little pink scrap, run grey at the heel, wrinkled his nose and chucked it into the corner.

'Oh, stop it,' I said. I'm not famed for my mad house-keeping skillz. And, luckily, I'm not one of those girls who meets clients at her own flat. Personal maintenance I can whip up in a jiffy. But hoovering in advance of an appointment? Not my bag, baby. And it would make having a regular boyfriend infinitely more complicated. 'You know you're not dating your mother.'

'No, it's sweet,' he said, wrapping a strong arm around my waist. 'Problem is, we've yet to fully christen the place.'

'What do you mean? We've done it on the sofa, in the shower, in the bed . . .'

'Mmm hmm?'

'Oh, you mean the kitchen? Okay, but I thought looking at pots and pans was probably the antidote to sexy.'

'True enough, but I've been dying to see you model those oven gloves.'

mercredi, le 06 juillet

Please don't misunderstand, I like the heat of summer as much as – if not more than – the next person. But if and when I make my millions, I'll retire to life as a mad inventor. First innovation: an antiperspirant dispenser specifically designed for attacking the under-boob area.

vendredi, le 08 juillet

Working in an office is an attenuated form of servitude. It's sharecropping for the modern world. With all the time and effort that goes in to normal modes of employment, where do you end up at the end of a year? Are you ahead, what have you achieved? You work for a salary because you have a car payment, a mortgage – why do you have those? You need a car to get to the office at the hour prescribed by your superiors. You need a house because you're told you do, because there is inherent insecurity in your world and turning your sweat into capital over thirty or more years seems like the right thing to do, even if you're not sure why. In contrast, my body is available for rent but when the job is done I still take it home, it's mine. Your time and your potential are what your employer takes from you; ask yourself, when you go home, do you still have them? What lifestyle equity has eight or more hours at a desk bought you? Was it worth the exchange?

Maybe even then the thought of sex as a transaction still bothers you. Maybe the knowledge that marriage is a plain and simple business contract still does not convince you. Ask yourself, then, what sort of a person you are. Are you a humanist? Then blame the social structure, not the sex worker. Are you a Christian? Then love the sinner, hate the sin. Who I am, and what I am doing is a rational response to the current economic and cultural climate. Deal with it.

samedi, le 29 juillet

'Who are we meeting again?' the Boy said, spritzing his pits with deo.

'L,' I said. 'Remember? She's the one who was at school with me.'

'Oh, one of your posh friends,' the Boy said. This is a bit of a joke; the Boy's family are far more posh than mine or indeed than of anyone I know. He's always pegged me as a bit of a social climber. It's not true, though – L and I were friends at school because we were equally bookish, lousy at social niceties and unpopular. Nowt to do with money. 'Is this the one who's a barrister or the one who hates me?'

'Both,' I said, slipping on a pair of satin heels. 'She's a barrister and she hates you.'

'Two great tastes that taste great together,' he said and grabbed his keys. 'Am I driving again?'

'As you're the one with a car and zero alcohol tolerance, I'm afraid the answer to that question will always be yes.' I pecked him on the cheek and turned off the hall lights. 'I'll stand you lemonades all night.'

'One of these days we should go out with my mates,' he said.

Wow, it's been years since he even offered. 'Ah, there's the rub. Your friends hate me, but aren't posh enough to hide it behind a veneer of polite chatter. L is.'

'If that's true, how do you know she doesn't hate you, too?' he said, waiting for me to lock the door. 'She's ever so polite when you're together.'

'If you think friends aren't out to destroy you, then what do you know about friends?' I smiled. 'Come on, or we'll be late.'

dimanche, le 10 juillet

Cleaning out old files on the computer, I ran across my CV. Been a while since I updated the thing, not since the last time I tried looking for work. But I told myself that once the sex-work gig was under way, I'd wait until it looked like there were more jobs in my sector. Then I left it because the money for entry level didn't look very good, especially when I found myself peeling pinks off a roll of cash on a very regular basis. Finally I stopped looking at it altogether – though I can't say I never looked back.

They say the past is another country – but sometimes mine seems like another planet. But I wonder, was it worth it? Did I make the right choice?

lundi, le 11 juillet

'You're a dirty girl,' the client said. 'Dirty, dirty girl. Do you want to suck my fingers after they've been inside your pussy?'

Honey, I want whatever you want me to want. 'Oh yes, I want to suck them.' There was the familiar tang of my own juices, the slight sweetness of lube – many of them, particularly the edible ones, contain glycerine – and the not-so-faint taste of latex, as we'd already fucked once this hour before he started fingering me while wanking himself back to hardness.

'God you're filthy. Why don't you come on my hand, you dirty girl, and then you can taste it.'

Meep. Always a slight problem there, as I have a policy of not coming with clients. To be honest, when you're concentrating on what he wants, and how it looks, and how it sounds, and thinking ahead to the next assignment, plus keeping half an eye on the time, who can let go enough to orgasm? Every call girl has a repertoire of faking which is honed over many clients, and there's always the safety valve that if he doesn't believe it, well, he doesn't have to book you again. Serves them right for wanting orgasms on demand anyway.

Step 1 for faking: the audio
'Oh, yes . . . yes yes yes . . .'

Step 2 for faking: the visual
I arched my back and shuddered, rolling my eyes back into my head and thrashing against the bedsheets.

Step 3 for faking: the internal
Especially if his hand is inside you, clench, baby, clench. Rhythmic or solid? Doesn't much matter. Just tighten those pelvic floor muscles for all they're worth.

Finally, step 4: the follow-through
Remember, your world has just been rocked. Breathe shallow and quickly, and look away – a direct eyelock is the number one tell-tale sign that you've actually been pulling a Meg Ryan. Oh, and you're a lady, when you finally catch your breath and come to, don't forget to thank the gentleman.

'No, it was my pleasure to watch you,' he said, smearing his fingers over my cheek. 'You dirty, dirty girl.'

mercredi, le 13 juillet

Scenes from a working-girl's history, number 1:

There was this regular customer. Sunday mornings, every week without fail. He'd sigh, and sweat, and there was always a moment when it looked as if he would refuse to pay – and I just wanted to scream, you idiot, you ordered this, it's here, you pay for it. But I didn't; my job was to smile sweetly.

'You'd think they could send the current issue, I'm always a week behind,' he'd say, irritated.

Every week. I put his *New York Times Book Review* into a plastic carrier bag, unfolded, and laid the receipt in his palm. Why are you telling me, mate? Like I can do owt. They have to send it from New York after all.

'Yeah,' I shrugged. For goodness' sake. It's a book section, not state secrets. Get over it already.

That was when I worked in a bookshop. That job was about ten per cent worse than being a call girl.

jeudi, le 14 juillet

The Girlfriend Experience (GFE) is bread and butter to girls like me.

There's no shortage of men wanting a filthy fuck in a hotel room, but to be honest, at least as much business comes from home calls. And for some reason when going to a man's actual house, nine times out of ten they want the GFE.

I guess it's part of their ability to compartmentalise: if in hotel, kinky romp; if at home, relationship sex. And I appreciate that it's easier to stay in rather than go out – why get takeaway when there's delivery available at no extra charge?

Like tonight. Smiles, chat, bottle of wine, straight suck and fuck. Okay, so maybe it was on the living room floor, but that's the sort of variation that hardly requires the intervention of a pro to fulfil.

Still, I'm surprised they can do this, particularly the married ones. Don't they get cuddly, face-holding sex often enough from the wife? Then again, maybe they're not getting it at all.

He kissed me deeply at the door and pressed another fifty in my hand. 'For the great conversation,' he said. I pinched his cheek and walked away. As the door clicked shut, leaving me on the street alone but for the taxi, I was struck by the strangeness of it. God, how long had it been since the Boy and I sat in one night and really talked, setting the world to rights like we used to? Here I am, someone with a boyfriend, treating strangers probably better than I treat him. But then, nine times out of ten, I never see them again. Once or twice the Boy has hinted at moving in together, but if I can't sustain the good feeling on even our irregular basis, what would it be like if he were around all the time?

vendredi, le 15 juillet

Scenes from a working-girl's history, number 2:

Oh. My. God. There must be what, twelve of them? Not a single one who knows what he wants, nor even thought about what they might do when I turned up. Why do I always get these idiots? One's given up altogether and is just staring at my tits. Another one looks at me, eyes begging for some sort of direction. I'm going to have to figure out what they want, and do it fast – or else stand here for twenty minutes waiting for them to decide.

Right. Start them on some booze, maybe things will improve. Either way, if they don't like what they get, in the end they'll blame me to try to avoid paying. I'm already counting on no tip from this group. Happens every weekend.

According to the dates on my CV, for almost one year, I was a waitress. That job was about twenty-five per cent worse than being a call girl.

samedi, le 16 juillet

Midday Saturday? Who wants a call girl on midday Saturday, I wonder?

The possibilities occupied my mind on the way over. According to the manager, he was young, fit . . . 'veeery good customer, always so polite to the girls, wanted something new'. So if he's not a first-timer, what's with midday Saturday? You can more or less guarantee that the popular girls will have been out the night before, maybe even doing overnights, and will hardly be at their best.

Maybe that's exactly what he's after. If the manager was right and he was looking for a new regular girl, maybe he wanted to see what she was like at her worst, in anticipation that it could only get better from there. I scowled. I was used to meeting new people, but I distinctly felt that this time I was going to be judged, assessed, graded and possibly found wanting.

'Do you know what he's into? Are there any props I should bring?'

'Take your usual bag,' the manager said. 'As far as I know the standard will do for this one.'

Ugh. The other thing that bothered me was that this broke up the weekend in a terrible way. I'd lose having the day to myself to potter, and if I ended up having another appointment Saturday night, I'd be in a panic to shower, do hair and be out the door again on time.

I sighed as the taxi pulled up to the door. Like I said, who requests a hooker for midday Saturday, anyway?

A junior doctor on shifts, that's who.

dimanche, le 17 juillet

'I love your taste in anonymous coffee bars,' I said as L sat down. God, I cringe at myself sometimes. Why do I feel like an awkward loner making an approach to a woman at a bar? Maybe because I have about as much experience of friendly female company as your average unlucky-in-love Joe. Your average woman may as well be from another planet from me, and I'm not leaving my mother and sister out of that judgment, either.

L smiled at my bad line. Clearly she knows more about the early stages of feminine friendship than I do.

'I know, right? They're like the crappy, pseudo-French restaurants of yore.' She nodded at the walls, always painted orangey-brown in these places, decorated with indifferent nostalgic prints that were probably trying to invoke a kind of café chic but are really the modern version of Athena. 'We could be surrounded by spies, philandering husbands, and creatures from another planet but are so lulled into a coma by bad background music and abysmal lattes that you'd never know.'

'Speaking of which, is that Genesis? Again? Is Phil Collins getting a cut from this place or what?'

'I'm on a Wham count, so far today we're up to three,' she said archly. 'Death by bad eighties pop.'

'I can think of worse ways to go.'

lundi, le 18 juillet

Scenes from a working-girl's history, number 3:

Cold wind, rain, hail . . . we stood outside every day regardless of the weather. Pasting on a smile for the people who walked by, hoping just one would stop to talk. If they did it was a two-minute chat before I was asking for money; however, most people saw us and crossed to the other side of the road.

The fellow in charge looked after about five of us. He'd cruise by a few times a day to make sure we were still out and, more importantly, not pocketing cash on the side. If you didn't make money, you were gone. Simple as that. There was no such thing as an hourly rate – you got a very small slice of what you brought in, and that was all. Other benefits included pitying looks from bell-ringers and the risk of frostbite. My heart wasn't in it and I lasted two weeks. A girl I met back then is still doing it, though she's moved up the ranks now and is managing her own team. Apparently she's one of the most successful women in this field. Saw a recent photo – she looks incredibly worn-out for her age.

That's one I'll never dare stick on the CV. We were euphemistically called canvassers, but I believe they're more commonly known these days as charity muggers. A job which is one-hundred per cent worse than being a call girl.

Home from another appointment. I checked my personal phone and sighed – three missed calls from the Boy. I ring him back.

'How's things?' he said, with the air of studied disinterest. It's our well-practised code for him to ask about my work without actually asking about my work.

'Fine. Boring,' I said. My well-practised answer. 'I'm pretty tired, see you tomorrow?' There's an unspoken agreement that we don't get together after one of my appointments – how on earth would that work out if we lived together?

The man had been unobjectionable, and actually a nice chap. Once upon a time that would have been precisely the sort of client I relished, because I knew how to get along with them. Now, it all seems as if it's been said, heard and done before. The bottle of good-but-not-extravagant wine. The well-appointed bachelor pad with signs of a harried and overworked life. The comparing degrees, friends, travel plans. And the sex, of course – the sex, vigorous but not kinky, with a touch of affection here and there but no love. When I look up at him while giving a blowjob to see if he's watching, his eyes are closed. He's probably thinking about his most recent girlfriend and how she compares to me. When he comes, I make the right sounds and the right faces.

But there's nothing wrong with the client; I know that. It's not them. It's me. It's the fact that as much as I enjoy sex, as much as I am comfortable doing this job, there's little mental stimulation. Sometimes you get lucky and have a rip-roaring conversation, but to be realistic, those sorts of chats only happen with regulars or overnights. Otherwise it's just eating up valuable time on the clock. And nice as the men can be, there are some conversations I am sick to death of, such as:

- Why do you do this when you have a degree?

Sorry, but have you perused the job market for recent graduates lately? You could make more money selling salt to slugs. But the matter of fact is that hookers come from all walks of life, and we all have our reasons.

- My wife/girlfriend/partner doesn't understand me.

Well, duh. That goes without saying. That you've decided to call in a professional pre-empts further discussion of the topic. If the woman you pledged your troth and sex organs to for eternity completely understood you, I wouldn't be here. Unless that's what turns her on.

- I'm single, but my job is stressful/time-consuming.

Also goes without saying. Why belabour the point?

- Tell me about your manager/the other girls/your other clients.

Why, they're shining examples of humanity, sir. Impeccably behaved jewels among the dross.

The reality of the situation is that we meet but rarely, and I like it like that. Sure, maybe I miss the stimulation of being able to chat freely with co-workers, but from what I remember offices are not exactly hotbeds of intellectual debate and who wants to get closer to women whose direct relationship with you is as your rival? They're at arm's-length and there they stay.

And the men? Noble laureates each and every one.

• Have you slept with anyone famous?

I have, it was unremarkable, and no, I will not name names.

• What do you think of politics?

Are you kidding? I have a degree, buddy, not a lifelong yearning to discuss the finer points of the London mayoral race with someone who's about to come on my tits. Unless that's what turns you on, I mean. Bottom line: just because your dick is currently entering my pussy does not give you access to the whys and wherefores.

vendredi, le 22 juillet

Why I love N, number 54,807 in an infinite series of texts:

> Ah, Waitrose, so cool inside. Now would madam like cucumber, large cucumber or torpedo???

Ah, the hijinks we'd had with salad vegetables once upon a time. If by hijinks you mean sticky double penetration sex, which of course I do.

> No dice – Boyfriend over for the weekend. Try me again Monday xx

And the reply:

> Oh I will.

samedi, le 23 juillet

Scenes from a working-girl's history, number 4:

Our shift starts when everyone else is going home. If anyone asks our names or where we're from, we lie. There's a script and you'd better remember it. The manager may not be watching you in person, but she knows what's up. If you don't pull down enough cash on a weekly basis, get ready for the sharp end of her tongue, and even worse assignments at dreadful hours.

You never know who you're going to get – someone who's lonely and keeps you too long because they want someone to talk to, or a controlling jerk who likes nothing better than abusing girls like you.

One day I just never went back. The manager didn't even ring me to find out what happened. There was always a queue of people ready to take my place – younger ones who would work harder, later and for less.

I'd rather get a straight shot of come in my eye than ever go through that hell again. If you guessed that I once worked at a call centre, you are correct. It was easily two-hundred per cent worse than being a call girl.

dimanche, le 24 juillet

'I'm going to the toilet,' the Boy said. 'Before I do, do you want to go first?'

'Depends,' I said from the sofa, pushing the last sticky scraps of breakfast around a plate. 'Is "going to the toilet" code for reading your comic or farting?'

'The first one. It's a new Megazine, I may be a while.'
He's redirected his comic book subscriptions to my address

now. Might as well, he said. Since I always end up leaving them at yours anyway.

'Nah, we're good, enjoy yourself.'

Do you know what I love about this man? It's that now, because of me, he knows about Rufus Wainwright and the *Story of O*. And because of him, I know about *World of Warcraft* and that I should leave cooking eggy bread to the experts.

mercredi, le 27 juillet

'He's in town for two days and would love to see you. In fact when he rang he mentioned you specifically. He asked to see you so nicely.'

'Which days?' I flipped through my diary – booked. Fully booked. 'Sorry, wish I could say yes but I'm too busy and it's too short notice – planning meetings like this takes time, you know. Where did you say his hotel was? Kew? That's nowhere near me.'

'Honey, don't let me down on this one.'

Not my agent, my mother. Her older brother was in from abroad – a conference or something. 'What's so important you can't make time for family?'

'Um, work and stuff? Life? Come on, it's not as if we've been in constant contact.' And my uncle was cool – he understood life's ebbs and flows. My mother, on the other hand, would put off her own death for a minor family obligation to some second-cousin-twice-removed if they asked nicely.

For almost my entire life, this uncle has lived in a different country, on a different continent, even. The de Jour family diaspora is huge. He's been married three times and I honestly don't even know how many children he has. His second oldest is J, the one I was closest to, who is almost exactly my age – J's hardly seen his father any more than I have. It's sad, but my uncle had to leave J's mother because their combined problems were too much for one couple, and I cannot blame him.

And when I left the UK for a few months to visit J in Mexico, where he was in drug rehab, he had a lot to say about his mother. The way he'd grown up. The things she'd said and done. But one subject that was sacrosanct was his father. Whatever else had gone wrong in J's life, he would not blame his father. And then it occurred to me that J would not be seeing him on this visit. Or in fact any time soon.

I tapped my fingers impatiently on the table. Maybe I could put off one regular appointment for another day; maybe my manager could make sure she didn't book anything this week without checking with me first.

'Fine, okay. But I'll really have to squeeze to make it.'

'Oh, honey, good,' Mum said. She didn't say 'thank you'. Thank You is for the weak. Thank You is not for closers.

vendredi, le 29 juillet

Scenes from a working-girl's history number 5:

Come on, come on. How are you not done already? The amount of energy expended in the last hour could power Birmingham for six days, and still you're carrying on, dripping sweat like a fricking rainforest? I try to think of encouraging things to say, to make the time pass, but end up staring at the far wall, the ceiling, the carpet a lot of the time. I've perfected the I-don't-really-mind smile, in fact, I should copyright it. Sell that off to all the other girls I know are doing the same thing, while the men are panting away.

No, on second thoughts, I don't go to the gym with that boyfriend any more, it's all a bad memory now. Funny how little things like club memberships on the CV always make me think of him. But for the record, being in that relationship was eight-hundred per cent worse than anything that happened to me in the sex trade.

dimanche, le 31 juillet

It was a posh hotel, not in the centre of London but not far away from it, either. I had the time to spare and made a quick mental calculation: price of a taxi vs. time on the Tube. I opted for the Tube.

The lobby was full with men in suits, just off some conference or other. When it's a business trip, their drinking tends to start early. I navigated past them to the desk at reception.

'Hello, I'm here to meet someone, but I'm afraid I don't have the room number. Can you ring up and ask him to meet me in the bar?'

'The name?'

I give his surname.

'Yours?'

I give my first name. The man at the desk looked me over, taking in the dress, the high heels, the handbag. I rolled my eyes. If I were here on business you can be certain I wouldn't just bounce on up to reception asking stupid questions. That is not how I roll.

'It's my uncle,' I added unnecessarily.

'Mmm hmm,' said the man at the desk, placing the phone back in its cradle. 'He'll be right down.'

I waited in the lobby, idly fingering the heavy curtains. For some reason I wanted, needed, the man at the desk with the arched eyebrow to see my uncle, how we resembled each other. Except that we really don't. He's dark, with a creased, narrow-eyed face; his hair is kinky, not just any old Jewfro, but kinky like African kinky – I mean there are photos from the 70s where his hair is physically blocking the people around him. My uncles kept black power-fist picks in their 'fros until well into the 80s.

A hand lit on my shoulder. I turned, and my uncle buried me in a bear hug. He was rounder than I remembered, a little shorter.

'Let's get something to eat,' he said. 'I'm already tired of this place.' The sun was still bright. 'I love long English summers. So, what are you doing these days?'

'Ah, things,' I said. 'Stuff.' Anyone else and I would have lied, made up another ludicrous office job, but somehow I knew with him there was no pressure and thus no need to lie.

He stopped and looked at me. 'That's cool,' he said. 'You're a smart girl. But don't let things and stuff become all you have.'

We found a pub and I ordered pints. We sat outside (he found it cold, I thought it rather warm) talked about ourselves (his business is doing well, one daughter is a chess champion, another had surgery for scoliosis), our memories of each other (several angling outings when I was twelve or thereabouts, where I was the only one to catch any fish), the future (I promised to visit, he promised to write).

And he was cool. Even cooler than I remembered. He made a few decisions that got him a lot of flack when I was young, but now it all seems to be working out. He has gone, in the space of my memory, from a man with few prospects and a lot against him to a settled, serene patriarch with the world at his feet. Leaving home matters. It changes you.

Yes, you can go home again Thomas Wolfe, but only a fool would expect it to be the same.

He told me about his farm, the menagerie of pets and semi-feral animals. We walked to the Tube platform and he squinted at the network map. 'Are you sure that's your train? Positive?' We postulated an inverse relationship between the corruptibility of the government of a country and the reliability of its transport schedules. He was warmer than I remembered. Less angry at the world, having found a place in it.

The train moved away from the platform steadily, and I saw him wave and turn away. It might be years before we meet again.

I wondered how different J's life would have been, if his father had stayed.

Ten Call-Girl Commandments:

You may be surprised to learn I'm a closet fan of hip hop, not least because it is a limitless font of street wisdom. Take, for instance, the Notorious B.I.G.'s Ten Crack Commandments. They have been words to live by in my line of work. For those among you not already familiar with his oeuvre, by all means do spare the tune a listen – you won't be disappointed. So with apologies to the learned Mr Biggie Smalls and without further ado, I bring you the Ten Call Girl Commandments:

1. In the first rule, Biggie advises discretion on the matter of one's income.

No one knows the truth but my accountant. Everyone else gets generalities and hints, but it is never, never, never worth dishing your financial details. Those who make less will use it against you; so will those who make more. This is particularly true if you happen to be dating someone who knows you're a working girl. Just lie to him about your income, okay? Just lie.

2. Secondly, he advises keeping your own counsel on the matter of future plans.

Whether it's deciding to let a client go, change agencies or quit the game altogether, don't talk about it, just get on with it. Waffle about moving on too long and you'll look like someone who is all bark and no bite (and attract the ire of your agency manager, if you have one). Let your actions speak for you.

***3. I couldn't live without rule number three, which in
short runs, trust no one.***

Or as Prince Humperdinck put it, 'I always think everything
could be a trap, that is why I'm still alive.'

Biggie goes on a bit about your Moms nicking your crack
and lighting up. Can't say it was a problem for me as such,
but the bigger message is that 'loose lips sink ships'. My
father has a favourite saying – two people can keep a secret
if one of them is dead. Much as I hate to admit it, he's right.
Don't want the world and its dog to know what you do for a
living? Then don't tell nobody, fool.

***4. Now, number four is an odd one for some to grasp:
don't use your own source of income as a vehicle for
getting your personal kicks.***

Controversial. Some people insist that they enjoy work sex
in the same way as the unpaid variety, but like Biggie I beg
to differ. Work sex is performance art, with emphasis on
'performance' (and also 'art', but only if you consider *Penthouse Forum* 'literature'). Orgasms are for boyfriends.

***5. In rule number five, it is revealed that as with sex work,
crack is best kept out of the home. Good man.***

Again, some would disagree, and these are the ladies who
are happy to entertain you in their 'central London flats'. I,
on the other hand, am not down with the idea of anyone
coming to visit my home. I am a fan of the out-call system,
not least because if worse comes to worst you will be on
someone's CCTV somewhere. If you don't fancy sitting in
taxis and negotiating hotel reception, find an agreeable
brothel or pay timeshare on a flat with other girls you
know. But don't take that shit home. You want your
neighbours to know you're a prostitute? Might as well stick

a neon sign above your door because, sooner or later, they'll figure it out.

6. On rule number six, we are advised that extending credit to those whose involvement is in the client side of the relationship would be, well, a bad idea. For crackheads this is certainly true – and for johns it is as well.
. . . or to put it another way – no money, no honey. Cash up front. Always. Every time. Everywhere. No exceptions.

7. Keeping your family and business apart seems like a natural rule, no? If you said yes, welcome to Rule #7.
Wow, I like this man! Shame he died before he could write the next self-help bestseller. Again, I so totally agree. Interviewers always ask whether my family has ever found out – the answer is no. I want my parents to know their eldest daughter accepted money for sex . . . err, why exactly?

8. Now, number eight may be more relevant to the drug trade, but it also applies here: watch out for the people you pay to look after you.
At some point you may need heavies. Oh I've forked over a pink once or twice for someone to sit outside a hotel room for an hour 'just in case'. But you have to listen to your instincts and trust your judgment. And a word about your agency? Trust them, but not too much. Never give them your real name. Be aware of anyone about to make trouble for the girls – maybe another call girl burning her bridges on the way out, maybe the manager. Never let your reliance on outside help be a substitute for knowing when to cut your ties.

9. Number nine, which Biggie lists as his most important rule of all, is to stay away from the police. Unless, of course, they're providing you with product. As I come fully equipped with my own internal apparatus necessary for the job, this rule is an easy one to follow.

Unfortunately, I did once have the pleasure of the company of the Met's finest. But they never became regulars, and not for lack of desire on their part. I would also counsel staying well clear of politicians and celebrities if it possibly could be avoided.

10. And finally: Don't put too much trust in people you meet; the longer you've known someone, the more you have an idea of whether they keep their word.

The phrase 'call girl', in case you'd wondered, means you're on call. Available. When the phone rings, you're already preparing yourself to say yes. So, keep this in mind: one date does not a regular make. Not even two at nine p.m. on consecutive Wednesdays. And if someone wants the right to reserve your time, he has to prove himself trustworthy. You don't want a late cancellation to mean you can't pay the rent that month.

Août

'So, do you watch much porn?'

Like, does the Pope shit in the woods? Hells, yeah. 'Sometimes.'

'Do you have a lot of it?' The client unzipped his trousers. He hadn't even touched his wine. He was busy touching something else.

Do I have porn? I have an entire section of my closet strictly for the storage of cardboard Ikea boxes. Inside of which are plastic bags. Inside of which, categorised roughly by type, is porn. 'No, just a few things I found in my ex-boyfriend's things . . .'

'Tell me about them.'

Okay, now this is weird. A man hires a woman to come in person and tell him about porn? Takes all sorts.

'Well I was doing the laundry one day when I found a magazine he was keeping under the mattress.' Did that sound true or not? This is fantasy territory. Doesn't matter. All that matters is you keep going, keep him hard.

'What was the magazine?'

Um, think fast. What does this one like? 'It was one of those foreign ones, with the stories written in German. There was a woman and two men. She was younger . . .'

He started thrapping harder. Bingo.

'. . . they were both big, and her mouth, it just looked so tiny. Her hair was pulled off her face . . .'

His fingers pulled the foreskin back and over the head

rhythmically. He didn't close his eyes, but focussed on my face, my mouth.

'What did they do to her?'

'. . . by the end she had them both in her mouth at the same time . . .'

'You filthy slut. What a dirty mouth you have. Get over here and suck me off with that dirty mouth.'

mardi, le 02 août

We were driving back from the edge-of-suburbs, everything-and-then-some hypermarket, the Boy's car packed to the gills with industrial amounts of bog roll, washing powder and tinned tomatoes. By gods, if there is one area where my Jewish heritage suits his natural proclivities perfectly, it's in the urge to stockpile. I could hoard for Britain, me.

'Hold on, just going to make a stop,' he said, turning off the main road.

'What for?'

'There's a storage centre over the way – they sell boxes.'

'Why do you need boxes?'

He gave me a smile, the silly-girl-we-discussed-this smile. The smile that only makes an appearance when he's had entire conversations with me of great importance and hammered out a solution, save one crucial detail – they stayed entirely in his head.

'For when I move in, of course,' he said.

'Uh, we talked about that when exactly?' It had been on my mind of late, after all we had been a couple on and off – mostly on – for years now. But that was a step for someday, not right now.

'Oh, we haven't talked about it as such. But it really is

about time, don't you think?' His fingers curled around my clammy ones.

Post-midweek shopping is really not a time for such discussions. I smiled back with my silly-boy-I'm-screaming-at-you-now-in-my-head smile.

'Fab.'

'Cool. I'll be, like, ten minutes, okay? You wait here?' He smiled his I say ten minutes, I mean an hour smile.

'No problems,' I said, and smiled my I'll-be-going-through-any-and-everything-you-leave-in-the-car-while-gone-especially-your-phone-and-sat-nav-history smile.

'Great,' he said, opening the door. 'Oh, almost forgot this,' he said, leaning back to grab his phone and kiss me on the cheek.

Ooh, the cheek.

mercredi, le 03 août

For the record, I wouldn't classify anything I do as kinky.

As far as I'm concerned, normal is what I want to do, and kinky is whatever I don't want to do. Golden showers? Normal. Smack me about the face and neck? Normal. Texting photos of my breasts covered in bulldog clips to someone I've not seen in person for almost a year? Normal. Scented candles and having face-holding anniversary sex? Eww, kinky. You won't catch me doing that. Not often, in any case. And definitely not for free.

Rather alarmingly, there are a lot of people – many of them with access to newspaper columns, Amazon accounts and the minds of children – who are happy to label anything that wouldn't pass muster in the third act of a Richard Curtis film as kinky and abusive. Random strangers labelling anyone who enjoys vigorous roughhousing as sick and damaged usually angers me, but only fleetingly, because it is quickly replaced by pity.

Pity they spent their formative years cooing over *Four Weddings* when I was watching *Urotsukidōji*. Pity they think short skirts and thigh-high boots are for Halloween. Pity they might not have earth-rocking sex until, as the song puts it, 'thirty when a girl starts getting dirty'.

Respect and equality and soulmates are jolly nice ideas, but not what sex is about. It's the sensation that matters. Orgasm is extreme sensation, but so are many other things, from slap and tickle to pinch and singe. Out of the context of actual violence, these sensations can be surprisingly pleasurable – even more so when administered by someone whose company you particularly enjoy.

So if you're one of these people – one of these you-can-come-inside-me-or-not-at-all-types, one of the legion who don't do doggy style because you want someone gazing into your eyes at all times, a girl (or boy) who's never even felt the warmth of come on her (or his) face, then I pity you. You are missing out. Really, you are! Sex is fun, people! Remember what it's like to be a kid, the butterflies in your stomach as you queue for the roller coaster? The building tension as you are strapped into your seat? The feeling of the world dropping out from underneath you, and the buzz afterward? It's like that. It's awesome, it's life-affirming, it's beautiful and soulful and real and normal. And not at all kinky.

jeudi, le 04 août

The manager said, 'He looks like Daniel Craig and tips like a merchant banker.'

'Ooh,' I said, 'Yes, I'll take that one then.' I'd love some

Daniel Craig. Granted, the Boy is like a bigger, darker version, but you always need a pocket-size for emergencies, no?

We met in the hotel bar. He was blonde, and possibly fit (couldn't tell for certain, it was one of those suits that is cut so well it would make Phill Jupitus look like Mr Universe). He was also three inches shorter than me. And I hadn't even worn the highest heels.

Ah well, let's see how she does on the second point then.

Hmm. Well, looks like a banker – just that touch around the middle that says he gets to the gym, but also gets to long lunches. Acts like one – impatient on the blowjob (relax, honey, you'll come faster; but no, they'd rather micro-manage the appointment). Thrusty on the main event. Talked the talk – rather a lot of the dirty talk, in fact – but it was straight suck-and-fuck all the way. And I wasn't ultra-convinced that he actually came. At any rate, I know I didn't.

And the tip? Like a merchant seaman.

vendredi, le 05 août

'For reals? For really reals?'

'Yes, really. It's next week. It looks like a good one, as well. I don't remember even posting a letter, because I'm sure I would have thought this job was well out of my reach.' I bit my lip. I was lying, of course – would never have admitted it to the Boy but what my uncle said had been bothering me.

You see them sometimes, perusing the sites of other agencies and independent escorts – the Hooker for Life. Tanned, over-blonded and the wrong side of forty, undoubtedly with a clientele comprised mostly of moneyed, sixty-ish regulars and young men looking to scratch their MILF itch. Not, I hasten to add, that there's anything wrong with that. But I am getting on, at least in mainstream-escort terms – the agency had shaved three years off my age to begin with, and hadn't updated that part of the profile since, making the believability factor just a little beyond the boundaries of credibility.

And while I love the life – love the money, love the dressing up, the access, the fact that I don't have to set an alarm for six a.m. – was that really what I wanted to end up as? A Hooker for Life?

'Holy . . . wow. That's amazing. I'm so proud,' the Boy said. 'Are you . . . are you ready?'

'I don't know. It's been a long time since I was out there. Any suggestions?'

What a mistake that was. He launched into a twenty-minute diatribe about the Do's and Don'ts of the modern workplace. I put the phone down and went away to make a cup of tea, only to come back and find him still rabbiting on. From the sound of it you'd think I'd got an interview to be an astronaut with NASA or something.

Still, as far as I was concerned, this was akin to a whole new universe. One in which the quality of my oral sex abilities will not feature.

For the most part, anyway.

samedi, le 06 août

I did it. I really did it. I thought I never would. I mean, I'm up for almost anything. Almost. But everyone has to draw a line somewhere and for me, that was always it. As far as I was concerned, any girl who did this was a tramp, no questions asked, no exceptions.

Sigh. I suppose lines were meant for crossing. I had my tips done. (Note for men: this means I went to a salon and had fake nails put over my real ones.)

Why, you might ask? After all, as a call girl, one of my trademarks is real everything: hair, tits, nails. And generally speaking, my nails are in very good shape. I'd managed to stop biting them with the thought that if I were going to make a living off my looks, I had to have the total look. You would have thought that two decades of tooth-based assault on the nail-beds would have left them irretrievably lost, but no. They were fine. Great, even. To the utter surprise of anyone who's known me since childhood, my nails grew out long, strong and perfectly manicurable.

It's the worry about the Boy's push to move in. In less than a week, I'd bitten them down to nothing.

Problem is, I have a job interview this week for a job I'd like. Something a bit of a step up on the career ladder from your usual entry position (on all fours, gripping a horsetail plug in my – hahaha, no, I meant work position), something that would put my prestige and income roughly where those of my age who took the more normal route to full employment now stand.

I know, I know. I'm buckling to pressure from the Boy. But deep down, I only started as a call girl because I couldn't get a job in my preferred field before. The fact that I ended up liking sex work was just the icing on the cake. It really only ever has been an extended temp job.

That's what I tell myself, anyway. That's what I'll tell my accountant, too. And that's what I'll tell the nail technician when I can't come in anymore, because these little trips to the salon won't be tax-deductible for very much longer.

lundi, le 08 août

Makeup? Done, sorted.

Suit? Sorted.

Shaving, et al? Unnecessary. Sorted.

Transport? Tube. Damnation.

Correct address? Ah, shit. Either the piece of paper dropped out of my bag or more likely it wasn't in there to begin with. My memory has got me as far as the correct street but how do people handle getting from point A to point B without a manager texting them the details? Note to self, land this job then see how quickly I can get a PA. Decide to ring A4 who logs in to my email for me and reads back the details, which I have no choice but to write on my hand.

Licking the address off my hand in the ten seconds between the smiling receptionist leaving the room and being led through to the interview? Just managed it.

mardi, le 09 août

For once, I've nailed something that wasn't another human being, or a sex toy, or whatever.

I nailed that interview.

Of course, I can only say that now – it's not a done deal yet as I've a second interview on Friday – so if anyone asks about it, I'll limit myself to: 'I think it went well . . . they were very nice.' What can I say? Superstitious runs in the family.

Unfortunately, getting the job would put me in a bit of a bind with the agency. The new position doesn't start until the end of the month, which is good, as it would give me time to work out how to tell the manager. Obviously, jumping up and down on the table yelling Boo-yah! Take that, you hamster-faced dullards! for the benefit of the rest of the agency girls next time we have a meeting is an attractive option, but probably not the best way to announce any good fortune.

And there's the fact that once you make public your plans to move on, no one takes you seriously. The Americans have a great phrase for this in politicians – the 'lame-duck'. Once you tell people you're going, you're not expected to be using your time wisely but rather to be taking long lunches (in Mustique), charging things to the company account (like a pair of Ginas for every day of the week) and ignoring all emails (as they would interrupt your midday holistic massage). But that just don't fly in the sex biz. The manager of the agency knows well there are thousands of girls just waiting to take my place. I'm as expendable as a Stalin crony.

I am in fact planning the opposite; now that I think I'll be moving on to something better, I can relax and throw myself into my work, which I have been, frankly, less than enthusiastic about lately.

Bring on the crack wax!

mercredi, le 10 août

'Did you come?' the client asked. We were lying in the tangle of sheets, sweaty and spent. Or he was, anyway.

'Oh, yes. Of course.' They don't always ask, but they do often enough and my answer is always the same. I figured with the amount of effort and groaning, there was no way he could tell otherwise. And, even if I've come close once or twice, it's like I said – I never reach climax with a punter. And never intend to.

He looked at me. 'Are you certain?'

I laughed. 'Believe me, a woman knows.'

'Oh, okay. I couldn't feel it, is all.'

I smiled lightly and rolled out of bed saying something about the shower. Honey, I thought, there are many things that can be ordered with confidence on the internet these days, but a woman's orgasm is not one of them.

vendredi, le 12 août

'Well don't leave me in suspense, woman,' N rolled his eyes. 'How did you do?'

'Quiet, I'm setting the scene,' I said. 'Picture me, suit, heels . . .'

'I can picture it – in fact it's what you're wearing right now,' he said.

'Oh. Right. Anyway. City, afternoon, the interviewer is . . . how shall we say . . .'

'A public school twat?'

I shot N a look. 'We're talking about my future boss here.'

'Aha! You did get the job.'

'Will you just let me tell the story already?' He shrugged. 'Okay. So he's there, Pink shirt, Ferragamo shoes . . . you know the type.' N nodded, and we said in unison: 'Client.'

'You didn't . . . you know, make him an offer he couldn't refuse?'

'Nah, he was impressed enough with the CV, apparently.' I'd covered the long period out of work by calling it a family illness in the end, and adjusted a few dates either side. Hopefully that didn't raise too many red flags. But it must not have done because he made no mention of it. 'And of course the usual by-the-book manager crap: "Where do you see yourself in five years' time?"'

N hooted. 'What did you tell him? Playboy?'

I shook my head. 'Is this what fifty per cent of my clients are like in their real, working lives? If so, I can see why they feel the need for erotic relief. This must get so depressing.'

As it happens, the young man didn't wait for my answer. Because like fully half of my clients, he was the sort who liked to talk at, rather than to, you. 'You can imagine, right?' I said, deepening my voice in imitation. '"In this company, we're interested not simply in the bottom line, but in our people. We expect anyone we take on not only to work for us, but for themselves. Developing their skills. Tackling new challenges".'

'Fucking hell,' N whistled. 'You almost sound like you believed it for a moment.'

'He was checking out my cleavage while he said it, mind.' Yes, that young man was every inch a professional.

'What did you say?'

I crossed my legs at the knee. 'That improving client relationships has always been a priority for me.' If you know what I mean. And I think he did. And any woman who is scowling right now, who imagines she has never, ever used her feminine wiles to get ahead, is a liar who can fuck right off.

'So when do you start?'

'In a fortnight,' I said. 'Apparently his name is Giles.'

samedi, le 13 août

'My god, that's great news!' the Boy said. 'Why didn't you say so earlier?'

'Um, because I just got home five minutes ago?'

'You know what I mean,' he said, picking me up by the waist and spinning around.

'Stop!' I squealed and struggled, but we both knew that meant don't stop.

He set me back on my tip-toes. 'This calls for champers. What do you say to a bottle of bubbly?'

'Love some!' I said, clapping. We stood in the middle of the kitchen. 'Um, are you going to get it?'

'Sorry, do you have any?' he asked.

'I don't, no,' I said. 'I thought you were implying you did.' After all this time, a part of me still held out some hope that maybe someday the Boy would surprise me, give me a gift that wasn't half-eaten, or anticipate what I'd like. But after so many years, it was churlish to be disappointed now. 'Hey, it's okay, tea and telly will do.' I kissed him on the cheek. 'Come on then, it's your turn to make the brew.'

dimanche, le 14 août

'You what now?' A4 gaped at me, unbelieving.

'I used him as a referee, of course.' We were talking about A2, who is (surprisingly to anyone who knows him as we do) something of a name in the world of business. Not like Trump or Sugar exactly, but recognisable to the right set.

'But he's your ex. I'm the one who works for him, and he's not even one of my referees!'

'Have you ever asked him to be?'

'Well, no . . .'

'Then that's not my fault.' I sighed and looked at the fake nails. I'd lost two on the Tube after the interview and another, I think, is in the duvet somewhere. 'Membership has its privileges and so on. Use the connections you have.'

A4 shook his head. 'You really have no conscience, have you.'

'I like how you put that as a statement, not a question.'

mardi, le 16 août

Who knew having female friends was going to become second only to work in the stressful-social-situations stakes?

L's finally given up on ever attracting the attention of her one-and-only love, Robbie Williams. 'So I've signed us both up for a singles party.'

'It might have escaped your notice that I actually have a boyfriend?'

'Honey, who cares? Has he never heard of a girls' night out?' L said. 'Let him have a Friday on his own for once. Besides, you need more champagne in your life, and if he isn't delivering, then it's down to us XX's to get it when we can.'

Actually, I thought, he had loads of Fridays on his own – it was a popular day for some of my regulars. But of course there was no way L knew that, as I'd used him as the excuse to turn down invitation on Fridays from her before. And I was tempted to do so again – but my uncle's words came back to me. Did I want things and stuff to be all I had? Or was it not finally time I made some proper female friends, like every other woman seems to be able to do?

'Okay,' I said. 'But I'm going strictly as an interested observer.' I suppose someone has to be the sane partnered chaperone, no?

'Of course, darling, of course,' she said. 'Dress to impress.'

Which, of course, means do not dress to upstage me. There are a few things I know about women.

Girl's Night Out: A Review

Preparation . . .

. . . took a bloody age. Can't go out in work gear; can't go out in slobbing-around-the-flat-clothes, either. Where's the middle ground? I finally settled on a black dress and silver heels. Boring, I know. Like a fricking office-party outfit. I shuddered at the thought that I'd probably pull out the same ensemble again, soon.

Location . . .

Not only did it take us ages to find where the bar was (who plans events like this in an infamous mobile black spot?) but having ascertained the location of the party we could not get in the door. Literally. L and I walked round and round a glass cube watching the action inside before finally finding the way in. I felt a right twat.

Situation . . .

Once inside, though, the feeling changed; not simply because no one had particularly noticed our late and rather inelegant entrance but because all but a handful of people in the room were stripping off, preparing to do bodyshots, demonstrate sex positions, and the like. Luckily L and I were not stripping; we were watching.

'The nice thing about this,' L said, 'is getting to see the goods beforehand. Some people just look better with their clothes on, and it's useful to know who they are before making a move.'

I nodded. As someone who considers herself better-looking unclothed (and is generally surprised that most women don't think the same of themselves, especially when they are still young enough to be in the age-range when everyone looks at least half decent), it's good to know the difference between dressing well and looking good in the buff is appreciated and factored into any future decisions.

'Mind you, I haven't seen any I particularly want to follow me home,' L said.

'Honey, we're just watching, not shopping!' And this is the point at which, if the music had been a little less loud and the naked girls and boys not half so distracting, I would have recommended Michel Houellebecq to her, perhaps *Platform* to start with. Oh for a world where it could have been so. I hopped off to the DJ booth, but the troglodyte contained therein was a self-important turd with terrible taste in music who could not be convinced that bleepy reach-for-the-lasers shite was not going down so well with the nonperforming members of the congregation. Not at that volume at least.

Contemplation . . .

Later, both admiring one girl's especially enviable midsection: 'I would love to lose this weight. Go home and surprise people. Show them,' L said. While I think L is perfectly lovely, she does have self-image issues and will not be convinced that she is, in fact, one of the very few women who, honestly, would be hot at any weight.

'No, what you really want is success. Losing weight doesn't take talent, only initiative,' I said. 'Any boring fuck can go on a diet.'

'You know what I like about you?' L said. 'Any other woman would have started telling me about her month on Atkins.'

dimanche, le 21 août

We sat on the sofa together, the Boy leaning against the armrest and I resting between his legs, my head propped on his chest. The radio was on some weekend comedy show, with clever-clever guests trying to outdo each other on whatever obscure topic was up for discussion. The Boy loves these things; I find them just this side of tolerable. A cup of tea cooled on the table next to us and we took turns sipping from it. The Boy sighed and shifted back against the sofa cushions. 'This is like heaven.'

'I was just thinking the same.' Actually, I was thinking that I was glad we'd showered straight after sex this morning, what with my head being practically in his armpit and all. It was a good shower too; we took turns cleaning each other and I couldn't resist going down to check that his cock was adequately hygienic.

'You've made this place quite the little nest,' he said.

'Yes, it is very domestic, isn't it?'

'Perhaps now's a good time to move in, now that you're about to start a new job. Clean slate and all that rubbish.'

I stiffened. We hadn't talked about my current working arrangements explicitly, but I assumed the Boy knew I hadn't yet quit going to appointments with clients. Or maybe he did know and thought I'd surely give it up soon after the first day at the new job? To be honest, everything had happened so quickly that I'd not had time to plan and was going to play it by ear. I had mentioned to the manager that I wouldn't be available daytimes anymore, and would like about half as many evening appointments, but she took it in her stride and hadn't even asked why.

'I thought you liked your place,' I said, barely suppressing anger.

'It's okay,' he said. 'But J' – his housemate, whose hatred of me is so strong I very rarely see the Boy's flat as a result – 'is moving in with his new girlfriend . . .'

'The one he started seeing three weeks ago?' I said. 'Bet she's thrilled.'

The Boy pursed his lips. 'Yes, well, I think his ex getting married hit him very hard. Anyway, it's coming to the end of our lease, and I can either try to find someone to move in there, or . . . I mean, it's really a glorified student house over there, this is so much more . . .'

'Like a home?'

'Yes.' He took a mouthful of tea, swished it around a bit and swallowed. My anger sat in the air between us. It's been something I've always hated about the Boy and his kind – the sense of entitlement, the absolute conviction that nothing they say and do, no matter how thoughtless and self-centred is wrong, ever. His eyes held mine, then flicked away. He set down the mug and leant towards me, gently taking another tack. 'Please, don't make this into an argument.'

'Just the fact that you pre-emptively accuse me of making this an argument is turning this into an argument, you know.' I wrinkled my nose and looked away. It was always like this, every important decision, fought over with heels dug in, both of us so stubborn that nothing ever happened. Nothing between us had ever really changed, ever moved forward, for years.

'Please,' he said, softly. 'I love being here on the weekends. I'd love to come home to this every day. And . . .' I waited for him to say something else, but he didn't, and minutes passed before he finally stood up. He kissed me on the head, breath hot and damp in my hair, and went to the kitchen for another cuppa.

It was the first time he'd ever given ground. My anger

deflated, leaving me with a strange mix of love and shame. Maybe things between us were changing after all.

lundi, le 22 août

I'm very good at first impressions.

I'm accustomed to it, you see. The stilted conversations, the awkward questions as you negotiate your way around a new person and a new set of rules, the breakthrough when you discover you've something in common after all and you both smile thinking, yes, we can make this happen, we can get along.

The crucial few minutes between a first glance and getting down to work? It takes a lot of effort and you have to be on top of your game at all times, but genius, as they say, is one per cent inspiration and ninety-nine per cent perspiration. Though in my case there's an awful lot of deodorant involved, too.

But to make a long story short (too late), meeting people is something I consider pretty easy. So as Giles showed me around the offices, introducing me to Jane and Audrey the admin ladies, the clutch of temps gathered around the photocopier, the suited men and tidy businesswomen I would soon know as colleagues, I smiled and chatted and generally charmed their socks off. I'm a polite, well-groomed master of intelligent conversation as long as you only see me for an hour.

Having to come back every day and do it all over again? Now, that's going to be a problem.

mardi, le 23 août

As per the manager's recommendation, am keeping a bag in the bottom, locked drawer of my new desk – and hope I'll never have to use it. It contains an emergency kit of makeup, a pair of high black shoes, a racy set of lavender silk lingerie and a capsule wardrobe of condoms, vibes and lube. The thrill of carrying on with a secret second life is not at all what I expected – in fact, I'm mortified my co-workers might find out.

mercredi, le 24 août

'Don't you want to know how my day at work went?' I asked, bringing the bottle back to the table with three glasses.

'Unless it involves giving blowies to hedgies, not really,' A2 said. 'You're a civilian now like everyone else. Boring.'

'Hey, I still have an edge,' I said. 'How many office workers do you know who can change into a push-up bra at their desks with no one the wiser?'

'Um, all of them?' A1 said. 'Come on, you have to admit it, you're a face in the crowd now,' he said. But his eyes were twinkling.

'Nice try,' I said, clinking glasses with the lads. 'But you can't wind me up that easily.'

jeudi, le 25 août

Okay, so maybe other office workers have long-since mastered the art of tarting up in the office for a night out, but how many can tart right back down again? In the fourteen minutes I had after a lunchtime appointment in the back of the taxi, I managed a quick-change that would have done a Catholic schoolgirl on her way home proud. Went in a gleaming groomed call girl and came out the other end prim and ready for the afternoon slog at work.

Apart from the bow-back heels and lingering whiff of lubricant, I mean. Ah well, practice in future cases will no doubt make perfect.

samedi, le 27 août

And suddenly it's as if our relationship was new all over again. The Boy hasn't brought me flowers in years – he's sent roses to my work already. And we rarely meet in the middle of the day, but he rang Friday and we walked to a park near my office and ate packed lunches.

Saturday morning was an epic lie-in when he literally wouldn't let me out of bed. Not only with the rude stuff, but also fetching the paper, cups of tea, the best batch of eggy bread ever. My head was nestled on his shoulder as we both read the paper (me: style, he: sport).

His breath ruffled my hair. 'I could do this forever,' he said. And when he said it, I knew I could, too.

'Then let's do it,' I said, flipping over to look at him. His eyes, so blue, were softer and more crinkly around the edges than when we met, but his chest was still broad, his hair still curled softly around a face that I always had loved.

'Really?' he said, sitting up. 'You're not . . . going to change your mind?'

I smiled tightly – the way he said that would have sent me into a rage before. But no, this was the New Us. Things were

58

going to change, I was determined. 'I'm not. Come live with me.'

'Oh, you little thing,' he said, holding me tightly, so much so that I gasped. 'I want us to grow old together.'

dimanche, le 28 août

Manager rang at eleven. Last-minute appointment scheduling.

'Sorry, can't,' I said. 'Isn't anyone else free?'

'Eef I had any options I would not have called,' she said. 'Charlie has a hair appointment and Sophie is on holiday in Blackpool.'

'What, again?'

'I know, I'm beginning to think I should send her to Paris next time. For her own good.'

'But I'm at work,' I hissed from deep inside the cleaners' closet. 'I can't sneak off for the sake of a client.'

'You've done lunchtimes before,' she said. 'It's only Bayswater and it's double the usual price. In, out, done. You will hardly interrupt your busy schedule.'

'No!' I squealed. 'Absolutely not. Ring him and cancel.' And yet, I was thinking, I probably could make it. Just. There was the bag in my desk from the last lunchtime client after all, and the money . . . well. But I also knew the risk was high – it would be difficult, maybe impossible, to get in and out of the foyer without being noticed.

'This is a very good client, he's seen several of the girls before, and always tips well . . . basic suck and fuck, nothing taxing. You could be having your nails done and you wouldn't even notice he was there.'

Wow, there's a testimonial. 'No.' Well, maybe not. I thought about the house, and how we really could use a few things here and there . . . 'Fine. But from today on I don't do short notice.'

I sighed. Pick your battles, right? I went back into the office, grabbed the bag, and changed in the toilet down the far corridor. My work clothes I stashed in the cleaners' closet. Was walking out the door to meet a taxi when I passed a co-worker.

Giles. Shit. In my peripheral vision, I saw him do a double take, but I continued straight on and didn't look back.

Fuck. Fuck. Fuck.

mercredi, le 31 août

Missed calls: 5
Voicemail messages: 3
View now?

And every one of them from the agency manager. Shite. Giles was droning on about something or other, leaning across my desk. I shuffled around in my handbag.

'Sorry, darling . . . I'm just off to the loo.' Giles nodded and I scampered towards the stairwell.

There was a queue for the toilet. I sighed. The phone started going again, grunting like a little insistent rhino in my hand. The woman in front of me turned and smiled. 'Is that your phone?'

'Yes. Yes, it is a phone.'

'Are you going to answer it?'

'Probably. Yes, probably.' She nodded, gave me an odd look, and turned away. Stupid bint. Her biggest problem at that moment was trying to keep from wetting herself in public. I was a prostitute trying to manage her appointments.

The queue simply wasn't shifting. What on earth are

people doing in there, their own hysterectomies? I dashed back out and stood in the stairwell and dialled the manager. 'Darling, hello,' she barked. 'There is a laaaaaaarvely man who wishes to meet you this week—'

'Yes, yes, yes,' I said impatiently, smiling tightly as three chattering secretaries pressed past me on the stairs. God, how long does it take a group of women with the combined IQ of a salad bar to descend stairs? It ain't hard, princesses. Forward, down, repeat. I lowered my voice to a whisper. 'I've been thinking that, well, perhaps it's time I . . . I mean we . . . what I want to say is, well, I'd like to consider, you know, quitting.'

The girls on the landing went suddenly quiet. Jesus, ladies, get a move on already. It's not going to turn into an escalator.

'Darling, I'm sorry to hear that. Is there a problem?'

'Well, yes. My schedule outside of work has been very busy lately, and I'd like to . . . consider . . . other options.'

'Haven't we already talked about this, sweetie?' the manager purred. Oh, she knew how and when to turn it on, she did. But like they say, I knew all the games she played, because I play them too. 'I'm sending only the most exclusive, hand-selected clients now . . .'

As if they had previously been chosen by machine. 'And I appreciate it, I do.' For fuck's sake. They're still there. Must be some sort of secret lesbian romp and I've interrupted. 'I think however that it's time I stopped for good.'

'Oh, sweetie. If it's a matter of more money . . .'

I understood. In the unwritten etiquette of the call girl, 'I want to quit' virtually never means that. It means the girl in question isn't feeling valued highly enough, whether it's because her rates are significantly lower than some of the other girls', or her profile isn't featured at the top of the listings any longer. Hookers who want to walk, nine times out of ten, just walk. But I'm not the sort of person who just walks. 'It's not about the money, it's the conflict of work with my personal life—'

'Darling, every profession has that—'

'—and I don't want to risk my privacy.' Though with the KGB setting up ten metres down goodness knows how long that would last.

'Sorry, bad connection. Your what?' the manager enquired sweetly.

'My privacy,' I said a touch louder.

'Phone must be going, I can't hear a word you're saying.'

'My privacy!' I shouted. 'I'm concerned about privacy!'

'You might consider taking your phone calls elsewhere,' one of the dippy girls giggled, and they finally moved on. Finally!

'Oh, darling, if only you'd said,' the manager cooed. 'I can blur your face on the photos a little, to make it less recognisable. Good. Great. I'll text you the details of this new man. We'll talk tomorrow,' she said, and hung up.

'Brill. Talk tomorrow,' I said to the dead line.

How to balance life and work:

1 Pace yourself. Don't take on too much in the first few, heady days of office work. The men aren't going anywhere; they can be worked through in due time (such as the office Christmas party).

2 Say no to the unimportant. Including, but not limited to: answering the phone on your desk; answering all emails on the very day they arrive; and attending the various workshops and inductions designed especially for new employees. No one will notice you've not done it anyway.

3 Take care of yourself. Granted, your officemates may get a little annoyed at hearing the emery board constantly grating, so keep such activities for home. But plucking is completely silent and fluorescent light is brilliant for finding stray hairs.

4 Get a check up. Your co-workers, particularly those with small children, are a source of infection in the office, especially during flu season. If your office doesn't give you free time for medical appointments, consider wearing a face mask.

5 Stop being a workaholic. On the rehab coolness stakes, workaholic is somewhere between glue-sniffer and habitual tissue-eater. Alcoholism is so much more you.

6 Simplify your life. If you normally walk to work in one pair of sensible shoes, changing to more office-appropriate footwear on arrival, your routine can be considerably simplified by not walking to work.

7 Find a friendly workplace. See comments re: office Christmas do above. As they say, an awkward morning beats a boring night.

8 Get a handle on your finances. Don't be tempted to spend away your new earnings before the pay packet's even

arrived. Beat off the temptation to treat yourself to expensive gewgaws on a weekly basis by beating off in the toilets during breaks.

9 Define success for yourself. A day in which I managed eight hours without a single work-related email? Success!

10 Raise the bar. Try for two days in a row of no actual work-related activity. Who dares, wins.

Septembre

jeudi, le 01 septembre

On the last shred of energy. Today I went straight from one job to the other. Was already tired from the office but had a turnaround of thirty minutes – shower, change, higher shoes, better knickers, slinkier suit and shinier lippy – then back out the door.

Note to self, must remember to check whether the manager has actually changed my profile on the website. But haven't yet had enough spare time in order to do so, and certainly can't check it from work!

The client was mid-thirties, dark hair, Northern accent. Geordie, in fact. He looked tired around the eyes, as if he too had just dashed in from work in a mad rush of preparation in order to meet me, but I know that wasn't so. His creased shirt and the rumpled suit jacket over the edge of the sofa said exactly the opposite. This was a way of life for him, only just starting to realise that the long hours and manic pace of a twenty-something go-getter start to catch up with you eventually.

'Wine?' he asked, taking the chilled bottle from the fridge. I nodded and looked around.

It was bachelor pad par excellence – a little creepily so, in fact. Everything was precisely where you would expect it to be. The sleek, expensive stereo system. The flat-screen television. The exotic hardwood furniture and worldly tchotchkes. All the boxes were ticked. It looked like a room in a boutique hotel, and then it occurred to me why. The carefully curated music collection was too neat, as if none of the CDs had ever been played. The spines of the books on the shelves, not a one of them embarrassing or in anything other than perfect taste, were uncreased. He probably spent as much time here as in hotels.

'Gorgeous flat,' I said.

'Thank you,' he said from the kitchen.

I spotted the contents of his refrigerator before the door closed: olives and four wine bottles.

I'm glad I don't take clients at my own house; I'd never manage to make the place look neat enough in time. Going out requires a certain amount of organisation. In the last few minutes before the taxi arrives I'm usually digging around looking for the stockings I'm sure were clean but if so, where the hell did I put them? Having that extra time to fiddle in my own space would spell disaster, surely.

Unless I was like this fellow and never at home. Which, in the last few weeks, it was certainly starting to feel like. I watched his feet as he walked back towards me, glasses in hand. His socks didn't match. One brown and one black – I wondered if he'd even noticed.

The client slid the glass of chilled white into my hand and smiled. He'd already quaffed his, I saw. I took a ladylike sip, set the glass down and followed him to the bedroom.

Naked, he was soft. Not his cock – that was sizeable, and ready for action – but this body, it had seen better days. He probably even had been pretty once, the sort of man who rode high on a wave of potential and bedded women like they were a limitless resource. He didn't ask me what I wanted, what I liked, just went to work. I wasn't offended; it clearly was far from the first time.

But I did wonder what he saw in the mirror. There was something about him that reminded me of . . . no, girl, don't think it, don't even mix the two . . . of Giles. A loneliness couched in long hours and endless striving after a dream he already knew was not nearly as big or as bright as he once had hoped. Oh, he'd be all right in the end. We would have competent, even sexy, sex; he would come and tip well and I'd never see him again. And someday he would end up with a woman, a good woman, not the A-woman but certainly pretty enough and nice enough to look good on his arm. And he would always, secretly, wonder what happened to the strippers and models he'd once dated.

And the woman he'd marry? Oh, I knew the type well. She'd give up her job, or work part time in consultancy. Prepare the food, keep the house, send out the laundry. Collect his paycheques and dole him back out a stipend of spending money. Her friends would come round for coffee mornings and wonder how does she do it, how does she keep this running so well? She'd nod sagely and tut and intimate that without her help, her husband simply wouldn't be able to get by.

But from where I was standing (as he knelt between my legs, flicking his tongue over my clit) I wondered whether I agreed. It's a lonely life, yes. But food can be ordered in, cleaning ladies hired and as for the sex . . . well, mine was very much a customer service position. Having the same person do it every day, does that make you any less lonely? Having a wife who patronises and infantilises you and fills the flat you've carefully arranged with moustache bleach, shoes she'll never wear and back issues of *Heat*, does that make things better somehow? If I had to lay a bet either way, I'd say he'd keep using prostitutes, only in-calls at lunch instead of out-calls in the evenings. 'Honestly, sweetheart, I don't know where the money goes. A few too many espressos probably.'

He moved on to my nipples and sucked them with a contemplative air, as a man who was compiling a top-ten list of nipples in his head. It was hard not to laugh. Some people just never turn off their analytical brains. Granted, when on the job, I tend not to because the client's experience is paramount. But I had the feeling even at a moment when he should have been enjoying himself his pleasure was nothing more than another exercise in good taste. Another ticked box.

We finished with him standing and me bent over a chair, at the last moment he pulled back, and I looked round – to my horror he had taken the condom off. But it was so he could ejaculate on to me, which is something I am very fond of as it happens. His sigh sounded half fatigue, half relief. 'Wait, stay there,' he said, and fetched wipes from the bathroom (sterile as a hotel's, with matched toiletries) to clean the mess from my back, arse and the backs of my thighs. He didn't seem to notice the droplets sinking into the carpet, or if he did, wasn't concerned. Doubtless the cleaning lady sees more of the room than he does.

'You've got great tits,' he said, and smiled gently. The taxi was outside and he'd opened the door to let me out, his chest showing through an unbuttoned shirt looking almost like a young man's in the light. 'Don't lose an ounce of weight, they're perfect.'

A connoisseur. I nodded and promised to take the advice seriously. It was three minutes, tops, between when the taxi dropped me home and when I hit the pillow, still in full makeup, already mostly asleep.

samedi, le 03 septembre

Checked the website from home finally, and the manager seems to have kept to her promise and altered my profile. As in, the photos are so blurred you can hardly tell the image is of a human, much less a woman. I rang her.

'This is insane – no man in his right mind will book a flesh-coloured blob,' I whined.

'Honey, you should be thanking me,' she snapped. 'You're the one who wanted to be anonymised.'

'Anonymous to possible co-workers, yes. Unidentifiable as human, no.'

She sighed. I could hear a buzzing in the background that sounded like her other phone. 'Fine, you do the alterations. Edit your original photos and email them back. I don't have time for you girls and your complaints.'

mardi, le 06 septembre

'He's gorgeous, he's young, and you'll love him, I just know it,' she trilled.

Not the manager. My mother.

I rolled my eyes and tucked the phone between my ear and shoulder so I could finish the pedicure I'd started. 'Mum, please. You've been divorced, what, half-a-minute now? Is this really the right time to be diving headlong into another relationship.'

'Don't you mother me,' she said. 'Besides, none of us are getting any younger. Yourself especially.'

The orange stick hovered in midair. 'What's that meant to mean?'

'Oh, nothing honey. Really, nothing.' Word to the wise: when a Jewish mother says it's nothing, it's definitely something. Related: when she says it's nothing to do with you, it most certainly is.

'Sure. Nothing.' Ugh. I had made the mistake of thinking that because my sister had gone and got herself married and knocked-up (and not, necessarily, in that order – I may only have an arts degree but I can still subtract) this would take the pressure off me, the elder daughter, for a few years. At least until I turned thirty. No such luck. And as for bringing her around to the idea that maybe, just maybe, the ring and the brood of children and the yummy-mummy, yoga-lite wardrobe were not reliable indicators of personal achievement, well – forget it.

'Just . . . it would be nice if I could tell everyone both of my girls were happily settled.'

'People in hell want ice water,' I snapped, jabbing the orange stick viciously against my cuticles. Ow.

'I wish you didn't have to be so rude about it,' Mum said. 'When I talk to your sister . . .'

'Yeah, I'm sure when you talk to her it's all singing birds and politesse,' I said. 'Why shouldn't it be? She's landed on her feet without ever having to try at anything. Sure, I'd probably be nicer too if I could afford to swan around in a country cottage playing house.' Now, I had the small inkling I should have stopped there, but I ignored it. 'Oh, I'm sorry. She doesn't really afford it herself, does she? What's her salary these days? I've completely forgotten. Is it nothing, or is it zero?'

Mum sniffed. God, the art of the sniff. The impatience, the rage, the smothering love. She could convey the entirety of the *Brothers Karamazov* in a single sniff.

'Well, at least she's happy with her life. And I'm happy. Are you, dear? Are you?'

jeudi, le 08 septembre

If there is any phrase in the English language more horrifying than 'work drinks', I've yet to hear it.

It's not the prospect of seeing those I work with inebriated that troubles me. After all, I survived university. Rather, it's the unwritten rules of going out with workmates: never drink more than anyone else, pretend you don't notice anyone who is, and for goodness sake, never crack on to someone you work with.

'Do you like real ales?' Giles asked.

'Like them? Why as a student there was this challenge called the Beer Monster, and I practically . . .' Quiet, now, this man is your boss. He doesn't need to know how quickly you can do ten pints. 'Er, yes, I could enjoy a nice ale.'

'Good girl,' he said. 'It is a school night after all.'

Three pints in and I was starting to wonder whether Giles shouldn't be following his own advice. For every round of beer everyone else had, he was having a cider, sometimes two. For every giggle that arose among the slightly stilted attendees, he was guffawing. In fact, he appeared to be really rather drunk. Someone should have called a taxi, but he was our boss – who dared?

Apart from how to down a pint of bitter in less than six seconds, there was something else I learned at uni, and that is when to call it quits. All the unsuccessful nights out had one thing in common: there had been a point at which I could have stopped drinking and gone home, and didn't. There's little or nothing to be gained in closing a pub down. What's more, most people probably won't remember you'd gone anyway. Showing your face matters. Face on the floor? Less so.

And someone should have told Giles. I was just outside the ladies', buckling a strap of my shoe, when he came up behind and put a hand on my hip. Scooting past to get to the gents', perhaps? Ah, no. It was definitely a suggestive grab.

'You all right?' I asked.

'Are those what I think they are?' Giles said, palpating my upper thighs.

'Afraid so,' I said, teeth gritted. You can't mistake a real garter belt and stockings. I was struck with embarrassment for him, but also horror: what must he think of me? Seeing me going out at lunch the other week, now the stockings – it wouldn't take a genius to suspect, and not much digging to put it all together.

'I know you have a boyfriend, but . . .'

Fuck. It wasn't that he wasn't attractive; he was. Sexy, in fact. But he was also the boss, and if there is anything I'm good at, it's compartmentalising. There is recreational sex and there is work, and never the twain shall meet. Even if work doesn't strictly revolve around sex any longer.

'It's not a good idea, mixing business with pleasure,' I said, edging away from him. His cheeks were flushed, his shirttail had come untucked. He looked suddenly younger, like a student at a ball.

'Tell me, wontshoo,' Giles said, teetering slightly, 'what you do mixsh your pleasure with.' His body rolled and lurched towards mine in slow motion. I pushed him gently away just as Audrey came round the corner.

'Call him a taxi, would you?' I said to her. 'I think he's had enough.'

'You're a beautiful lady, you know that,' he said, stumbling away from his secretary and towards the bar.

vendredi, le 09 septembre

'He's out sick,' Audrey said. 'I'll ring him at home and ask if he can reschedule your meeting for next week.'

'Giles? He seemed fine last night,' I said.

The secretary chuckled. 'Yes, well, some of us can handle our drink, and others . . . you know.'

I shook my head. 'Not as hardcore as he'd like to be.'

'Well, we can't all be as nails as you,' she said.

'Me? Nails?'

Audrey smiled in a funny way. 'Oh, you try to hide it, but I notice things. You're a party girl of a whole other calibre.'

I wondered what she'd noticed, exactly. Also how secure the door and desk locks were in this place. 'God, Aud, please don't think I come to work just to—'

Audrey waved a hand in the air. 'I don't mean anything by it. Work hard, play hard. I think it's funny. You're a dark horse, you are.'

Hmm. Well, as long as she didn't seem to actually know. There are dark horses, and then there are dark horses.

lundi, le 12 septembre

A tap on my shoulder. 'Hey, beer monster.'

I jumped, and hastily removed my earphones. 'Giles, hi. Sorry . . . you startled me.'

'Can we chat?' he said.

'Sure, of course,' I said. 'Now?'

'Tomorrow or the next day,' he said. 'I'll have Audrey book something.'

Ah, for the days that would have instantly meant a dirty romp in a hotel room. But of course he meant lunch. I smiled. 'Great. See you then.' What the hell is he after? I wondered as he left the office. A chat? Or something more?

mardi, le 13 septembre

Going up:

Shell jewellery. Rocking the seasonally inappropriate is so my bag, baby: wool in summer, grockle-shop crap and flip-flops as the weather cools down. You know you love it.

The air-dry. Suddenly, the hairdryer seems a superfluous addition to my day and to be honest, I'm not sure anyone has noticed the difference. (The GHD, however, remains.)

Instant soup in a packet (tomato and basil, or minestrone). If I have one more cup of tea, I may very well turn into tannin. This provides an alternative excuse to visit the kettle. When I was a kid, it was all about Bovril and Marmite (or sucking on undiluted stock cubes, actually). Whatever happened to hot, savoury drinks?

The current shoe moment. My preferred style of shoe (patent leather, round-toed, extremely high) now seems to be everywhere. Seriously. The petrol station is giving away cute shoes with every top wash. What shoe diet?

Going down:

Watches. The repairs on my preferred personal chronometer all but require a mortgage (I stupidly left it in the shower at the gym and, although someone miraculously turned it in to lost and found, it appears to have been flushed, kicked, and used to nail up a few walls). I'll be wearing the emergency backup Oyster for a while, then. Le sigh.

Lipstick. The amount of tea I drink, I probably digest about half a tube of Stila a day.

Pop socks. After 'herpes lesion', the most horrifying two words known to (wo)mankind. I can not even begin to explain what happened, except that M&S was involved . . . with the pop socks I mean. Not herpes.

The commute. Ugh, how do people live through this? Oh, how I miss taxis.

mercredi, le 14 septembre

Giles messaged to say he was running late, so I waited at the restaurant in South Kensington. It was in one of those lovely creamy terraces on a street going up to the park. Inside, the room bustled with student servers and local suits jostled for position at the rough-pine tables. The hostess smiled and handed me a menu. Roast loin – 'of pork' no less. Organic, locally sourced, free-range, poached duck eggs. I wondered what they were going for here exactly: a gastropub, only no pub? Some sort of upscale caff?

Giles arrived. He ignored the menu, smiled at the waitress and just ordered a fry-up. Ah, so a caff then – or at least what passes for a caff down Kensington way.

Giles didn't mention the work party so neither did I. He probably didn't even remember what happened . . . I hope. Our still waters were brought to the table with a flourish as if they were fine wines.

'And coffee,' Giles said. The pretty waitress beamed at him and scampered off. 'Meant to mention, saw you going off to lunch the other week,' he said.

I stiffened. I should have known it. Now what? He invites me to a local boutique hotel for . . . a chat? A threat? A come-on? Can the end of my career really have come so quickly?

'Did you?' I said, voice shaking.

'You looked . . .' Giles seemed at a loss for the right word. '. . . very nice,' he said finally. 'Were you meeting a friend?'

'Er, yes, just a friend. An old friend. Someone I've known years in fact.'

'Your boyfriend?'

'No, not my boyfriend. Someone I've not seen in some time, ha-ha-ha.'

'I see. Just a friend then?' he asked suspiciously.

Jesus, was he digging?

'Not to worry, he won't be dropping by the office.'

'That's a pity,' Giles said, cocking half a smile at me. 'I'm curious what a woman like you would find attractive in a man.'

I cough. Is there any way to answer that?

'Yes, well. That being as it is . . . just what did you bring me here for?'

'Which do you want first, the good news or the bad news?'

Was this some sort of trap? Was I going to be fired over a plate of bad fried eggs and indifferent black pudding?

'Bad news, I guess.' I'll always play true to type. Glass half empty and all that.

'The bad news is I'm moving to a new role in a few months' time,' Giles said. 'After that, until there's someone new I'll still be managing the day-to-day, but I wanted you to know about the upcoming vacancy in the new year.'

Uh, vacancy? I still didn't quite get it. 'Whose?'

'Mine, you silly girl. As in, I think you should apply for the position.'

'For your job? But I have no experience in this field. I've been here like six nanoseconds.'

'Basically, I have a good idea of who might apply for the

position. There's Ray from downstairs,' – I knew Ray, he was the sort of person who scratched himself a lot and never let anyone get a word in edgewise – 'there's Mark, but he's just got his wife pregnant again and I'm frankly beginning to doubt his commitment—' to Sparkle Motion '—to his career. And then there's you.'

'What about anyone who might apply from outside?'

'Doubtful. The pay rise is negligible. The hours are painful. And, frankly, we never hire from outside.'

'You hired me,' I said.

The eggs really were like rubber. Like rubbers, even.

'You have . . . energy,' Giles said, pushing a burnt tomato round his plate. 'Your background is different. You bring a new perspective into the group, and you get things done without belabouring the point.'

If that's management-speak for rushes-jobs-through-so-she-doesn't-have-to–stay-at-the-desk-a-minute-later-than-required then I guess, yes, I do fit that description. Sort of.

'So what's the good news then?'

Giles swallowed his coffee and grinned.

'Well, I had rather thought the prospect of immediate promotion would be the good news. And also that once this is settled, we might go for a . . . more social . . . drink sometime.'

Ah, yes. The classic. Never ask a woman when you can just state. And for chaps like this, it's a ploy that often works.

'No beans. But I will let you pay for breakfast.'

'Shame, it's on expenses,' Giles grinned. 'Sure I can't buy you breakfast another time?'

'You're a great boss,' I smiled, getting up. And what you really need is to get a call girl and stop bothering your subordinates. 'But I don't do slumber parties. Ta anyway.'

Never had much time for people who stand around pointing fingers, accusing others of 'selling out'. There is a significant shortage of people living unconventional lives, and the name-callers are seldom they; also, as Robert Zimmerman so eloquently (if tunelessly) pointed out, you got to serve somebody.

But I see friends whose temporary jobs somehow became permanent; couples who marry because they're supposed to after two years' dating then have children just to get the in-laws off their backs; single men who have never had to change a nappy talk about their desire for a family; and a generation whose previously self-satisfied mocking of the 1970s has transformed into a genuine desire to recreate that era, complete with disposable and horrific fashion, permanent confusion on the topics of sexual promiscuity and working mothers, and a disturbing attachment to scented candles.

Fucking hell, is that what my life's becoming?

'Hmm, car park looks nearly full. I'll drop you by the door and go park somewhere else, okay? Wait for me by the paints?'

'Interior or exterior paint?'

'Um, interior. It's nearer the door.'

'Okay, see you in there.' A quick peck on the cheek, then he's off in the Ford Focus.

In the last few years acquaintances and people I was at uni with have coupled off, produced babies, acquired mortgages and generally started on a settled and proper life. Anyone who suggests maybe their effort could have been used for something more unusual or interesting is told, 'Oh, just grow up.'

In the other hand are the older people I've met (generally clients) whose marriages and careers – often not even the first ones – are falling apart, whose children hate them and who spend whatever they can to try to regain a trendily dressed, fast-driving, surgeon-tightened facsimile of youth. Why do the younger ones think they're exempt from this fate?

Where do these/ Innate assumptions come from? Not from what/ We think truest, or most want to do:/ Those warp tight-shut, like doors. They're more a style/ Our lives bring with them: habit for a while,/ Suddenly they harden into all we've got/ And how we got it . . .

I should talk. I'm out with the Boy comparison-shopping for curtain rails this weekend.

'When I move in, we'll get the place properly sorted,' he says. 'There's the dining table that's been in storage, the desk from the old house . . .'

The people I admire most are those whose motto is 'Live Forever or Die Trying', because at least they've looked at the abyss, acknowledged their fear of it and are doing whatever they can in the meantime.

Everything else is just middle-middle class, middle England, middle-of-the-road. Fine for some. Is it fine for me? I can't remember what I wanted to be when I grew up.

dimanche, le 18 septembre

'What's the occasion?'

'No occasion,' he said, reddening. 'I saw these and thought . . . I thought of you.'

Hmm. Well if the Boy's trying to sweeten the cohabitation deal, buying me lingerie is a brave choice. Men buying bras and knickers will always be difficult. If they get the style right, that's great; if they get the size right, it's a miracle.

The matter of bra sizing is, in an ideal world, standard. But who's ever standard? My bra size is not so unusual that I have to shop from those desperately awful mail-order catalogues featuring torpedo-breasted ladies in industrial strength nursing bras, yet not so common that I can easily find it anywhere apart from M&S or online. Actually I suspect a conspiracy by Marks to measure you up for bras that only they among all high street vendors can supply, and thereby be obliged to spend far too much on what amounts to a very plain, very itchy, altogether dissatisfying offering from their stock . . . and while any of their bras labelled 'balconette' is usually acceptable, the 'padded plunge' does nothing, nothing, nothing for my figure . . . damn it, why couldn't I have been a 34C?

The agency has always been particularly prone to exaggerating the girls' profiles. A cup added here, a band-size shaved there. So imagine my – and probably a few clients' – surprise to see myself listed as a 30DD. That's not only wrong, it would have taken a KFC bucketful of chicken fillets for me to approximate. I appreciate as much as the next girl the power of exaggeration in the matter of one's figure, but that's a bridge (or a cup, as the case may be) too far.

I checked the label, I hoped, discreetly. Whew, he'd got it right. So I knew at least he hadn't searched my online profile for the size.

'These are beautiful,' I said. The Boy beamed.

Bottom halves, however, are another kettle of fish entirely. I'm a size eight to ten, but women's sizes are notoriously open to interpretation, and where bottoms come in small, medium or large, where does that leave me? And will they fit?

The boyfriend twisted the bag in his hands nervously. 'I think I might have gone a little too small on those,' he said.

'You think so?' I held up the knickers and peered at them. 'I don't think my arse is that big.'

I checked the label. Medium. And what looked to be a generous Medium, at that. Let me emphasise that there is nothing wrong with Medium. Medium implies normal, usual, neither gifted with built-in thigh panniers nor a bottom that may be mistaken for a boy's. Medium is good . . . and yet, there is a tiny voice inside me that will always prefer Small. Small implies cute, toned, not quite so heavy-handed with the butter at mealtimes.

'There's only one way to find out,' he said.

I tried them on. Perfect fit. Damn, my arse is that large. Ho-hum. They look pretty swish, though, if I do say so myself and are very silky. Though I should really have checked whether they were safe to put in the washer before suggesting I masturbate him with the damp gusset.

lundi, le 19 septembre

For every woman, there are certain conversations that mark milestones in her life.

Like telling my mother I wasn't a virgin anymore. In retrospect, I could have got away with not telling her, but if something had happened – if I'd got pregnant, or . . . well, anyway, I've always been one for fretting – I thought she needed to know. I don't know what I was expecting, sympathy maybe? She cried. We never talked about it again.

Explaining myself the first time at the GUM clinic, that was another one. I like the full everything-everything. And if it were up to me, there would be smears every year, not once every three. Like to know I'm getting my money's worth out of the NHS, right? But there was a little awkwardness, even though I'd no doubt the nurse had heard it all before and then some. I'm still concerned someone might be judging me. Can only guess what's written in my patient files. 'Surprisingly conscientious for a hooker' would be my guess.

And the most recent one. I finally told the agency no. Maybe I'd take Giles up on his suggestion – the work one not the sex one – and maybe I wouldn't. But either way, it was becoming unworkable. It was somehow easier to keep work and life separate, when life didn't also include another job.

I went back to the stairwell (empty of giggling secretaries this time). It took me three tries but I finally worked up enough bottle to make the call. The manager took it well – crisply. I think she knew I meant it this time. Also, a month or so and I'd wager she won't even remember my (working) name. One thing London doesn't lack is pussy. Provided you're willing to pay, that is.

mardi, le 20 septembre

Came to work still buoyant about the conversation with the manager. The bag in the bottom drawer of the desk? No need for that any longer! No need to work extra-strength condoms into my weekly budget, or keep two separate underwear drawers, one for clients and one for everyday. I sent a text to the Boy:

Did it. Love, your newly legit girlfriend xx

No answer. Well, it was breaking our unspoken agreement to never mention my work, but I thought he should be among the first to know.

mercredi, le 21 septembre

Dropped something like my monthly salary on a bit of shopping. Oops. What can I say? The shiny window fronts of Old Bond Street were calling and I was powerless to resist. Am already imagining what the Boy will say when he notices (and he will notice), so had to cover my tracks by forking out for some baubles for him as well. Also attempting to devise a justification (to myself, the Boy and most importantly to my bank manager) wherein I forgo buying shoes for the next decade, or something.

Met with the A's for a meal and a much-needed setting to rights of the world.

'Now as a man I realise this is borderline grounds for expulsion from the sex,' A2 said. 'But if I see one more pap photo of Paris Hilton's cooze*, I may go off the concept for life.'

'Gash flash is the new mooning,' A1 said. 'And you're right, we'd better book your sex reassignment now.'

'Fuck, that's harsh,' I said. 'Couldn't he just go gay?'

'That seems reasonable,' A4 said.

'Also, can you do it too?' I said. 'And obviously I'd have to watch.'

Am now fully topped up on booze and hot goss, but couldn't help feeling a touch melancholic on the bus back.

---

* At university A1 and I decided that 'cunt' had lost its power to offend – largely because we used it so often and with so little regard for context. So it was necessary to come up with a word that could be deployed when one really wanted the object of the insult to take offence. A nuclear option, if you will. That word, friends, was 'cooze'. And I defy you to come up with an insult that makes the skin crawl quite like that one does.

Between the Boy, the one job, and now the new one, there's so little time for friends. I miss my men and wish I had them on tap at all times.

vendredi, le 23 septembre

The topic was football at Friday coffee. It's always the bloody football. Sometimes a moment or two is given over to the consideration of rugby, or cricket, but never in any depth, not that it would matter. I am so fucking sick of smiling and nodding about sport. Not just sport, but the same damn sport topics over. And over. And over again. They say women aren't interested in sport; in my case, that's not the truth. I like sport just fine, ta. What I'm particularly uninterested in is listening to people spin the same cogs week after stagnant week.

After the usual grumbles (favoured team perilously close to relegation, new coach who was last week hailed as saviour will probably turn out to be rubbish), the talk turned as it always did to the subject of money.

'They're paid more than I earn in a year for kicking a football around?' said one chap, whom I happen to know has a season ticket, but no matter, I've learned where football is involved there is no such thing as a logical conclusion.

Much tch-ing and sucking of teeth from the gallery.

'Criminal.'

'Beyond belief.'

'And they charge how much for a child's away kit?'

I smiled and, as is the habit, nodded. But honestly if that's the going rate, that's the going rate. It's probably unethical that I once earned more in a hour's fucking than most people earn in a day, but so long as someone is willing to pay it, is that wrong? It's not as if there were public funds involved – I for one was never involved with politicians.

'What the fans ought to do is go on strike,' Jane said. 'But that would never happen.'

'Actually it has,' I said. 'Apparently once the women of New Orleans stopped having sex with the men who were fans because of something to do with the football team. Now that I think of it, it was rather like that play . . . you know, by what's his name?' I looked around the room, to blank faces. '. . . the Greek one? Euripides? No wait, he was dead then. I mean Aristophanes. The play with the women who stop having sex in order to end a war . . .' Hmm, lot of mouths agape here. 'You know the one . . . not the Frogs. Er, Lysistrata. That's it, Lysistrata. It was like that apparently.'

The room broke out in guffaws as my co-workers – each one of them with a degree, and a considerable number with two or three – barraged me with ridicule.

'The who what now?'

'Are you joking?'

'God, how random was that?'

In the corner of the room I saw Jane mugging at Audrey, using the universal expression for Pompous Blowhard, in an impression of what I can only assume was me.

It's been probably a good decade or two since I ran out of a room crying at having been roundly ridiculed by my peers. Thank you, office life, for making me feel twelve again.

samedi, le 24 septembre

This weekend: Come Anywhere but There theme weekend.

For reasons best explained by my GP, I am off the pills this month. And the Boy is paying the price. When I was a teenager, condoms were not so easy to get hold of – not like today where they hand them out to six-year-olds at lunchtime, or something. So I'm familiar with all the old tricks . . . examining mucus, the week-two anal, and so on. Because let's face it, no one really likes to have to use a condom if they don't have to.

'Stop,' I said, grabbing his shaft and pushing his insistent cock away from between my legs.

'Please, just a minute. I won't come.'

His glans was telling another story, sticky and shiny with pre-come. What are we, sixteen? I've heard that line before. I turned over and around quickly, and offered him my cleavage instead.

Next weekend: A blood test, the painters come in, and hopefully straight back on the pills.

Can't wait.

dimanche, le 25 septembre

Can't take it, really cannot. Absolutely unbearable &c. Am convinced if not actually physically ill, that there is at the very least a course of therapy in order.

It's that time of year. The time of major sporting events and reality shows, of the long, lonely run up to Christmas, when the women of the country are collectively oohing and ahhing over this or that sweet piece of totty recently brought to our attention – someone a bit ruffled and unsuitable – a Russell Brand, say, for the arty ladies; any of a hundred footballers for the rest of us. Cricketers and rugby men. An entire country of hot man-tarts just ripe for the fancying, in short.

Meanwhile I am plagued every night by a lack of fantasy material.

See, my boyfriend and I love Sunday night television. Until very recently, *Monarch of the Glen* was the guilty secret chez Belle. He'd provide the cider, I'd provide the Scotch pancakes, MotG would crank up the twee to suitably Sunday-night levels, and I'd coo and giggle and go all mumsy over cute, non-threatening men.

Then the show ended. We tried to find a replacement for it in our hearts (and schedules), but nothing fit. We've hurtled from this show to that – and a few back series of DVDs. And I must admit, *Lost* is absolutely infested with fit bodies. But not a one of them is wearing a kilt or stalking manfully through the Highlands. I have, quite simply, nothing to fantasise about.

So I've turned to that oldest of retreats. Skulking around the newsagent, hoping the shop empties by the time I go to the till, holding in my sweaty hands the shameful bounty. I'll laugh it off, try to hide it under a bag of crisps perhaps, and claim it's for my nonexistent teenage sister.

I'm talking about buying *Sugar*, of course.

It is disturbing and wrong. And makes me very nervous about what I might inadvertently yell out when me and the boyfriend are having sex.

vendredi, le 30 septembre

I may be on a shoe diet (and as of last week, an Unfeasibly Expensive Bracelet diet), but one thing will always claim its share of my budget regardless of finances, and that is books.

Unless running for a train I find it nigh on impossible to pass a bookshop without stopping in. Used (usually), new (why not) and, yes, I even browse the book aisle at Tesco. My library cards (for they are legion) are worn to a sliver and I always have a book or three on the go – usually too many, and going past too quickly, to remember to update here. It was with some surprise, and not a little heartbreak, that I learned the profession of literary editing – one which I had always admired, and still do – actually involves less reading for pleasure rather than more. I'll keep this as an avocation, I think.

So a few days ago I was in Oxfam books. I picked up Paul Auster's *The Invention of Solitude*. I've read most of his books, more by accident than by design, so wasn't terribly keen to take this one home. Long meditations on the notion of fatherhood are so not suitable for travelling. Or pre-bedtime reading. Or for flipping through in the loo. Or, in fact, for any activity short of planning your own slow, drawn-out, futile demise. But a stack of handwritten cards fell out as I was flipping through the slim volume. I stooped to pick them up off the shop floor and was amazed. Recipes! Yorkshire pudding. Scotch pancakes. Hotpot. Moules marinières. The hand was small and neat – a man's writing, I'd wager. Maybe amassing a small repertoire of culinary skill in order to impress a lady friend? Whatever it was, I hope it worked and that he wasn't in some kitchen now, frantic with the beef about to go in, wondering where he'd left those recipes. 'Cause I sure as hell wasn't handing them in to lost and found.

This is the Holy Grail of charity shopping: like finding the perfect handbag with a wad of twenties tucked inside, except of course without the nagging guilt that you really should have handed over your unexpected find in the name of charidee. At any rate, the pale scraggly chap at the till didn't look as if he cared for mussels anyway. I read the book on the train, put the cards away for another day, and am planning to get the Boy all wet and salty in the kitchen sometime tonight. He does love his mussels.

Top Tips for making the transition from sex work to 'the real world':

10 Brush up your CV. Add a month here and there to narrow any awkward gaps. If all else fails, claim an illness in the family.

9 Choose your wardrobe carefully. Dressing for the office is nothing like dressing for clients: it's far more casual than that. And if anyone asks about that killer suit, say M&S, not Dior.

8 Put away your best watch, at least for everyday. You never know what sort of riffraff you'll meet in the office.

7 Remember, you're among civilians now. Waxing regimes are no longer normal water-cooler conversation.

6 Even in the event of a Tube strike, resist the urge to take a taxi to work.

5 Eat in public, even if it's only half an apple at lunch. Office girls are vicious gossips and anyone shy of a size 22 risks being labelled anorexic.

4 When in doubt, bring the conversation back to *X Factor*.

3 You may be invited to colleagues' homes; coming with a bottle in hand is still considered good etiquette. But make it wine instead of lube.

2 If you must keep condoms in your desk . . . actually, just don't.

1 Be nice to your boss. But not that kind of nice, okay?

Octobre

samedi, le 01 octobre

It is a truth universally acknowledged that if you're going to have sex with three men at once, you have to get the angles right.

This all depends, naturally, on what arrangement of junk in holes you'll be going for. Some favour the exotic: double anal with oral. Me? I'm a modest, old-fashioned type – one cock in each orifice. Best to keep things simple really.

The vaginal comes first, woman on top. Thus arranged the anal can insert himself from behind. Careful – if both men are sizeable, and these ones are, it's all too easy for someone to get squeezed out here. Then, with the more complex pieces in place, you can have blowjob man slot in wherever it's convenient.

'Mm-mmm-m-mph.'

'Sorry?'

I cough. 'Careful, you three.'

'Oh. Okay.'

'Whoops.'

'Little carried away there . . .'

One other thing I forgot to mention: you can't have all of them thrusting away at once.

And the guys can't be afraid of a little sweat, nor the pong of other vital male bodies. I'm lucky to have found three such impressively fit men who are always up for it. We start again, more slowly this time.

Once the foursome gets going proper, it's only minutes

until blastoff. I come, every time without fail, and I come hard. The sensation is made all the more intense by being virtually unable to move, much less cry out.

Sated, my body sinks into the damp warm sheets. I reach out and caress my boyfriend's shoulder. He grunts, sighs, rolls over and resumes snoring. It's been weeks, maybe months, since he was interested in whether or not I masturbate in bed.

dimanche, le 02 octobre

'What's the difference between a hooker, a mistress and a wife?'

I sighed. Daddy's jokes have been geologically dated to at least the Cretaceous period.

'I don't know, what's the difference?'

'The hooker says "faster . . . faster . . .". The mistress says "slower . . . slower . . .". And the wife says "beige . . . I think I'll paint the ceiling beige . . ."'

'Very funny, Daddy.'

It wasn't at all, and it made me a little sad, because it's starting to come true.

When you and your sweetie started dating back when Tony Blair was still riding high in the opinion polls, it's inevitable that your sex life might have diminished in the meantime. In our case we've tried to keep up the bedroom acrobatics but while frequency is still acceptable, the heat has dissipated somewhat. Usually it's a quick slap and tickle, a poke at anal and a pearl necklace to finish before lights out. Still, no complaints from the Boy's end as yet, that I know of.

'Morning foxy,' a voice said from the door.

I looked up and grinned at Giles. 'How goes it, boss-man?'

He crashed into the seat opposite my desk. 'Not bad. Last month was a corker.'

'Work-wise, or . . . ?'

Giles has an eye for the ladies, and the more inappropriate the liaison, the better. In spite of that he always manages to pull longer and harder hours than any of us.

'Work, of course, you minx,' he smirked. 'Unless you're going to tell me you've shaken off that deadweight of a boyfriend and are going to meet me at the nearest available hotel for a champagne lunch?'

Oh, if only. Not for the first time I thanked the Internet Gods that my image was well and truly off the agency's site.

'Keep dreaming, gorgeous. So why the personal appearance this a.m.?'

'Can you run up the ex-regional stats for the last six weeks and give me a trend summary in PowerPoint slides?'

'I can do that. Unless you need them today.'

He dropped his jaw in false shock. 'Would I do such a thing to you? Would I ever? Oh no no no.' He idly picked at his fingernails, which I noticed had been looking rather manicured of late. 'Lunchtime if you please.'

'Do I have a choice?'

'You always have a choice, darling,' he said, scooping his long frame out of the chair and heading back for the door. 'Especially if you want my recommendation for that job. My way, the highway, and so on.'

I winked at him, and to my surprise, he blushed. 'Just this once then. But you owe me,' I said.

'Add it to the list,' he said.

'Hello, are you still there?' I was on the phone to A4 and the Boy was rubbing my feet. That's the deal: he gets his Scrapheap Challenge repeats from 2002; I get pampered. Only he's very easily distracted, and every time a hovercraft is mentioned, he loses concentration.

'Sorry, I . . . wow,' A4 said on the other end of the phone. 'It's a bit of a surprise. Ah, I mean, I always thought you'd be the last of any of us to . . .'

'Oh, me too,' I said as the Boy stared slack-jawed at a fat man welding a crank shaft to the larger portion of a rusted washing machine. 'But since the landlady's husband died, she's keen to sell up and has given me first refusal on her house.' As far as moves go, it wouldn't be too far: the land-lady's was all of thirty metres from the flat where I was sitting. 'The surveys are already done, so it's just a matter of paying up, really.'

'That's top news,' A4 said. 'Guess you'll have to start looking for a mortgage.'

'Um, yeah,' I said, cautiously. I'd managed to put rather a lot of money away when working as a call girl and could just about squeeze the price of the flat on savings alone. But I had been considering a small loan as well to carry out some much-needed interior updates. 'Wish me luck on that.'

'Good luck,' he said. 'And make this the last time you move for the year, yeah? I can hardly remember where you're staying as it is.'

'You mean, here in your old flat? Yeah, must be so con-fusing.'

mercredi, le 05 octobre

Morning commute arithmetic . . .

Bus caught in traffic
+
Go-Go's on the iPod
+
Tristram Shandy
=
Rock'n'roll!

jeudi, le 06 octobre

'You know what your problem is?' N said. We had dropped into his local for a swift half – he was meeting a hot date later, some supposedly gorgeous Irish athlete he kept going on about. I, of course wanted to get a look at the goods, even if would only be a vicarious thrill at best.

'No, but I'm certain you'll tell me.'

N smirked. 'Your problem is, everything's going your way, and you refuse to either believe it or enjoy it.'

'Oh, sorry, pot, kettle and black alert,' I said. 'Since when have you ever done anything but contemplate the empty half of the glass?'

'Fair dues,' N shrugged. 'But you really should step out of yourself sometime. Maybe I could come around and smack some sense into you?' He smiled in that sharky, sexy way that I never was able to resist – the smile that said, on the surface, I'm only joking with you, but you know I'm not really.

'Oh, the Boy would just love that,' I said.

'I bet he would. So how is he these days?'

'What, as if you care?'

'You're right, I don't.' N checked his watch and the door; no sign of his lady friend as yet. 'So, shall we have another?'

vendredi, le 07 octobre

'New face in the office,' Giles said, popping his head round the door. Only a moment later a second head popped round. 'This is Alex, she's our new intern for the next three months.'

'Hi,' I nodded, distracted. The bus this morning was caught in traffic and I was late to work; I was only just putting my bag down.

'Nice jacket,' Alex chirped, standing in the doorway. 'Is it a Vivienne Westwood?'

The jacket was a nice little wool and silk number I'd picked up because the odd cut of the sleeves meant it went just as well with jeans as it did with office wear. And, yes, it was a Vivienne Westwood and had cost more than I make in a week these days. 'What, this old thing?' I laughed. 'No, just some random piece I picked up in the sales last year.'

Alex tilted her head quizzically. 'Really? That's amazing, I could have sworn . . .'

'Love to stay and chat about clothes, girls, but you've the rest of the office to meet,' Giles said. 'Alex, I'd love you to talk to . . .' and with his hand in the small of her back, he guided her away from my door. I closed it behind me and exhaled loudly. Something about that girl smelled like trouble to me.

Despite being, on paper at least, the ideal-women's magazine consumer – I like knowing which nail polish comes highly recommended and tips on where to buy cute shoes and decent bras will never fall on deaf ears here – I cannot abide the things. This is because, apart from pictures of clothes and makeup reviews, the content is typically rubbish. And the models these days are so ludicrously young/skinny/airbrushed that they resemble nothing more than foetal telegraph poles with fish lips, which is not a good look to aspire to. So for the most part, I don't buy them (unless travelling or in a particularly self-punishing mood).

On the Internet, such things are harder to avoid. I can generally manage to steer myself past the pink-and-shiny section of WH Smith, but clicking through to a link is far too tempting sometimes. And then suddenly, without so much as a warning or preferably an 'All Hope Abandon Ye' splash page, you can find yourself smack in the middle of women's-magazine hell.

Take today: I clicked through to a quiz purporting to find out 'Are You a Babe in the Bedroom?' (I know, I know.) And was faced with the sorts of questions that were either written a) by a twelve-year-old, b) for a twelve-year-old or c) with the help of a specially designed Crap Generator.

Exhibit A:

In your bedroom, your optimum foot fashion is:

- Playful, fluffy slippers – perhaps with a stuffed animal head at the toe.
- Snuggly socks – or whatever socks I pull out of the drawer.

- Fitted, attractive slipper-socks, perhaps with faux-fur lining.
- My bare feet – with my toes between someone's lips.
- A fresh pedi in a sultry colour and toe rings.

I don't even know where to begin. Apart from the fact that uttering the word 'pedi' un-ironically should be a hanging offence. And since when do slipper socks come with 'faux-fur lining'? When Agent Provocateur started doing their Senior-Living range?

I mean, hello. Are we really meant to believe that someone who spends her time selecting toe rings is ipso facto a man-eater in the bedroom? That owning a faux-fur anything translates somehow to animal attraction? That buying 'flavoured body powder' is the cutting edge of sexual experimentation?

Hot fried Christ on a stick. If it were that easy, kids, we could all buy our way to sexual happiness (and, if the women's magazines had their way, a particularly cosmetically enhanced and satin-upholstered sort of sexual happiness complete with matching accessories). If perfectly painted and shiny things happen to float your boat, great – but good sex is precisely about what floats your boat. Not what someone else thinks should float it. Which, in some people's cases, might just be plain cotton socks.

What is really bothering me, of course, is that my answer would be B. What do I put on my feet in the bedroom? Whatever socks I pull out of the drawer. Why? Because sexy is a matter of what's in your head, not what's in your lingerie drawer. And because when I come in from a bracing walk with my sweetie, where we've been figuring out the best way to indulge in a quick anal session while avoiding the ubiquitous rambling fraternity, I want my tootsies to be warm, darling.

dimanche, le 09 octobre

The Boy wants a kitten.

'Kitten,' he says, whenever the conversation has died down, or we're in the car, or, in fact, anytime the thought crosses his mind: at last count, about once every two minutes. 'Kitten,' he says, and makes a face as if to say to me, why do you not love me? Why have you not provided me with kitten?

The reason is simple. If I wanted to provide cans of food and a toilet for something that otherwise contributed nowt to the running of a household, I'd adopt a teenager (my boyfriend also fulfils this spec in many ways). But the Boy, he loves cats. The mostly detached indifference of small female mammals entrances him – which probably goes a long way to explaining the durability of our relationship.

'Would you like me better if I got a kitten?' I ask. 'If I strapped it to myself, would you pay attention to me again?'

He ignored the question. 'Every home needs a kitten. Now that we have our own home . . .'

My face twisted into not quite a smile. Did he really say our home? Funny, I'd thought the lion's share of the purchase was coming from my account. As in, all of it. As far as the Boy's moving in was concerned, it seemed limited to a single carload of old comics and photos he'd stuck in the spare room. The rest was on hold until buying the new place was finalised. I was struggling to comprehend on what basis, exactly, this was now to be considered our home.

'. . . it needs a box of shit in it? I think not, somehow.'

'Just think', he said. 'If we had a kitten, we could take pictures of it. Then we could get broadband and put pictures of the kitten on the Internet.'

Like most people I have seen enough blog photos of

people's cats to last me the next few reincarnations. I also, in the interest of getting something done this year that is more worthwhile than reading email, am resisting signing up for broadband at home.

'Yes, because as everyone knows the Internet won't let you on without an offering of kittens and porn,' I said.

He nodded. 'I would go around saying "porn" at you over and over, but it's not as cute.' I laughed. Actually, to a girl like me, it would be.

mardi, le 11 octobre

Signs you're getting old, number 1: Before so much as packing a single box to move, you've already calculated the amount of packing tape required, purchased the appropriate number of blankets to cushion furniture, and prioritised the rooms of your current flat in terms of what should be moved first.

Signs you're getting old, corollary 1a: your boss takes one look at the dark circles under your eyes and asks if you've been up all night getting fucked silly. You're too ashamed to tell him otherwise.

jeudi, le 13 octobre

For the first time, the Boyfriend has invited me to a work do. He's been hinting broadly at a potential promotion in the works; thus, is eager to impress. When he told me about the event a few days ago, shyly, almost as an afterthought, I could tell what he was thinking: what will she do to embarrass me this time? Get drunk again? Dance on tables? Tell off the wife of someone important?

I'm a little nervous, not just because I'm more accustomed to working well in one-on-one (ahem) social interaction, but also because of the issue of competitive dressing.

(Boys, an update: women do not dress to please you. We dress to impress other women, or to please ourselves. If you want a girl to be turned out in something you specify, folding money or a holiday will probably be involved. Okay, now then . . .)

I scrutinised the invitation for clues. My man will be wearing a dark suit, but what does the vague statement 'evening attire' mean for the ladies? Sub-black tie is so complicated. Something smart but understated, the girl equivalent of a suit? A dress? A cocktail dress? I need something that says 'sexy' but not 'slutty' and definitely not 'ex-working-girl'. Additional sartorial subtext should include 'expensive' and 'back the fuck off, bitches, he's mine'. So I decided to vet my selection with the Boy first. Because the lad, in contrast to his rough-and-ready looks, is actually a frustrated artist.

'Hey, those are good,' he said, indicating the shoes. 'Are they new? I thought you were on a shoe diet.'

'These? I've had them ages.' I made a pact not to buy new shoes unless they were absolutely necessary, making my total shoe expenditure this year barely equal to a month's rent (one pair soft boots, one pair running trainers, one pair silver espadrilles). For me, that's progress.

'I've never seen them.'

They were pleated, red-satin Vuitton heels, with a tiny velvet bow. You know the ones I mean – two years ago, they were absolutely everywhere. Their success was based largely on the fact that they were all things to all people . . . i.e. fucking gorgeous.

Oops. These used to be work shoes. 'Ah. Well, you know what I'm like. They've never even been out of the box except when trying them on.'

Someone once said love is learning to bite your tongue at least six times a day. Thankfully, he did.

The rest of the outfit, in case you wondered, is a grey jersey dress, a charcoal velvet bolero, and an art deco diamond pin. Wish me luck!

vendredi, le 14 octobre

Executive summary: I didn't drink too much, didn't dance on tables, my dress kicked arse and I didn't tell my boyfriend's boss's wife where to stick it (largely as there is already such a large rod up her arse that finding spare room to insert anything else would be outside the boundaries of Newtonian physics).

We arrived at the Boy's works do to find the place already crowded. My grin fossilised on my face – the other invited guests largely ran to sprogged-up society housewives. While working as a call girl does give one a certain ability to talk to anyone about anything for an hour, my tolerance level on conversations about holidays and school fees is famously low. I told the Boy I was off to locate the G that was somewhat lacking in my G and T, and wandered off to find more sympathetic company.

Luckily, it's easy to find those people these days, as they are most often found outside with a fag. I don't indulge, but I've no quarrel with those who do, and have been known to find the act faintly sexy, especially now that it's about as transgressive as you can be without the law sticking you not just in jail, but under it. One giggly lady in hot pink sucking on a menthol as if it were her last meal turned out to be a football agent and we discovered we'd been at the same university at the same time. Small world. Laughing and gossiping, we went back in together.

It was so good to be able to unload to someone in that sterile room about putting up with our partners' strange hours, their constant stress, their work-related mood swings and especially the pathetic excuse for a salary they earn doing it. Unfortunately making allies is probably frowned upon in that particular corporate culture because it wasn't long before the boss's wife stalked over and looked on disapprovingly as we chattered away.

'You'll simply have to accustom yourself to being second best,' she said, looking for all the world like a woman who wears her martyrdom with the same casual ease as she wears her Liberty scarf. Her husband was the top of the food chain, making her, I expect, Alpha Wife.

Fuck that noise, I thought. I am second best to no one and especially not a woman whose idea of work is spending daddy's money. Plus her husband was exactly the sort of man I would have had as a client once upon a time. I smiled. My new friend the football agent piped up that she had always counted on being the breadwinner in the family, not her husband.

'Well, you're a very selfish woman,' Alpha Wife said, and turned sharply.

The football agent turned to me as we both pulled faces. What on earth was that about? If it didn't mean the end of my boyfriend's career, I would have been tempted to tell Alpha Wife what I used to do. There aren't, after all, many times when you get to say 'I once shat on a man's chest for money' in polite society.

I walked in to the bedroom. The Boy was standing over an open suitcase, considering two shirts.

'Plotting your escape already?'

'Ha, no,' he said, coming over to plant a kiss on my forehead. 'I'd never run away without at least leaving a note.'

I smiled. 'Business trip this week?'

'Er, sort of . . .'

'Sort of?' I was growing used to the last-minute trips with little explanation, and meeting other people he worked with at least helped put a few faces to the names I'd been hearing on various late-night phone calls from hotels all over the north. Still, it was one of the things I liked least about the Boy's job. What's the point of living with someone if they're always away?

The Boy sat on the bed and patted the duvet next to him. 'Um, no thanks, I'd rather stand,' I said, suddenly suspicious. 'What's going on?'

'Please, don't make this hard for me . . .'

'Make what hard? If there's something you need to tell me, surely it would be easier to just get it over with.'

'You're not going to be happy about this,' he frowned.

'Whatever it is just tell me already.'

'Um, starting next week I'm based in Birmingham.'

'Pardon?'

'You know, in the West Midlands, second largest city in the—'

'Yeah, yeah, I know what Birmingham is, I'm not stupid. Now what's this about being based there?'

'It's for work,' he said. 'Of course it's too far to commute, but I'll be home on the weekends—'

'Wait. You're going to be working in another city for five days of the week?'

He shrugged weakly. 'I took you to my work do because I thought maybe you'd make friends with some of the women there, have someone to talk to . . .'

I barked a laugh. I don't do female friends, not in the sense everyone else seems to. There's L, we were at school together, and she is a queen among womankind. There are a few allies in the office, but no one ever considers those to be real friends anyway. Otherwise women to me are either potential rivals or potential lays. 'How long have you known about this?'

'About three weeks,' he admitted.

'You knew and didn't tell me for almost a month? What the fuck?' I turned and bit my knuckle. Down, girl, be reasonable. This happens to lots of couples. Yes, but not lots of couples where you've only just started not sleeping with other people in the last year. Deep breath. Deep breath. You know his ex, Susie, she works only over in . . . Shut up, stupid. Go make a cup of tea. It'll be okay.

'Where are you going?'

'I'm going to join a shooting party in the Cairngorms,' I said. 'Where the fuck do you think? I'm going to go pour myself a drink. And then I'm going to have a bath. And then, if you're very, very lucky, I'm going to consider whether or not to ever speak to you again.'

lundi, le 17 octobre

Night number one of the new arrangement was mostly spent on the sofa, ignoring the Boy's phone calls and watching crap repeats on television. When I finally answered I said

I'd been so busy packing boxes I must not have heard the phone.

mardi, le 18 octobre

N phoned me at work. 'Have you seen that recent heart disease ad campaign?'

'The one with the girl drinking five litres of cooking oil?'

'That's the one. Is that just straight-up water sports or what?'

'Not to mention the girl is, like, twelve.'

'Reminds me of the advert for video phones last year."

'You mean the snow bukkake one? That was priceless! Hey, I have to go. Talk to you later, bye.' Hmm, seems unusually quiet in here.

Sometimes I forget when my office door is open. Oops.

jeudi, le 20 octobre

There is very little in life, the kitchen or indeed the bedroom that could not be improved with the liberal application of chocolate sauce from a squeezy bottle. Many an awkward occasion has been eased by the use of such. I believe it was Jerry Hall who famously said that men want a whore in the bedroom and chocolate sauce in the kitchen. She wasn't wrong. She was so, so right. Chocolate sauce has the power. In fact, I believe the solution to the Middle East Crisis may well be chocolate. And saucy.

Just so we're clear on this point – it does very little good to your washing machine. Note to self – wake up fully before tackling household chores.

So, the big day. The Boy is packing up the rest of his things at his old flat and putting them into temporary storage in advance of my move. So obviously I've decamped to York-shire for the duration.

Five things I miss about home when I'm not there:

The garden. It's not a huge garden; it won't win any prizes. But it's just the same as I remember it – a gloriously tranquil place to sit and read and watch the sun tracking across the sky.

The food. Sorry, not the food – The Food. Bagels. Knedlicky. Pierogi. Yeah, I love my carbs, and I have the bum to prove it.

The knowledge. Of where everything is, who everyone is, when everything is happening, what it was all like twenty years (or more) ago.

The birdsong. Only in the past few years has it become apparent to me what vast swathes of Britain are largely free of the twitters and chirps at home. I blame the fact that there are something like 2.3 cats for every woman in London.

The tumble dryer.

Five things I miss when I'm at home:

A lie-in. You'd think of all the places in the world, this is the one where you could truly shrug off all worries and sleep till noon as if you were a teenager. No such luck, especially with my mother up and crashing about from 5 a.m. If I want an undisturbed rest, I have to go to A4's mum's house – that's just sad.

The radio. It's telly or CDs at home, always, always, always.

My own cooking. My mum is a great cook. Her mum is a great cook. They've been practising for, like, decades. My cooking is merely okay, but hasn't it occurred to them that if I don't get a chance, I'll never improve?

The Advice Buffer. I don't need on-tap advice from my mother at a moment's notice. I like a little breathing space, and this far into buying a house, her opinion that the conveyancing is costing too much is Really Not Helpful.

Having private phone conversations (see above).

dimanche, le 23 octobre

I still don't know how to feel about the Boy's new work arrangement. On the one hand, we will be seeing each other on the weekends, so I won't completely dry up; on the other, what happens if I'm horny on a Wednesday? Yes, yes, masturbation and all that; but after far too much experience of long-distance relationships I can testify that sometimes nothing but cock will do.

mardi, le 25 octobre

Five things I have, but don't want:

Three spare beds. Don't ask.

Every note and handout and book from my degree, ever. It's not as if I look at them or anything, nor are they remotely relevant to what I do now. It's just that they might be, someday.

An entire cupboard filled with vacuum-packed and freeze-dried food (plus water purification tablets and stormproof matches). For camping. Or the war. Or that millennium-bug nonsense. Or an imminent zombie attack. Oh, who knows why any more.

A gmail account. I am slightly suspicious of Google; also, cannot be bothered to transfer contacts, etc.

The ability to detect aspartame at homeopathic-level concentrations. I don't care if you put vanilla, lime and a whole goddamn fruiterer in diet soda. It still tastes crap to me, though this doesn't mean I won't drink it.

Five things I want, but don't have:

A storage space devoted to spare duvets, pillows, sheets and so forth (see above, re: spare beds. Note to self, could poss put where camping rubbish lives now?)

A sensible system for organising makeup and various jars of girlystuff that is space-efficient, easy to dust, will fit on a smallish shelf and is both not pink and not made of f*!&ing seagrass.

More time in the morning, without the trouble of actually having to get up earlier. Half seven! That is the absolute limit and I will go no lower!

Someone who can turn my sale-bought fabrics into Roman blinds.

The ability to fly.

Five things I don't have and don't want:

A husband. Lucky I don't want one, as current arrangements make it an unlikely outcome of my current relationship anyway.

Fine china, though I did buy a set of crystal champagne flutes. They have never been used and currently reside in a box under the kitchen sink, next to the bleach.

A family member who is also my best friend. Don't get me wrong, I love my mum to bits, but how yucky?

A signature scent (unless you count 'mildly sweaty').

A kitten.

jeudi, le 27 octobre

The solicitor rang just before I left work. The contracts have come through and everything is tickety-boo. I should have been rushing home to pop open a bottle of champers and break out those never-used crystal flutes so we could have a celebratory drink amongst the cardboard boxes; instead, I'll be returning to a flat that feels just as empty as it looks.

'Hey, well done,' the Boy said distractedly. 'Listen, can I ring you back later? Some of us are going out for a bite to eat. Oh, there's the door, bye.' And he clicked off, just like that.

I rang my mum but no answer – probably out on a date; I couldn't bring myself to ring Dad. So I did what any reasonable girl would do: exchanged dirty texts with N late into the night. Happy Birthday to me.

vendredi, le 28 octobre

I went to see an ex-client at his place of work.

Terribly indiscreet, no doubt, under normal circumstances; but this ex-client is an author. I wasn't meeting him for an appointment – we were going to a book signing.

The Boy loves this writer, he's well into his crime fiction – the more hard boiled the better. I hadn't mentioned that I'd met the author before; it would be rubbing it in, wouldn't it? A certain amount of having a successful relationship while still a call girl, I think, is resolving to never, ever mention it. Or money. Or sex with other people. Or the drawers full of underwear he's never seen you wear. Or dropping a thousand quid on a handbag. Anyway . . .

It was at a hotel, not far from Piccadilly. The room was high-ceilinged, brightly lit. There were hardly any seats left and we'd missed the first few minutes, having turned up to the wrong place. After his brief talk and question-and-answer session, a book-signing queue formed.

'Hey, I'll get one for us,' I said to the Boy.

'Really?'

'Absolutely.' Another thing, pay for random things your boyfriend would ordinarily buy himself anyway. But small things, not too much – you don't want to start an argument.

At the front of the queue, head bowed over the open pages of my copy, the author asked to whom I would like the book signed. He hadn't seen me yet – this was probably, for him, the very last of a long line of fans, on what was the middle of a no-doubt gruelling book tour. Enforced eye contact probably has a way of making you blind. And if I must say so, I probably looked rather different than the last time we met.

It was a couple of years ago, in a London hotel. It was the

last time he was on a book tour, or possibly the time before that. I turned up having had very little notice for the appointment, and with a cold and, although he had given his real and full name when booking, it hadn't clicked that he and I shared any interests beyond my having sex with him and his paying me. I sniffled through the first half hour of the appointment – the Lemsip had yet to kick in – and turned down the offer of a drink.

'Do you like jokes?' I asked, stealing away to the toilet for a tissue.

'I do.'

'What do you call a whore with a runny nose?' I asked through the open door.

'I don't know,' he said. I came back to the bed, clothed only in knickers, stockings and suspenders. 'What do you call a whore with a runny nose?'

'Full.'

Now, some two years later, his fair head bent with fatigue, I could not help but smile. He had been a nice client, slightly more interesting than the usual – a pleasant memory of my previous life. 'To whom do I sign this?'

I said my working name. He looked up. Please, let him at least recognise me.

His eyebrows arched in mild surprise, but not shock. He smiled and asked how I was.

'Doing well,' I said. 'Still in London. New job.'

He smiled indulgently. Oh, they must get this all the time. Wide-eyed fans who pretend to have more of a connection with his life than they're entitled to. But they make conversation anyway. It was an offhand gesture of meaningless politesse of the sort that is the bread and butter of being a successful call girl.

He started to sign the book. 'Oh, sorry, I mean, sign it to my boyfriend.' He smiled and nodded. I was the last in the queue. As he ambled towards the hotel bar I watched his walk, tried to glean something from the way he moved. Was he going back to another call girl in his hotel room, I wondered? Or maybe just a drink and an early night? I grabbed the Boy and we headed out. He was dead pleased with the signed book. Though on the way home, I did wonder if we should maybe have offered to buy the author a drink.

lundi, le 31 octobre

'How do you feel?'

'What do you mean, how do I feel?'

'Do you feel any differently? Does it make you feel like a real grown-up? Should I come round and take a picture while you do it?'

'No, it's not different at all, really. A little anti-climactic. I mean, I've only moved next door.'

'That's why you're standing outside your new house in the cold for half an hour phoning me?' A2 said.

He had a point there. 'Yeah, you're right. It's like the big swinging dick of adulthood.'

'Great. Now get in there.'

Ten things that make a house a home:

1 Christening every room. You may think you know what I mean, but a room isn't properly initiated until the woman has come there as well. Quickies don't count.
2 Curtains. Seriously, consider doing this before following the last piece of advice.
3 A good, serious, oh-shit-I'd-better-ring-my-dad DIY crisis that you suddenly realise, for the first time, can't be solved with a simpering phone call to the landlord.
4 A good, serious, oh-shit-I'd-better-ring-my-mother argument.
5 Him Indoors finally figuring out where you store the tea-spoons rather than leaving them piled up in the drying rack. Her Indoors finally figuring out where he keeps all his porn, and nicking it for herself.
6 Your first home-cooked meal, shared at the dining table, with candlelight and fine wine and rarefied conversation. Failing that, a Chinese takeaway and bottle of cider in front of the telly while watching Match of the Day.
7 A general sense of unease and underlying panic at all times brought on by even the most fleeting thought of the housing market.
8 Careful consideration whether the spare bedroom would work better as a dungeon or a guest room, and whether they could somehow logically be combined.
9 His n' hers comfy chairs in the front room.
10 Inviting the neighbours round for a cup of tea and friendly chat, knowing full well they heard you going at it through the adjoining wall just that morning.

Novembre

mardi, le 01 novembre

'You think you're so clever, and classless, and free,' he says.

'You think I don't know the song you're quoting?'

He barks a laugh, and pats my right hand with his paw. His hands are browner – both parents are more olive than me, startlingly so, though if Mum's anything like me I'm probably the milkman's. But my hand, though fairer, is a tiny copy of Dad's, so I know that's not so. We're driving from the rail station to our house. I mean my mother's.

'I'm surprised you remember that,' he says.

'Remember? I have entire brain lobes dedicated to the complete post-Beatles outputs of John Lennon and George Harrison, and not by choice.' There's no need to be able to read minds when I can see what he's thinking on his face. How has his daughter ended up where she is, the one with so much potential, neither on top of the world nor tearing it down, a cog in the middle-class machine?

I wish I could tell him. What my life was really like, back when they were breaking up, when I was telling bald lies about looking for work in London and living on the knife edge of poverty. Would they understand? Would he? That it's not all about the sex – never has been – it's about the heart of darkness.

And yet, what would I gain by telling them? Nothing that can go in the brag book next to my university-graduation photos (black gown, wan smile, my thoughts: this is the last time I ever do something for the sole purpose of pleasing my family) or my sister L's swimming certificates (blue swimming costume, loads of medals and she's never stopped being a people pleaser). Nothing that would see our family name preceding an -ism. Nothing they would see as real genius, revolution or success. This is what it's like to be born to a generation who imagined they were changing the world – you live up to neither their hopes nor fears.

So as far as anyone is concerned, I'm just up for the night to show Mum some pictures of the new house, have a late birthday dinner at home, and stay up complaining about my boyfriend and job before going to bed in my old room and getting the first train back in the morning. As far as anyone is concerned, I'm another face in another crowd. Even as far as my family are concerned.

'Is that the turn? I almost forget where it is now,' Dad says.

'Have to draw you a map next time.' I smile, and keep the secret of his lie.

He nods. Whatever's going on in his life since the divorce, I don't know about it. He doesn't even switch off the engine this time when he pauses by the kerb to let me out. If he's happy or not, I don't . . . whatever. Dad kisses my cheek and, very briefly, we smile before I shut the car door and go inside.

Here I am, what am I supposed to do?

mercredi, le 02 novembre

Some days resemble films. The new intern, Alex, has been having a *Dude, Where's My Car?*-sort of day, while the fellow whose desk is diagonal from mine will soon be finding out all about *Coming to America*. For me, though, today was definitely *The Good, the Bad and the Ugly*:

The Good: 'You have a very nice arse . . .' Oh, cheers Giles.

The Bad: 'Care to re-enact the opening scene of *Lost in Translation*?' Eek! Noooooo!

The Ugly: Losing a day's work because I was so spaced out by the music I was listening to, I inadvertently closed all my windows without saving. Note to self: no more Sun Ra at work.

jeudi, le 03 novembre

Sigh. My boys love me, they do. And do they ever know what sets my tiny heart a-racing. The last two of my birthday gifts have finally come through: from A2, a gift voucher for Figleaves; from A4, a subscription to the *London Review of Books*.

vendredi, le 04 novembre

'God, it's good to be home,' the Boy said, curling his arms around me from behind.

I smiled and pressed into him. He seemed more tired than usual; he said it had been a long week. 'I'm glad you're here,' I murmured.

'Yes . . . always good to do the things you can't do during the week . . .'

I pressed against him harder. 'At least you'd have a lie-in tomorrow if we stay up all night tonight . . .'

But it was too late, he was already asleep.

samedi, le 05 novembre

You know what no one ever mentions about buying a house? That you won't just be picking out curtains, you'll be spending your much-valued Saturdays with the boyfriend picking out curtain rails, the hardware needed to attach said rails to the wall, the 24V cordless-hammer drill needed to make said hardware functional and that buying a drill will take longer (if such a thing were possible) than picking out a curtain fabric that does not make your boyfriend involuntarily grimace.

You know what else no one ever mentions? That you won't be breaking in each room by having dirty sex on your OMG-I-can't-believe-I-own-this floor just yet, because there are boxes everywhere and, in case you forgot, you have no curtains.

On the bright side, now you can ask me anything about masonry drill bits. Anything.

dimanche, le 06 novembre

Ooh, some days the entire world annoys me. You know, like when you get a skinny heel caught in a crack in the pavement and it snaps off? Then you turn up at the shops to find that Really Normal Things (such as washing powder and mozzarella) are sold out? And then you miss the last bus not by minutes, not by seconds, but by nanoseconds?

Yes. One of those days.

Only, my shoes are fine, being the thick heels so of this season. And the shops seem to be stocked with all the usual things I buy. And I made the bus with time to spare and, even better, it was nearly empty. Found the umbrella I thought I'd lost. Under normal circumstances, I would chalk it up to time-of-the-monthiness, but for goodness' sake, a) I'm practically thirty now, do I really have to refer to my bodily functions using giggly euphemisms? b) apart from the day or two a year/month/week I want to rip my boyfriend's head off, I don't really believe in that hormonal garbage, and c) I generally try to treat my cycle the way it ought to be treated, i.e. with as little anticipation and fuss as possible, just whip out the appropriate product, slap it on, and done. There. Like my mum with a plaster when I skinned my knees. Now stop crying, you silly girl.

Still, for whatever reason, I'm feeling right tetchy.

Exhibit A, I walked into a young man on the pavement because a) he was the end-person of one of these four-abreast-on-the-pavement monstrosities that comes only of children who were driven everywhere in their short lives, therefore never understanding the notion of Giving Way and b) there was a puddle and I am a lady after all, so I go to the far side. End of story. Also, I called him a twat as he walked away after refusing to acknowledge me, also because I am a lady.

Exhibit B, I snapped at my boss (I did feel bad about it after – he's only little).

Ugh. Gr. Must source some chocolate.

mardi, le 08 novembre

Things currently weighing on my mind:

1 I am ever so tired of over-inflation in speech. Shuffling between home and work (both in the dark) is not a 'great day'. Being paid in the mid-thirties, while the less clever but business-minded of your year at uni pull down

salaries larger than the entire value of your profession's pension fund is not 'well-paid'. Sitting at your desk fifteen minutes before I arrive in the morning does not make you a 'hard worker'.

2 If after five years a man doesn't know when your time of the month is imminent, it may be time for him to reassess any claims re: being a very sensitive and sympathetic sort of person.

3 Nine months of slogging through more long-distance relationship purgatory is not 'soon'.

mercredi, le 09 novembre

He, on the phone from a hotel: 'Have you read the stack of 2000ADs in the bathroom?'

Me, picking at the remains of my last pedicure, circa 1066: 'Not really, just flipped through.'

'I think you should read this Judge Dredd, it's really good.'

'Wow. Funny how you pick out the one about prostitutes for my perusal. Cheers.'

'This is so symbolic of how we see things differently. I thought you'd like it because it's a very adult, self-contained story.'

'It's about murdered hookers.'

'It's also about how Judge Dredd has depth of character and how he's sympathetic to the woman at the end.'

'What, he only gives her six months imprisonment? You call that sympathy?'

'For Dredd it is.'

jeudi, le 10 novembre

Drawbacks of the Mainstream Workplace Number 1:

Admin assistants (these were once called secretaries) who sneer when I ask for help submitting expenses on our new-fangled, online system. Correct me if I'm wrong but, back when they were secretaries, wasn't this their job?

Also, they have truly shiteous taste in clothing. Don't hate me because I'm working the fiercest cashmere this side of the Himalayas.

vendredi, le 11 novembre

Surprisingly therapeutic things to do when you can't sleep:

- Count sheep
- Make plans for the next day
- Scrub the bath
- Stab a needle through each condom in the pack you found in your boyfriend's briefcase
- Ring his phone every ten minutes until one a.m. with no answer before deciding that maybe a Valium or three is a better idea
- Listen to music. Preferably Will Oldham, Leonard Cohen, Elliott Smith . . . you know, something cheery.

samedi, le 12 novembre

'Run that past me again?'
   'It's not just that it's her wedding, it's that . . . I promised I would give her away.'

The mind boggles. So he's not only met secretly with his ex while he's been in Birmingham, but they've been planning her wedding? It all started when he left his phone on the kitchen table. There was a missed call, and I didn't particularly want to look – that's just not a road I care to go down anymore – only it was ringing over and over. I picked it up, and saw the name on the screen: Susie

The ex. Or rather, the woman who officially would have been his ex, if he hadn't been dating me at the time he was screwing around with her. When he came back downstairs I was waiting for him. 'Explain this, please?' I said. He stammered and evaded, but there were no legs in it. I had him, and he knew it. What I wasn't expecting was the wedding twist.

'So when is this shindig, then?' I asked. 'I'll need a new frock, of course.'

'It's next weekend,' he frowned. 'Umm . . .'

'No, I know I'm not invited.'

'Please don't be mad at me.'

'Oh, it's far too late for that. I'm beyond angry now. I'm actually past core meltdown and into year three of nuclear winter. Wait a while – the neighbours will start having children with two heads.'

'She doesn't have anyone else,' he said. 'Her father died when she—'

I put a hand up. 'You know what? I don't care. I don't care if she single-handedly saved sixteen soldiers from a firestorm in Iraq, lost both legs in the process, and has no one to carry her up to the Queen when they award her the fucking Victoria Cross. I know you're going to do whatever it is you want to do, as usual.'

'I don't, you know I—'

'Oh, stuff it. So who's the chump who gets to watch as the man who used to fuck her delivers her up the aisle to him?'

'Stop it, you're being nasty now. As it happens he is actually very nice.'

'Spare me the etiquette lesson,' I spat. If there is one thing that has always driven me over the edge regarding the Boy, it's his insistence that his mode of passive-aggressive politesse is somehow a more acceptable approach to conflict than mine is. He can be as much of a bastard as he likes, but in his mind, so long as no one says any rude words, no harm and no foul. What I can never believe is that he doesn't see how infuriating this is. But I was beyond caring. 'You're god-damned right I'm being nasty. You screwed around with this woman for two years and your entire family knew. Two years! You fucked her without a condom, you told her you were going to marry her and now you're pimping her out to some idiot who thinks you're some sort of daddy stand-in for her?'

'I can't talk to you when you're like this,' he said and crossed his arms.

'You mean, exactly as angry as any other woman in the world would be?' I said. 'Tell you what: you, the sofa. It's my fucking house and you're not welcome in my fucking bed.'

dimanche, le 13 novembre

I cave; I always cave. He did what he does – goes in to my room in the wee small hours and slides in. I put a hand on his back, between his shoulder blades, lightly. I promise myself – as I have done a thousand such times in the past and will probably continue to do indefinitely – that if he says nothing before I take my hand away, if he makes no move, loving or otherwise, that it will be the last time I ever touch him. Ever. I know that as we lie on the bed in the early hours of morning, still as tombs, sitting out the last few hours we have together, we are both thinking and doing the same thing: wanting to not be the person who breaks first. Wanting to not be the one who admits defeat.

After almost six years, this is a ridiculous way to carry on. But I put a hand on his back, and I make myself empty promises.

lundi, le 14 novembre

Drawbacks of the Mainstream Workplace Number 2:

When working as a call girl, I prided myself on a certain ability – shall we call it talent? – being able to suss out what a client wanted even with minimal hints. From the way some of the men reacted, you would have thought it was white magic. They were terribly impressed.

They needn't have been. It was sex. They were men. It's not hard to make someone hard.

Alas, it is only recently that I have started learning this impression of men as bears of very little complication is not entirely accurate. Unfortunately, this also coincides with an occupation in which my boss expects me to read his mind.

Like, when he sent me a month's worth of work. Today. And it needed doing two weeks ago. By someone whose qualifications are entirely different to my own. So, what does he expect me to do? Build a Tardis, go back in time, and do the work then?

Left wanting for answers, I did what my career in the sex trade trained me oh so well for: I went to his office, mildly verbally abused him, and he quickly agreed to do it himself. Result.

mardi, le 15 novembre

Was waiting at a bar in South Ken with a G&T. Sent a text to L:

Where are you? Bxx

Ten minutes passed, then fifteen. The phone finally beeped.

Hi there. Think your msg may have been aimed at somebody else. How's the new job and house? All well here. baby & husband gr8. I go back to work 2moro. Xx

Eep. I'd sent the text not to school friend L, she of the Gillian Anderson looks and Stephen Hawking mind, but to my sister L.

Ha! Sorry about that. New house okay, still unpacked. Back at work already? That was fast! How's tricks?

(It's worth mentioning that I'm older, she's younger, and we were last close circa season 2 of *Friends*.)

Lol. Don't ask. Wish I could wrk pt time 4 full pay so I could play w/ baby more. How's ur love life?

My boyfriend has always been a subject of much mirth to L. I've always suspected her of secretly fancying him, but no mind.

Oh, you know, the usual! Now he's talking about getting a kitten, and we know what that means, yikes.

I hate putting on girly talk, but L has always trumped me in the femininity stakes: accomplished, modest, cute. I bet I give a better blowjob, though.

Shit. That's nearly as serious as reproducing. If he starts wanting to take trips 2 Ikea, u should start 2 panic a bit :)

Uh-oh. We. Did. That. Last. Week.

In my defence, I absolutely hated shopping at Ikea. It's like being trapped in . . . well, it's like being trapped in Ikea. There is no analogous experience. Trapped with a manic, doughnut-eating boyfriend who thinks that arguing over curtains is the best way to spend time ever.

I'll start checking for your names on Selfridge's gift registry then. Would you prefer linens or glassware? hehe

Sigh.

mercredi, le 16 novembre

'You know Alex, I think you would benefit from shadowing me for the rest of the week.'

Uh-oh. Voices outside my office. Specifically, Giles and our new intern with bedroom eyes and a piercingly irritating giggle.

'Really?' Alex trilled. 'Wow! I'm soooo grateful . . .'

I got up and pointedly closed my office door. If there's one thing I can't abide, it's women who are blatantly walking into a bad situation. Still, she was young, and it was in no way my place to tell her. Largely because if experience proved correct, it wouldn't stop it happening anyway.

jeudi, le 17 novembre

1 gig with A3 – because that went so well the last time. Ended up sleeping in his spare room. Still irritated with the Boy so left my phone off all night. Let him fucking wonder.

5 minutes standing in Milroy's of Soho before realising the portly chap in the back did not care whether I was buying anything or not. So I didn't buy anything.

10 minutes standing in Harmony before realising I own that particular stainless steel buttplug already, the one that is a

sort of a large bullet on a stick – kind of looks like a toilet plunger. So I didn't buy anything.

1 impromptu lunch on Old Compton Street because the café name was identical to my working name as a call girl. Yes, now that you ask, I was called Wok N Roll.

4 batches of truffles delivered to friends and associates – made using the recipe below.

1 discussion of how awesome truffles are with C (who makes super-batches and freezes them!)

1 awkward moment when going the GP to talk about girly things only to find the new partner is someone I know from uni. May be time to register with a new practice . . .

Rum truffles

This is the recipe that makes it look as if I can actually cook. In reality, it's dead easy, but never fails to impress. Perfect for the girl who keeps little more than chocolate and hard liquor to hand at all times.

Ingredients:

150g (5 oz) dark chocolate
2 tablespoons dark rum
150ml (¼ pint) double cream
24g (1 oz) butter
The peel from 1 orange
2 whole cloves

2 teaspoons of ground cinnamon
1 tablespoon of plain flour

1 tablespoon of cocoa powder
toasted chopped nuts (optional)

Break up the chocolate and melt in a saucepan over very low heat along with the cream, butter and cloves. The lower the heat the better – if the mixture goes grainy, you've had it on too high. Chocolate starts to melt at body temperature so doesn't need much heat . . . I'll wait here while you test that fact on the nearest available man.

Ready? Good. Next step.

Grate the orange peel directly into the saucepan and add a squeeze of juice if you like. After a few minutes, stir in the rum and add 1 teaspoon of cinnamon.

Keep stirring for about three minutes, then pick out the cloves, transfer the mixture to a bowl and place this in the fridge overnight. I'd say an hour but I've usually opened a bottle of wine by this point and often forget to check how it's going. Eight hours won't kill it.

The next day, dust a wooden board with the flour, and sprinkle some cocoa powder and cinnamon over it. If you're using toasted nuts, keep them on a plate nearby.

Roll heaped teaspoons of the chilled truffle mixture into small balls with your hands. Roll these in the flour/cocoa/cinnamon mixture (and then in nuts if you like) and plop into petit-four cases.

Chill until ready to serve. Or, eat them now!

The night of Susie's wedding. My phone is still off; no way he'd ring anyway.

'Jesus, you act like this is the worst thing in the world,' A2 said to me over cocktails. I shrugged. I knew what he was implying: A1 had been married only a couple of years ago and I was in his wedding as a groomsman. The only woman invited to the stag do. And I didn't take my boyfriend to that.

'That's different; I never hid what was going on.' Also, A1 and I haven't had sex at any point in the last ten years at least. That definitely qualifies someone for Proper Friend status in anyone's book.

'He's not going to get off with her at the wedding,' A2 said. 'Shit, he's probably staying in some crappy B&B tonight, drunk and passing out in his dinner jacket, wondering why you're not answering the phone.'

'You think?'

A2 shrugged. 'If it were me, yeah. I'd be sneaking out of the reception right now, leaving drunk messages on your answerphone, getting all soppy about weddings and couples.'

'Really? How come you never did when we were together?'

'Eh, that was a long time ago. You stop eyeing up the bridesmaids after about age twenty-five, and start getting all weepy like a woman. Biological fact.'

'That men are more broody than women, when it comes down to it?'

'No, that after twenty-five you can't pull the bridesmaids anymore.'

I smacked him in the shoulder, hard. 'Cunt.' But we were both smiling.

samedi, le 19 novembre

I love my family, and I wish them well in all endeavours. Even after the divorce, I still wanted my parents to move on, do good things and be happy. I believe in the sanctity of family – that no matter what happens, nothing can make you stop loving them (not, hopefully they you, though as yet I've not fully tested the theory).

Meeting the Jason Lee-alike toy-boy Mum is currently schtupping, well, challenging these beliefs.

dimanche, le 20 novembre

There was only one thing I wanted for my birthday. I'll give you a hint: they come in pairs, they go on your feet, and they're the last word in glamour in some circles.

You got it: wellies. Now that I'm a fully paid-up member of the garden-pottering elite, or theoretically could be some-day, I have a need to accessorise and in this case that means wellies. Preferably those nifty pink, breast-cancer-charidee Hunter ones, but actually, any cute pair would have done.

I like a gift that satisfies the girly instinct while still being practical (and no, an ironing board does not qualify). So I ooh-ed and ahh-ed over the wellies in the shops, tried a pair on when he went shopping for his own, mentioned how it would be Really Useful to own a pair instead of stomping around the muddy garden in old trainers. I mentioned the wellies in conversation to him and to assorted mutual friends and acquaintances, in case he thought to ask any of them what I might want.

All things considered it should have been fairly obvious that what I wanted for my birthday was a pair of wellies.

What did I get on the day? A half-eaten bar of white chocolate (I hate white chocolate) that came from a skiing trip he took last year (I hate skiing) in the Alps (I fucking hate the Alps). But I was good, I didn't complain, I just stuck it with the rest of the rubbish at the kerb the next Monday. He's never actually bought me anything that wasn't something he wanted himself. At times, this works out fine (i.e. lingerie); at others, not so much (i.e. Grand Theft Auto San Andreas). The Boy doesn't quite understand how gifts work; that's part of his charm.

He came back the morning after Susie's wedding looking sheepish. I was on the sofa and his hands were behind his back, holding what looked like it might be a wellies-sized box. 'I've got you a late birthday gift . . .' he said, smiling shyly.

'Oh, honey, you shouldn't have!' I sat up eagerly. Finally, he'd seen sense, and was coming to me, hat in hand, with a peace offering! Perhaps an old dog might learn new tricks after all.

But really, when I said he shouldn't have, that turned out to be the truth. There were no wellies. I started to get suspicious when I noticed the box had air holes and was mewling loudly.

The Boy got me a bloody kitten.

lundi, le 21 novembre

'It's mewling again,' I groaned, lifting my head from the pillow. Ah, crap, forgot I was alone in the house. I got up and opened the bedroom door. The kitten squirmed under the duvet in the warm spot lately vacated by me.

'Well, at least someone's jumping to get into bed with me.'

mardi, le 22 novembre

Giles, bless his cotton socks, has recently suggested that I go to a conference for the sole reason of spying on a competitor's product 'in purdah'. Which Is Not Getting It on so many levels, I can only smile.

mercredi, le 23 novembre

'So I take it your mum's still single then?' N said, sipping his pint.

I grimaced. 'Stop that, you know it gives me goose pimples. And even if she was looking, you're far too young for her.'

'Like Mae West said, you're only as old as the man you feel.' He cackled evilly.

'Seriously, stop it. What if I wanted to date your mother? Wouldn't that make you uncomfortable to even joke about it?'

'Oh, you're never her type. She's more a butch-lesbian fancier.'

jeudi, le 24 novembre

So, the cat. How's that working out? Fine, as it allows me to make not-very-nice jokes about my boyfriend's attachment to pussy. And (so far) the new cat lit seems to be living up to its 'Controls Odours' guarantee. [Note to self: A1 and his wife have an automatic cat lit tray that sweeps itself clean after a cat has finished and seals any waste in a tiny plastic bag. Poss not so great for the old carbon footprint but neither is burning a hundred candles to get rid of the stink.]

And as the Boy will see that cat only at weekends for the foreseeable future (yes, yes . . . insert your own joke about the likelihood that he keeps another pussy at work here), this leaves me, a noted cat non-lover, with the dread task of having to empty a box filled with poo every day.

I'm not averse to bodily functions. I'm not frightened of the brown stuff any more than is normal – wash your hands, folks. I've done scat jobs as a call girl, and did not think twice about going through with them apart from what the professional mark-up for fulfilling such a fantasy might be. I am, to use the vernacular, down wit crap.

Except cat shit is possibly the most rank-smelling, caustic stuff ever to be willingly brought into a house. The kitten has not yet mastered either his bowel functions or an internal road map of the house, and I find poo in unexpected places on a daily basis. This is not cool. This is not cute. This does not match this season's neutrals nor score any points in the glamour stakes. Most importantly, there's no tip involved.

It has occurred to me that this is perhaps the single best reason I could see why a girl would want to get herself knocked up. Because when you're pregnant, you can't change the litter tray any more.

I'm not considering it seriously, but still.

vendredi, le 25 novembre

I used to love Fridays. When I was a call girl, they were guaranteed working nights, and usually reasonably good ones at that. Lonely men hoping to kick off the weekend. Single guys and fellows staying away from their families for the night. It was a good-tips night.

Now that my boyfriend is one of these, a man hundreds of miles from his home most nights of the week, in a hotel room, I try not to think about that.

I wouldn't blame him if he did. No, I would blame him; I just wouldn't be surprised. I've seen the inside of a lot of hotels myself. It's as if they're designed to destroy the soul.

I hate Fridays. I hate wondering where he is, when he'll be home, waiting for the phone to ring.

I hate not being the whore.

samedi, le 26 novembre

Things I thought:

- that friendship matters more than passion, in the long run.
- that my boyfriend had been deeply hurt by my time as a call girl, and I by his previous cheating, but that with patience we could get over it.
- that with some effort on both sides this could work out. I'm of the belief that no one is perfect, me least of all, so anyone who could put up with my past should deserve some understanding as he comes to terms with that. I'm a fan of trying.

Or as N always put it, I'm a stayer, not a goer.

So it's Friday, early evening. Only, because of the rain, it looks like he might not be able to get out of Birmingham. Everyone at his office is telling him the roads are closed. He says.

Right, okay. I'm a little steamed, because he should have left two hours earlier, the evening meal's already on the hob but whatever. He says he'll ring when he's figured out what's happening.

He doesn't ring for a while. Huh. So I ring.

No answer. Well, if he's in the car, maybe he doesn't have the hands-free on. I try again.

It picks up. 'Hello?' I say. But, no reply. No reply to me, that is. Because he's talking to the girl who's now sitting in his passenger seat. I guess he must have sat on the button, or something.

'Oh, little thing. Get in. You really are bust, aren't you?' he says, in the tone of voice that I hear only very rarely these days – the friendly, nice one. She replies in equally affectionate terms. He adjusts her seat. They giggle. He calls her a sweet tiny piece of fluff. She mentions my cat, my cat,

MY FUCKING CAT,

the cat I never wanted that he bought me as a birthday gift, the cat she just called 'our cat' to him, THEY'RE TALK- ING ABOUT MY CAT AND SHE'S MAKING COOING NOISES.

Then he refers to her using a pet name he uses for me.

My heart is . . . well, you know what. If you've been there you know what my heart was doing. If you don't know no description will suffice apart from to say that the phrase 'gutted' sometimes feels very literal. I screamed his name, over and over, down the phone, hoping he'd hear. He must have done because the connection cut off suddenly. I rang right back and it went to voicemail.

He rang me back ten minutes later – alone this time. He said it was someone he was giving a lift to. I held out – no it wasn't. His lesbian co-worker? Er, no, clearly not. Sorry, this time the truth and only the truth will do.

The worst part is, the woman who was in the passenger seat is his ex. The plain nonentity. The barren, middle-aged lack wit. The potato-faced giantess with a back end like two grunting pigs in a poke.

Who was just married.

And given away at the ceremony by my boyfriend.

I'm a stayer, but everyone has a limit, and mine was well and truly passed. Fucking hell. I have even said to him in the past, I do not object to porn, I do not object to strippers, I even think in a long-term relationship that the occasional visit to a sex worker is infinitely preferable to carrying on an emotional relationship with someone else. But he just doesn't get it. And, it's apparent, he never will.

It's funny, because I actually think being a call girl was a positive experience. Before, I hated men a lot more. In that work I saw the raw, tender edges of them and felt something like empathy. Having to negotiate everything that happened after with a partner made me much more sensitive to his view of what was going on. I think I learned how to manage my reactions to people, how not to fly off the handle at any little thing. A little perspective. I've changed a lot. And now I see he hasn't changed at all.

Fuck perspective. Some men really are life support systems for their cocks.

lundi, le 28 novembre

'You're looking particularly well-rested,' Giles said. 'Relaxing weekend?'

If only he knew. That my Monday morning glow was the product partly of an excoriating shower and partly of a half packet of Feminax. That at best I would be aiming not to break down sobbing at any point during the day and at worst that I would be aiming not to take to the roof with a high-powered rifle.

I made it to work this morning but am very much here in body not in soul. Suffice to say it wasn't a great weekend and not one bit relaxing. I screamed a lot. I punched the wall once. I rediscovered the joys of drinking spirits at 9 a.m. on a Sunday. I discovered, not for the first time in my life, that coffee and an upset stomach don't mix. Also which makeup hides the red blotchiness the best, and that the right mascara can work wonders. Just be certain it's waterproof.

'Yeah . . . you know,' I said. The veil of pharmaceutical assistance was just beginning to descend. Maintain an even strain, as A1 often says. My new motto. Maintain an even strain. Maintain an even strain.

mardi, le 29 novembre

'I'm glad you're making this easier by being such a bitch,' he spat at me from somewhere between the stairs and the car.

I was sitting on the sofa staring into middle distance and had long since given up arguing. There was no point; nothing he said even remotely approached what I might have needed to hear. He uttered a lot of 'I'm sorry but . . .', which is rubbish; no real apology ever includes the word 'but'. But implies that in fact you are the one responsible for his cheating. But implies someone incapable of growing a pair and taking responsibility for his own mistakes. And 'I can't believe you're throwing everything away over something as small as this', which is the last refuge of a man so damn guilty he can't even be bothered to deny it. And I think, I didn't throw anything away, I'm just carrying the rubbish to the kerb. His car isn't so big, so it's going to take a few trips.

But the locks have already been changed. One thing – I'm glad I own this place.

mercredi, le 30 novembre

There's still salmon in the fridge. I hate salmon, so scraped it into the cat's dish. He took a single sniff but didn't want it either. Good boy.

I couldn't bring myself to take his pillows off the other side of the bed, much less stretch out into the middle.

I woke in the night dreaming I was being kissed, but it was the cat, touching his wet little nose to my cheek. I fell asleep again, the cat curled tight against my body.

I would cry, but have already done so much crying over the length of our relationship, I think I've run dry.

Ten Steps to Getting Over Him:

1 Whatever he's left in the house, burn it. Yes, you could drag things to the kerb for recycling. You could donate them to a deserving charity. I tell you now nothing, but nothing, satisfies like naked flame.

2 Speaking of naked, isn't it time you renewed your gym membership?

3 Rename the cat 'You Bastard'. 'Get off the sofa, You Bastard; Stop humping the table leg, You Bastard.' Feels good, no?

4 Masturbate once a day, whether you need it or not.

5 There comes a crisis in every woman's life when she must admit she can't make it on her own. This is where personal shoppers at Harvey Nicks come in.

6 Forget location, location, location. Your new mantra is: manicure, manicure, manicure.

7 Now is a good opportunity to ask your friends what they really thought of that idiot. Be certain to say 'that idiot', alerting them to precisely what flavour of truth you want to hear about him.

8 Did I say manicure? I meant Chablis, Chablis, Chablis.

9 Find a karaoke night, preferably one you have never been to and will never visit again. Request 'I Will Survive'. You know what to do.

10 When all else fails, like my friend L says, the best way to get over one man is to get under another.

Décembre

jeudi, le 01 décembre

Your friends will ooh and ahh. They'll wonder how you managed to do it, after all this time. They'll even sneak over to you and press for details on what the secret was. They'll admire the newfound sparkle in your eye, the zest for life, the transformed figure of a woman you are. And it's true, things really will be different. The air will seem sweeter, the birds will be singing. Men's heads will turn when you walk by. You'll feel, and look, younger. And to think all it took was losing sixteen stone.

Sixteen stone of useless boyfriend, that is.

The dust hasn't settled – not as yet – but everything is on its way. It's surprising, after so much time, that it really does come down to three carloads of his crap and a short phone call to the council.

Luckily I never went in for the full ball-and-chain of co-habitation. Something I learnt from my mother. Even when they were married, my parents always had separate accounts. Yes, it's true, I'm only a half-hearted romantic, the sort of woman who believes in prenuptial agreements and starts to fidget whenever divorce-style 'rights' for co-habiting couples comes up on the news. I reckon if you want to go whole hog, get thee down that aisle. Otherwise, what's mine is mine, and . . . well, you can figure the rest out.

The irony is, it just feels – I don't know, clean. Inevitable. The right thing at the right time.

I'm keeping the cat. The fucking cat. Got to have a man of some stripe about the house, right?

vendredi, le 02 décembre

I met A1 and his wife for coffee. She suggested Starbucks and unthinkingly I said yes even though I hate that place. But sitting in there – the interior devoid of any charm whatsoever, horrible background music of Sarah McLachlan or whomever pretending to play the guitar – I thought it was just as well. If I'd actually been somewhere with decent coffee and muffins I'd have felt bad for letting it all go cold.

'Sorry, just need to pop to the loo,' I said and excused myself. The single bite of yoghurt I'd had in the morning came back on me, and a mouthful of coffee, and a nibble of the hated horrible muffin. The rest was just bile. I could just about hear A1's voice through the door – I hoped they couldn't hear me.

I washed my hands, scanned my reflection in the mirror and realised with some horror that it increasingly looks as though I've raided Cherie Blair's wardrobe. A colleague even asked if I were losing weight, to which my answer was, no, I've traded in everything I own for a wardrobe of capacious M&S trousers. Vanessa Feltz would look like Paris Hilton in M&S trousers and probably just scrape a size eight, as well.

Note to self: if a bra doesn't fit, get rid of it. Otherwise there will be inevitable laundry day quick-grab regrets and quadro-boob. Not a good look in the office.

I'm feeling down. So much so that even the thought of a Matt Dawson/Ben Cohen sandwich does not cheer me up.

This is wrong, kids. Very wrong. Something must be done.

samedi, le 03 décembre

I picked up the phone without even glancing at the number. 'Hello gorgeous,' a voice purred.

'Giles, hi. What's wrong?'

He laughed a short, sharp bark. 'Nothing my dear. Just checking on you. I heard about your recent bad news . . .'

'Thanks,' I said, and instantly felt stupid. Who thanks someone for acknowledging your breakup? Note to self, must stop reflexively apologising for things.

'I just wanted you to know, I consider you more than just an employee. I hope – on some level at least – you and I can call each other friends. And as your friend, please, don't hesitate to let me know if there's anything at all I can do.'

Good god. Had he rehearsed that? 'Cheers, Giles, I think I'll be okay for now. See you on Monday?'

'Yes, I . . . yes. See you on Monday.'

dimanche, le 04 décembre

'I'm coming over.'

'You're not. It's okay. I'm fine, really I am.'

'You're fine?' L sounded incredulous. 'You're all alone in the house, you're not picking up your phone until the twentieth ring and your voice is distinctly slurred in a way that speaks more of the bottle than the bed. You're not fine.'

'Honestly, it's nothing like that. I just woke up,' I said, and looked over at the clock. The red digital face flashed on and off. Power must have gone off in the night; it was a grey enough day to be any time at all. 'Uh, what time is it?'

'Right, I'll be over in fifteen minutes.' I groaned. 'I know what you're thinking,' she said. 'You want your boys to come over, and tell you you're foxy, and get you drunk. But drunk ain't gonna solve anything right now. What you need are girlfriends. In lieu of that, what you need is me and a dozen back issues of *Cosmo*. And don't even think about saying no.'

lundi, le 05 décembre

Every breakup needs breakup music, right? But it's not so easy. You can't go out and look for a breakup theme. It has to happen organically – be a song that's currently popular, or else something that enters your life by accident, not design. Also, it has to speak to you on a fundamentally aesthetic level. No dedicated Kylie fan will find herself sobbing over 'Bela Lugosi's Dead' in the weeks after the love of her life has walked out the door, nor should she.

Well, g*d bless the spirits that dwell within my iPod, because today the shuffle function happened upon the best possible song right when I needed it. I was grumbling and angry about a phone call at seven this morning from my ex nattering on about whatever the hell he imagines is wrong with his life/his relationships/me (who rings before breakfast, except to annoy? Who I ask you? No one, that's who). As a result I desperately needed something a little bit up-lifting, a little bit fuck you, a little bit sistas-doin-it-4-themselves, though perhaps on a scale from nought-to-'I Will Survive' something that measures only about a 0.8. I Will Survive.

Enter Pulp, and 'Bad Cover Version'.

Best. Thing. Ever. Thank you, iPod, for getting me through the morning.

mardi, le 06 décembre

I tapped on Giles's office door and it swung open. A flurry of activity on the other side settled itself before I realised what was going on – there was Giles on one side of his desk, smoothing his hair and giving me a look that said 'So?'

And there was Alex, blushing madly.

For the love of . . . she's half his age. 'Hi, sorry, I saw your door wasn't closed, and I . . .'

'No, no worries, just showing Alex the new quarterly report formatting.'

I looked at his Mona Lisa smirk, and at the rumpled front of her shirt. 'Of course, but, wouldn't it be more efficient to have one of the admin assistants do that?'

'Ah . . . um, yes. Probably. Only Jane's out today so I figured . . .'

'Naturally. Good of you to look after her so well. I'm off out to lunch, I'll email you the weekly summary, yeah?' I turned and left the office before either could respond.

mercredi, le 07 décembre

Picked up a women's magazine on the way home – yes, I know I've said I don't do that but there was a train involved and, what can I say, you do crazy things when you're heart-broken, and L had seriously damaged my shiny-magazine cred when she brought round the promised *Cosmo*s at the weekend – and came across someone whose job description, if it can be called that, was 'sexpert'.

Not writer. Not therapist. Nor even bon vivant. Not, in short, any of the many things that someone who knows a thing or two about sex and talks about that in public probably does for a primary occupation (such as, say, being an agony aunt or presenting a television show). Which leaves you to wonder where exactly this sexperting occurs. Jill Winterbottom, sexpert, call at my bungalow anytime between four and six, all questions answered? Can you put that on a passport?

Apart from my slight confusion regarding sexpertry, there is also the problem of envy. No one has ever (to my knowledge) called me a sexpert. Which is baffling. I've had sex with a statistically measurable proportion of humanity that even includes an error margin. And I daresay I've learned a thing or two about sex meanwhile. But this is not good enough for the world of sexpertdom. I think I know why.

It's about clothing. If you have sex then, later, with your clothes on, take money for talking about the sex you had, this qualifies you as a sexpert. If, on the other hand, you have sex and take money for the sex itself, this does not. To sum up: taking money with your clothes on, sexpert. With your clothes off, not. So basically sexperts are reporters about sex, rather than sex professionals. Or something.

Which is roughly akin to saying that Andrew Marr makes a cracking PM and Bill Bryson should be heading up a physics department somewhere.

But there is room for interpretation here. So rather than being a sexpert – has sex for free, charges for interpretation – perhaps I'm just the inverse of that – has sex for money, gives opinions for free.

Help yourself to a little of my wisdom:

- There is nothing sexier than a sense of humour. Apart from being really good in bed.
- You can buy a pregnancy test without embarrassment in today's world, but not at the same time as buying

laxatives. Also, don't give them your Boots loyalty card at the same time either.

- Any woman who says women can't have strings-free sex is stupid.
- Any woman who says she does have strings-free sex is lying.
- You should never date someone you met on the Web. Or at a club. Or at work. Or who is the friend of a friend (or friend of a relative). In short, don't date.
- If you have sex on a first date he'll never respect you.
- If you don't have sex on a first date you'll never see him again.

Right, consider me ready to be unleashed on the world of dating! Or at the very least the world of magazine columnistry.

jeudi, le 08 décembre

I've lost what it feels like, normal. My mind has only two states at the moment – one is lean and jittery, the lines of the world drawn sharp and tight, every voice a shout, every footstep a pounding. Then there's the other: cocooned in cotton wool unawareness, numb, unreceptive. Every voice sounds so very far away. Times like those I feel I could step off this crowded Tube platform in the way of the train and not feel a thing. And in the few lucid moments between them, I am ashamed. Ashamed at my grief. Ashamed that my gran saw half her family carted off to the gas chambers and I'm crying over some man. Not that such thoughts help; they don't. Can't.

'Coffee today?'

'Sure, Giles, what time?'

'Three?' I knew that really meant quarter past three, so I didn't hurry along. To my surprise he was already waiting in the queue when I arrived.

'Hello, how are you? Latte?'

'Thank you, yes, I'll find somewhere to sit.'

One of the more charming habits my boss has is never having got a handle on being in charge of other people, he still buys coffee. Hell, he still meets people for coffee. As far as I can tell, his diet is mostly comprised of coffee-based products. In fact, I think his contributions are single-handedly keeping Starbucks afloat in this country.

'You're looking well, considering,' Giles said as he sat down with our cups.

'Thanks. I like to hope this is only somewhere between a dead plant and the sudden demise of a parent on the grieving scale.' We both smiled.

'That's it, got to keep a sense of humour.'

'Um, G, did you really meet me for coffee in order to impersonate my father, or is there some ulterior motive here?'

'Oh, you and the honesty thing. That always kills me.' I smiled; somehow I've got a largely undeserved reputation in our business as a plain dealer. Not bad for a hooker, no? 'Listen. I like you, I like your style. I know you like me . . .'

'You're a great boss, Giles, no denying.' Compared to the manager I had at the call girl agency, he was in fact a sainted prophet.

He looked up at me through lowered lashes. I knew what was coming, but in such cases it's best to feign ignorance as long as possible. 'I mean I'd like to like you outside of . . . all this.'

'Outside this coffee shop?'

'Outside of work.'

I smiled sadly. So now I've seen it, I thought. Now I've seen his hand, his tricks, how he puts the moves on the girls in the office. He'd put himself out on a limb but it was nowhere he hadn't been before. Jane in admin knew him from a previous company, where apparently there had been the Canadian girl, whose engagement he ruined. The ladies in the office all clucked and shook their heads, but I kept my mouth shut. I couldn't blame him – she was the one who wasn't single and should have known better. Even so, once is excusable, twice is skanky. 'Giles . . . I know about you and Alex.'

He sat up, suddenly. He didn't deny it. Good man.

Now it was my turn to be out on a limb. 'This changes nothing between us, right?'

'Christ, no,' he said. 'If I lost you the place would no doubt fall apart.' He smiled broadly, but I know when a man's been wounded. 'Friends?'

'More than that,' I said. 'Colleagues.'

samedi, le 10 décembre

I'm so bored of . . .

- Television. When the best thing on is a craptastic adaptation of some Patrick O'Brian book (and I hate his books with a fervour typically reserved for hating people who shamelessly spread STIs), it's time to refocus the square eyes elsewhere.

- Christmas. Is it coming? Again? Really? Hadn't bloody noticed.
- Cocktails. Made for people who don't like the taste of alcohol: in a word, children. Want to know a recipe for the perfect cocktail? Take a bottle of spirits (your choice). Pour some in a glass with ice. Drink.
- Sex. No, not doing it. Could never be bored of that. It's reading about it. Or, more specifically, reading about how having an orgasm is taking one back for feminism or what-the-fuck-ever. It's sex. You don't have sex to score points for your gender. You don't have sex because that's what Major Feminist Thinker says you should do. You have sex because you're horny, lonely, bored or need the cash. It's a little like saying 'I'm breathing because that proves to the androcentric status quo that I deserve the air as well.' Wank! You breathe because it is a basic human function. Everything else is pseudo-academic twaddle.
- Mother-and-Child spaces in car parks. My dear mum and I were at a supermarket last week and she parked right up front. I looked at her. She looked at me. 'Well, you're still my daughter, right?' Ha! Love her.
- Japanophilia. Okay in 1994. Lame now.
- Fear of teenagers. Every morning I stand at the bus stop with a dozen gum-snapping, chain-smoking, under-six-teens. Big freaking deal. I'm more afraid of the grannies with the sharpened brollies.
- The widespread and seemingly unavoidable percentage of the population whose jobs consist of Giving Things Names rather than Actually Doing Something. (replace 'Giving Things Names' with 'Listing All the Things They Could, But Won't, Do' and there's another one.)
- Giant, sack-like handbags. Not only resemble bin liners but also have the organisational capabilities thereof. I like a big bag, me: just not a shapeless one that looks like you

might have three umbrellas, a sandwich toaster and a recent boyfriend lost at the bottom without you even noticing.

- Reading children's fiction/watching sci-fi for the life lessons. This is not an attack on sci-fi. I love sci-fi, even when it is high on 'fi' and relatively light on 'sci'. I think the new *Battlestar Galactica* is great. But it should not be the ham-handed means by which functional adult humans learn about social organisation, religious faith and political ethics.

Hmm, hatred of Japanophilia and sci-fi. I might as well just say: I hate my ex.

dimanche, le 11 décembre

I knew it had to start sometime. The drunk-dialling, that is.

Not me, sillies – though goodness knows I've a few reasons to hit the sherry of late. No, it's the ex. He rang last night an hour after I went to bed (not at 9 p.m., but thank you for the concern) and stupidly I answered. This is the problem of having a phone with an annoying ring you're too lazy to change – you're obliged to pick up.

I won't bore you with the details, because let's face it, every drunk dial that does not result in a booty call is more-or-less the same. The accepted stages are:

1 nervous greeting, followed swiftly by
2 I'm really enjoying life on my own, which leads inevitably to
3 I miss you, I'm lonely (subtext: I wasn't successful at picking up other girls tonight), usually swiftly chased by

4 I love you so why aren't we together, then usually a spot
  of
5 here are all the ways in which you are a bitch, then
6 another proclamation of undying love, and finally
7 the caller either urges you to ring back tomorrow, invite
  him over tonight or passes out.

The odd thing was, listening to him ramble on and on about this thing we'd done together, or that cherished memory or yet another way in which I Ruined His Life, it all seemed very unreal, as if it had happened to someone else. It was not unlike watching a film, or seeing one of those terrifically enjoyable reality shows in which you scream at the TV week after week for her to dump the motherfucker already. His voice was like the voice of someone I knew a long time ago, and all the things he said – they had no power. They were just words.

And that's why I didn't just hang up. I was so amazed by my reaction that I had to stay on the phone and see how long it lasted. If it lasted. It did.

lundi, le 12 décembre

Gah, it's definitely winter. There is no denying it. Only the chauffeured car set or the chronically idiotic are going around in those summer dresses now; although, with the party season soon to be upon us I reckon the ratio of jersey to exposed skin will soon be experiencing a reversal.

I despise winter. Much as I love this country I consider it a tragic joke that my family, nurtured for generations by Mediterranean sunshine and the occasional tropical out-post, should find itself caught in a land where one can, without particularly trying, go to and come back from work in the dark. And that's even true for people not working the sex trades.

Obvs, 'tis the season for my spending to ramp up a touch in anticipation of the height of winter – no, not the glitter-laden balls and bashes of Christmas and New Year but the dark, depressing bog that is January/February, when the only thing capable of putting a bounce in my step short of hot, wet, monkey sex is knowing I snatched up the new Mulberry must-have handbag simply ages before everyone else, and can enjoy its combination of ladylike structure and high capacity as a repository for woolly tights and waterproofs.

In fact, if such a thing were possible, this bag would be my philosophy in a nutshell: polite and polished on the outside, flexible holdall on the inside. Thank fuck for someone finally making a handbag that doesn't resemble a swing-bin liner with buckled pockets.

Have bag will travel: winter, bring it on.

mercredi, le 14 décembre

It didn't take long – the office gossips have already turned on Alex. Giles just announced that she was going to be joining us on a trial basis after graduation.

'You know what that means,' Jane hissed in the tea room. I raised my eyebrows and frowned slightly, not wanting to let on that I'd already known.

Then Elaine from downstairs came into the room, and they were off. It was T-minus four nanoseconds before they started ripping into her: her over-straightened hair; her try-hard wardrobe; her boobs; her artificially high voice. 'Alex is a fucking hag,' said Elaine, whom up to that point I'd thought was a fairly live-and-let-live type. But I know why there's so much hatred about this woman. It's bad enough being a minority around here. It's worse knowing someone else is working that to her advantage.

I know, I know. Pot, kettle and black, right? Except that while I could hardly begrudge another sex worker a more successful and varied clientele than me – hey, these things happen, and some people just give better blow jobs than others – in an area where favours are not supposed to be for sale, it really rankles.

The more they talked, the more worried I became. It's not as if I got my current job on my qualifications, more because I was keen and Giles fancied me. I've stayed in through hard work and I can see Alex is no fool. She's learned this place inside out in less time than it took me to figure out how the phones work. It's not that I think Giles is disloyal, but I know he's easily blinded by sex. As most men are.

The way I see them, my options are something along the lines of:

1   Beat 'em. Men paid good money to see me naked and as this lass looks something like a white, spotty Mariah Carey I reckon I could easily put her in the shade with a few well-timed flirtations. Though having already decided sleeping with Giles is strictly off-limits this may have limited effect.

2   Join 'em. She doesn't have female allies here from what I can see. Get in tight with her and ride the coattails? Maybe.

3   Poison the well. Not my style. But a nasty rumour could certainly have a chilling effect, provided it wasn't traceable. Alternatively, take a public opportunity – an upcoming team-building event, for instance – to embarrass her.

4   Ignore 'em. Sure, the men may give her air-time now but

in the long run they'll tire of her pushy ways. If I just keep my head down, and do good work, it will eventually pay off. Nothing is so sexy as competence . . .

. . . yeah, right. That's why I'm raiding my stash of push-up bras as of tomorrow morning.

vendredi, le 16 décembre

You know what they say: nothing gets you over the last one like the next one. So while my natural inclination is to wrap up warm and watch boring films with a cuppa in one hand and a purring cat in the other, it is – on paper at least – still the first flower of my youth and therefore not too late to discover a little romance.

A1 sets me up with a bloke. Numbers are exchanged; he rings first. We agree on a meeting time and place. It's a little stilted, talking to a stranger on the phone, but I have been assured this fellow – let's call him T – is interesting and nice. He asks what I look like, and I give him a brief run down: height; weight; hair colour. I ask what he looks like.

'Most people describe me as a cross between Kiefer Sutherland . . .'

yesssssssssssssssssss!

'. . . and Vic Reeves.'

Wuh? Maybe he's exaggerating so as not to come across as conceited. Maybe he means he looks like KS and acts like VR. Don't be an arse, I chastise myself. For all I know Vic Reeves is sex on wheels and a great conversationalist. Anyway, we'll see.

The appointed day and time arrives. I'm about to head out the door when I notice myself looking perhaps not quite up to scratch and in need of a touch of makeup and a general brush-up. So I ring T, to let him know I'll be a few minutes late. Unnecessary, you might say – men are used to waiting on women. Perhaps, but the two cardinal rules of being a call girl were 1) be on time and 2) look the part, and old habits die hard. So I call him.

'As it happens I couldn't find a place to park where we were going to meet, so I went somewhere else.'

Huh. He was going to drive to a location less than a mile from his house? No matter. 'Okay. Well, where are you?'

He names a pub I've never heard of. Turns out it's on the other side of the city.

Riiiiight. Gritting teeth, I make it there twenty minutes late. I'm not impressed. This smoking ban thing has been a nightmare, especially when the natural smell of a pub, as with this one, is of piss. I buy a pint and scan the room.

There – in the corner – yep, it's a Vic Reeves lookie-likey. I smile and walk over. We shake hands. He not-so-subtly checks his watch. Well, I'd have been mostly on time if you hadn't just picked some random other place to go. 'Everything okay?'

'Yeah,' he says, jingling the keys and change in his pocket. 'Only I've got to go put more money in the parking meter. Oh and I'm going to my mum's in an hour.'

Wow. Glad meeting me was such a priority. He comes back from the car, and we chat. Except it's not much of a chat. We have nothing, and I do mean nothing, in common. He asks about my work. I describe what I do, and my office.

'And what was it you did again?' I ask, struggling to remember our phone conversation. 'Something in music promotion?'

'Well, not actually,' he says. No, what he actually does is something creative. By creative I actually mean full-on, two fingers making quotes in the air, 'Creative'. I fucking hate creatives. I hate anyone who can't describe what they do in sensible terms and, when they finally manage to, have made it clear that come the apocalypse, they have no assets that would benefit a community of survivors whatsoever. I call it the 28 *Days Later*-test. Can you rig up a generator? No? Fire a gun? No? Read a map? No? Locate food and water? No? Run fast enough to not be a danger to the rest of us? No? Sorry mate, you're zombie fodder. Also, T probably makes sixteen-times what I do, but when he goes to the bar, doesn't buy me a drink.

'So, how old did you say you were?' he asks. I tell him, and he chuckles.

'Why, how old are you?'

'Oh, it doesn't matter. Old enough that your age makes me feel I should be in a Zimmer frame.'

Hmm, so he's obviously keen to get this started on an honest footing then. I'm guessing forty-five.

We spend a lot of time talking about Damian Hirst. Like, a lot of time. Almost exactly an hour of Hirst-based discussion. I don't actually like Damian Hirst. My eyes stray again and again to a newspaper someone's left on the next table, wondering if T would mind awfully if I started reading it instead of continuing this pointless conversation. He's constantly checking his phone, and soon (though not soon enough), it's time to go meet his mum. We shake hands and go out separate doors.

Analysis:

Boyfriend material? 2/10 – I like people to tell me their age and not be quite so attached to Mummy's apron strings in middle age (if indeed it was his mother he was rushing off to see). The last-minute change of venue was not a welcome sign.

Fuckable? 3/10 – I'm no great fan of Vic Reeves, and not

willing to stick around and find out which part of him draws comparisons to Jack Bauer.

Client material? 8/10 – Surprisingly high you might think but, actually, one hour's worth of conversation, and likes to get away quickly, and has the cash to afford me . . . loses points for changing location last minute but, otherwise, shame I'm not in the call girl biz anymore. He'd be close to ideal.

Would date again? 4/10 – Maybe a little harsh. I'm sure in three months' time, I'll look back on this as a golden age of eligible men. But I very much doubt it.

dimanche, le 18 décembre

'So how did it go with the—'
  'Don't.'
  'He said he thought you were—'
  'Don't.'
  'If you fancy I could set you up with—'
  'Please, stop it.' I glared at A1. 'I'm never going out with anyone recommended by a friend again.'
  A2 chuckled. 'Give him a break, he's only trying to help.' The boys were squished on my sofa, a three-seater which in reality only holds the two of them and me occasionally perched on the armrest between fetching cups of tea from the kitchen. Goodness knows when I became the char lady to my friends. And in my own house, no less.
  'Help? He set me up with the worst date I've had since . . . since I can't remember when.'
  'That's only because she can't remember when she last had a date,' A2 whispered to A1.
  'I heard that.'

'Well, if you're not going to let us find eligible men for you, then perhaps it's time to change tack entirely,' A1 said. 'Seriously, have you considered Internet dating? Speed dating?'

I stuck out my tongue. 'Ugh, that's for losers.'

'Suit yourself,' A2 shrugged. 'You're the one having your sofa monopolised by us of a Sunday morning.'

lundi, le 19 décembre

Just when you think you're through it, it comes back and hits you double. But I refuse to give in to the melancholy, refuse to sit replaying memories of happiness and holidays that once were with the Boy. Why don't we talk about a few of the things I've been actually enjoying this month?

- Mince pie anticipation. Am spending Christmas with A4's family and already looking forward to the tiny brandy butter mince pies they have every year. Although must get cracking on making the rum truffles or they won't let me in the door.
- Mulled wine at work. If you knew what I did for a living these days, you'd be writing an angry letter to the *Daily Mail* about the health and safety implications/wilful misappropriation of taxpayer money/danger to our lives and livelihood/won't someone think of the children? right now. Luckily, you don't.
- Long, long conversations with friends such as A2 who like all the same things I do (namely lesbian porn and jazz).
- Teaching the cat to act like a dog. So far: walking on a leash; sitting up for treats. Still to come: fetching; answering to its name – and no, its name is *not* the sound of a gravy pouch being opened.

'I love *Cosmo*. Look at this: "Hot Bedroom Ideas He'll Love. Twenty Key Pieces To Buy Now. The One Thing You Should Never Tell A Man",' L said.

'I know what that last one is without ever having to look,' I said, lolling on the sofa while flicking through channels. 'Never tell a man how many people you've had sex with.'

L flipped quickly to the page in question. 'Yes, that's exactly it,' she said. 'Funny, because I get that out of the way on the first date.'

I looked back over the arm of the sofa at L. 'Are you joking?'

'No, why do you think I would be? And I want to know his number, too. That way you know what you're in for.'

'I guess I just think . . . don't ask the question if you can't handle the answer.' If called upon to give an honest accounting of my number of sexual partners, I wasn't sure I could even give a good estimate. I'd stopped counting when the total hit twenty-two (well before I was twenty-two), and would struggle – especially since being a prostitute – to come up with a ballpark figure. Maybe if pressed I'd only count my long-term relationships (two at school, three at uni, N, the Boy) plus throw in a realistic two or three more for one-night stands. But it bothered me to think people were bothered – what would L think if she knew?

'But you'd have to tell him eventually . . .'

'Why?' I asked. 'It's not as if he's going to be The One. No harm in playing the field.' And even then, I might not tell anyone I dated in the future. Hadn't quite thought that one through yet – the Boy knew as it happened but how would I tell someone new about my past? There must be thousands of girls every year who wonder the same thing, especially as the odds of being found out once you're out of the business are low, provided you can be discreet. Honesty, I decided, was probably not the best policy.

'I love to flirt as much as the next girl, but I wouldn't go on a date with a man if I didn't think he could be The One,' L said. 'Would you?'

'Um, uh . . .' Who even believes in The One anyway? 'But you of all people? I mean, you're so foxy!'

L closed the magazine and pursed her lips. 'I've only been with four men in total,' she said. 'And two of those were in my Slut Fortnight.'

I quickly did the sums. Assume she was sexually active since uni . . . then her age . . . divide by four . . . 'That's like one man every four years,' I said. I was horrified. I'd be gutted if there wasn't every four months, at least. Oh, who am I kidding? One every four weeks. Four days. One every four hours, ideally. I turned back to the television. 'So, uh, anything on you want to watch?'

vendredi, le 23 décembre

Went into town to meet N for our annual Fuck Christmas, festive get-together. Being in the holiday mood, I promised to take him to one or three of Soho's finer strip clubs. Bless the man's evil heart, he pretended not to know where they were.

Meeting, late:

'Where are you?'
'Central . . . are you on the way?'
'In a few minutes. Pick a landmark and I'll meet you there.'

'Okay, I'll be outside the Dominion Theatre – under Freddie Mercury's crotch.'

Later:

'Hypothetical question: would you drink piss out of a bottle?'
'Depends.'
'What on?'
'If they provided mints for after.'
'That's what I love about you.'

Latest:

'I can't believe it. Three squid for a single journey? Three months of using the Tube is now as expensive as two hours with a call girl.'
'Yes, but a week of Oyster card is only twenty minutes in King's Cross.'

dimanche, le 25 décembre

'Happy Christmas, darling.' A4 scooped another chocolate truffle from the box.

'I can't believe your family went off skiing without you this year.'

'Leaves more truffles for me,' he said. Every year I make chocolate truffles for his family, who have been demanding them as an annual Christmas tithe. My family being Jewish weren't doing anything today but I did recklessly promise to see them on Boxing Day and, as there were no trains running, A4 agreed to drive. 'Plus I get to spend the day with you.'

'Frozen pizza with all the trimmings,' I nodded. 'Hand me the *Radio Times*, will you?'

A4 is such a sweetie, he collects snippets of Jewishness for me like some men awkwardly pick up smooth pebbles on the beach to impress their girls.

'Hey, look, Tony Blair on the telly wearing a Jewish hat and lighting a candelabra.'

'Do you mean a yarmulke and a Chanukiah?'

'Um, yeah.'

mercredi, le 28 décembre

Every year that passes I feel more apprehensive about the holidays, not least because of my parents' recent divorce. How do you steer a conversation so it doesn't come up? 'Sorry, Mum, can't have dinner with you tonight, because I . . . uh . . . have something else going on . . .' Talk about feeling like a borderline criminal – I would have felt more comfortable saying I was meeting my pimp.

And I so envy those friends whose families split when they were kids. Back then, the parents would feel guilty about the upheaval and try to buy your love. No such luck if you're an adult when it happens. Fur-lined jackets? Skiing holidays? Fuhgeddaboudit. The best you get is rolled eyes and the world's heaviest sigh when Dad's car comes up the street.

My mother's a savvy woman, she gave up long ago asking when I was going to settle down and produce a family like L***** (perfection itself expressed miraculously in the form of my little sister). No, she's moved on to working that rich seam all mothers in our family since time immemorial have mined so well, the passive-aggressive guilt.

And in such matters, she is but the padawan learner to my grandmother's Supreme Master Yoda.

So it's late and me, my mother and grandmother are sitting in the kitchen, eating chocolates – you know how it is. They manoeuvred themselves into the seats closest to the door, which in retrospect was my first mistake.

'It makes you think about things, doesn't it, this time of year,' Granny says, examining her stockpile of sweets. She's bagsied all the strawberry cremes since 1972. It's family law.

'Mmm. Yes, it certainly does.' My mother skips over the last dark chocolate caramel, favourite of both of us – she NEVER does that – and hands the chocs on to me. I pluck the caramel from the box triumphantly. Mistake number two.

'I always reassess at this time of year.'

Mum nods with considered thoughtfulness. 'You can't help but do.'

'I look back over my life and wonder about this or that little thing in the last year that made me angry or fretful.'

'Mmm.' (At this point, it starts to dawn on me that their purring exchange is not necessarily for the benefit of each other.)

'But it's all put in perspective – you can see now the things that really matter.'

'Family,' my mother says in agreement – and the caramel sticks in my throat halfway down – she never says anything like that. My mother is not a Stepford Wife. She rode motorbikes and smoked hash in Morocco and flashed her tits at a university don. Her youthful misbehaviour drove her family to prayer and countless men to despair. She is a good person but was most emphatically never a Good Girl. My eyes dart round, panicked, wondering where the pod people got in.

'Yes, I could worry about what I might or might not have achieved in life. But when I look at my children' –

glowing smile for Mum – 'and grandchildren, and now, great-grandchild, I know, that is really what this is all about.'

Now, for those familiar with my books, this would ordinarily be the point at which my father comes in and rescues me. But my parents are now divorced. There will be no saviour. I'm on my own here.

'I think my mobile's going,' I say, pushing up from the chair.

'Oh, honey, it's the holidays,' my mother says, all eggy puddings and sweet wine. 'Whoever it is will understand if they have to ring you back. Here, have another caramel.'

I don't remember much more of our conversation that night, but recall that mentions of JDate were made. Also some nice fellow with a son my mother saw in town recently.

Also the cost of freezing eggs. I think someone – probably me – uttered the words bride price. I don't know for certain.

All I know is, next time, I'm staying at a hotel.

samedi, le 31 décembre

Resolved:

• To make next year better than the last.
Shouldn't be a stretch. A twelve month coma would have been better than the last year.

Ten signs your sex-kitten powers may be on the wane:

10 Shoes that were previously in high rotation as office wear are now consigned to the 'fancy dress parties' area of the wardrobe.

9 Your night cream has become your day cream, your day cream is now your hand cream and you're slathering something suspiciously like nappy rash cream on your face before bed.

8 The phone rings at ten-past-ten on a weekday and the conversation starts, 'Sorry, did I wake you?'

7 That twenty-two-year-old isn't flirting. He is just being nice.

6 You know the difference between bio and non-bio and even hand-wash your scanties. Not that many people see them these days, but just in case . . .

5 Your sexual fantasies involve a shadow cabinet member (or two).

4 If they print one more article about utilising wind power to run the WiFi in your reclaimed-teak yurt, you're going to have to kill . . . wait, no, that was ten signs you need to start reading another paper. Sorry.

3 The last man who offered you his phone number was fitting your shoes at the time.

2 You've neatly solved the do-I-or-don't-I problem of getting those capillaries lasered by being too short-sighted to see them anymore.

And last but most certainly not least,

1 You're out of lube, and can't even remember when it must have been used up.

Janvier

dimanche, le 01 janvier

Empty gin bottles by the bed: four.

Not-quite-empty gin bottles elsewhere in the house: two.

Friends passed out on or in the vicinity of the sofa: also two.

Shoes I didn't quite manage to take off before getting into bed: one.

Other occupants of said bed: one (the damned cat).

The first fucking hangover of the year? incalculable.

mardi, le 03 janvier

'So now that you're available, presumably . . .'

'Presumably . . . ?' I was sitting on the edge of the bath, picking at the chipped varnish on my toenails. Essential maintenance has gone to hell, challenged the devil, passed through the other side, been reborn and dies another five times. I am practically a cavewoman now.

'Maybe you'd like me to come over and give you a good seeing-to?'

I giggled. I love this about N: that we can be perfectly platonic friends for months – no, years – on end, and as soon as we're both single again it's full steam ahead. It's like having the perfect man on tap at all times. If only that pesky relationship bit had worked out. But no matter – I know he plays Friends with Benefits like a pro. 'Honey, that's so sweet,' I said. 'Alas my schedule is rapidly filling with all sorts of pointless timewasters.'

'I'm hard right now, if it makes a difference?'

'I'm not ready. Not with you. Is that cool?'

'That's cool, you know that it is,' he said. 'Hey, that fit sister of yours divorced yet? They say the holiday season is the time of year when most breakups happen . . .'

'Stop it, she's my sister!'

'I mean, now that she's passed something the size and shape of a melon, maybe she'd be up for a fisting?'

'As if! You know that's not her style.'

'The fact that she would hate it just makes it all the better for my fantasies.'

'Shall I leave you to it then? Sounds like you've a lot, um, in hand . . . to deal with.'

click

mercredi, le 04 janvier

There's something about going back to work after an extended holiday that makes you see everything afresh. The clever co-workers. The helpful support staff. The high-flying clientele. The interesting and varied challenges of the job. Your smiling, capable, respected boss.

And how much you fucking hate them.

So when you're out there you might as well be out there, right? Or at least that's what I told myself cruising Gumtree late at night. Maybe a few years ago it would have been perfectly legitimate to sneer at people who met over websites but in the era of MySpace and absolutely everything being online, why not dating as well?

It being New Year and all, there were bound to be loads of eligible singles floating their stock for the first time. I wasn't going in with high expectations but one ad caught my eye. Athletic islander seeks serious girl for something not so serious . . . yes, sounds just the ticket. Hope springs eternal. Or midwinters, anyway.

We exchanged a few notes; he liked my photo. I said let's not drag out the talking and get this one the old fashioned way – with a face-to-face. He agreed. I just had a first name: Paul. We arranged to meet outside a bookshop; I'd mentioned a beer festival on the phone and he seemed agreeable. So far, so . . .

. . . Hmm. Shorter than I expected. Maybe shouldn't have turned up in the very high heels. Anyway.

He didn't drink alcohol, he said. Fine, I said. We don't have to go to that beer festival then. No, it's okay if you want to, he said. I looked at him, one eyebrow cocked. Don't you think that would be a little weird? I said. But that wasn't what I was thinking. Not weird, creepy. Very creepy. Apart from that, cute but dull. Northern Ireland. They say first impressions are everything and I suppose I'd already decided.

But, being in the habit of seeing things through, we walked on. He promised he was okay with me drinking, so we went to a bar, but not the one with the festival on. I ordered a half. He had an orange and lemonade. We sat on high stools and his feet were no closer to the ground than mine. 'Soooooo,' I finally said. 'Have you been single long?'

'Since before moving here,' he said. 'It's difficult to meet people, my job takes a lot of my time.'

Sure it does. I'd heard the same a thousand times before, usually from clients. A surprising number of the men who use call girls are young professionals who, you might imagine, wouldn't have any trouble attracting a woman if they only had the time or interest to pursue it. They're not all married men, losers and weirdos. I was tempted to ask if he'd ever been to a sex worker . . . but not so tempted I actually voiced the question. He would likely tell me in good time, probably without realising it. 'So you placed the ad then. How's that worked out?'

'Well, I met you.'

'Okay.' But seeing as I'd already ninety-nine per cent decided this was going nowhere . . . note to self, check the site when I get home to see whether his ad is still up. 'What gave you the idea?'

'Well a friend of mine used it and she was successful.'

'I see. So why didn't you and she date if you were both single?'

'Oh, she wasn't looking for a boyfriend. She was still a student and a little hard up, so she . . .'

. . . advertised for dates? Ah, a casual Gumtree hooker. Plenty of those these days.

'. . . put in an ad basically asking people to buy her dinner, which seemed to help her out a lot.'

'Heh. Great euphemism.'

'What's that?'

'You know, buying someone dinner . . .'

'I don't get it.'

'What's to get?' I said, and winked. 'As long as she offered value for money as it were.'

His eyebrows knit together in confusion. 'She said a lot of them were great conversationalists and that they took her to nice places.'

Was he kidding? Did this guy really mean to tell me he actually thought that friend of his was just offering companionship for the duration of a meal to strange men she hooked on the internet? Dear me, there really is one born every minute. Suppose that's the earlier question about sex workers answered, then.

vendredi, le 06 janvier

Thoughts, musings and goings-on of Belle de Office:

- Secretly wore push-up bra to quarterly-review meeting with Giles. Am wondering whether admitting this constitutes an unrealistic representation of working life.
- While I am ordinarily loath to burst anyone's bubble, it must be said that my boss is a balding, sub-Hugh Grant type with prominent incisors. Alas, it's not all chalk-stripe City boys like in the movies. Your boss might not be someone you'd choose in real life but it's part and parcel of the job to work for them – regardless of their appearance.
- Feeling v. guilty about my privileged position, as it's well known that one in five desk workers are not happy-go-lucky ladies of the day like me but underpaid temps forced into the industry in order to pay off student debts. Decide to forget it and bunk off for a champagne lunch instead.
- Unfortunately youth – or at least the impression of youth –

is paramount in this line of work. Am thinking of knocking three years off the time since my degree.

- Yes, it's a jet-set lifestyle. I get to travel between the break room and my desk, am fêted by secretaries constantly demanding my autograph and am paid almost a third of a living wage every year. But no one tells you about the unglamorous bits – like having to hand-wash your M&S jumpers and laying them flat to dry, for instance.

- Just discovered blog of anonymous lady accountant – hot stuff! Now that's easy money . . . would do it in a heartbeat if I had no conscience.

samedi, le 07 janvier

I work hard to maintain a hard shell of cool, but it's not really my way. I'm the person who always turns up just that bit too early and has to stand around wondering if in fact everyone is somewhere else while I sip a drink and try to look terribly interested in the football lest some forty-something bruiser decide I'm his target for the evening. I don't do late. It's not in my genetic makeup. It was a good thing when I was a call girl; I must have driven my manager mad with dozens of 'Oh no, I'm going to be late!!!' texts but was in fact rarely, if ever, not on time.

Still, fate has a funny way of making you feel a complete prat, and even the best laid plans fall foul of some cosmic schedule from time to time.

There is a saying, never attribute to malice that which can be adequately explained by stupidity. I suppose the larger view/global version would be never attribute to fate that which can be adequately explained by chance. But I can't help wonder if someone is trying to make a fool of me as:

- Important meeting yesterday; needed to make a good impression. Hair? Reliably neat for the last six months at least. The day of the meeting? Two words: 'Leo' and 'Sayer'.
- Finally cleared my schedule for a much-needed girly spa weekend with L when the boiler decides to break and, this being winter, must be dealt with post haste.
- This week, waiting for the British Gas people to turn up, scheduled on their marvellously impersonal phone system ('your appointment is scheduled for between twelve p.m. and six p.m. – goodbye'), I had one five-minute errand to run. Obviously at the very moment I was absent from the premises the man arrives, sees no one is home, and moves on. Genius.

dimanche, le 08 janvier

This may be an appropriate time to mention that I have had a long-standing masturbatory fantasy involving a gas man, i.e. I am administering oral relief to one when my husband/boyfriend/whatever happens to turn up and catch us in flagrante. As punishment, am required to service all the British Gas service contractors in a twenty-mile radius while said partner looks on (preferably from the vantage point of knacker-deep in my arse).

Probably best not to mention this to the chaps flushing my radiators, I suppose.

lundi, le 09 janvier

The hot Jewish list New Year's list (aka Take Note, I Won't Pair Off With Just Anyone):

1 James Callis, the mad scientist in the new *Battlestar Galactica* (also I think he played some minor role in the Bridget Jones movies but it's a minor flaw like that which simply highlights how perfect he otherwise is)
2 errr . . .
3 that's it.

I may be fatally picky here. A girl has to aim high, no?

mardi, le 10 janvier

Colds. They're really like the first flushes of lust, aren't they? You spend all day in bed, you can't concentrate on anything serious, you never put on your real clothes and you don't eat very much.

That said, I'd rather be having a man this week.

mercredi, le 11 janvier

'Is there anything you need from the shops?'

'Guh. Can't even think about food right now.'

'Now, now, that's exactly when you need to eat something. Get your energy back up. What was your resting heart rate this morning?'

'What are you, my GP? Fuck off.'

'Speaking of which, they say orgasm is the world's original analgesic. Maybe we could find a way to get rid of your aches and pains?'

I love N. There are few enough men in this world who would follow up an entreaty to fuck off with a sexual come-on, and fewer still who'd populate my life and drop everything to make up a Lemsip.

jeudi, le 12 janvier

Day three of a cold is officially melancholy day. Falling half in and out of sleep all day, twisting the bed-sheets into damp ropes, having dreams – were they dreams? memories? – of my ex.

It never hits you when and where you'd expect. You'll be fine, running a bath, checking your email and suddenly it overcomes you like . . . like what? A shroud maybe, only I wouldn't know. Like drowning but, again, I wouldn't know that for certain either. Do people who are drowning think it feels like melancholy?

Oh, I'm skilled at the art of breakup. I have all the coping mechanisms down: ringing friends to meet for drinks, throwing myself into work, listening to rock music at full volume. Only this time I couldn't get to some music or email or ring up a friend, I couldn't get away while memory had its dirty way with me.

Something my friend Tomás in Mexico said once: *Mejor sola que mal acompañada.* Better alone than with a bad companion. Of course, Tomás also said that it was good for a woman's eyesight if she wore earrings bought with money stolen from her husband and that a white cricket signifies doom. But he was right – not just about the cricket – and I had to keep telling myself over and over, weaving it into my neural pathways alongside the sex, the holidays, and the endless, endless arguments the Boy and I had together.

vendredi, le 13 janvier

'Oh, cat,' I said, scratching behind its ears. The cat let out a squeak and rested its little head on my thigh. 'Do you know, you're the only man in my life who hasn't left me so far?'

The cat sat up and licked its crotch. 'I know, I know, that's largely because I had you fixed. But still, aren't you happy here? Don't you have everything you need? Being with me isn't so bad, is it?'

The cat looked up and mewed. He cocked his head to one side and looked at me with wide, clear eyes. 'Your needs are so simple. A bit of kibble, a bit of lit to scratch around in and you'll love me forever.'

The cat mewed again, more insistent this time. 'Yes, it's like we have an understanding. I feel that we communicate without even having to be the same species. You're sorry for me, and trying to comfort me.'

The cat nibbled my finger gently. 'Aw, like that. You're trying to take my mind off things.' The bite went quickly from exploratory to sharp and I jumped.

'Or, our food bowl might be empty.' I sighed and shuffled towards the cat's cupboard. 'Typical men, you're all alike . . .'

samedi, le 14 janvier

Browsing men and books with L at Foyles. Lost myself in the graphic novels, where I came across an old friend.

No, not a man – a comic.

It was *How Loathsome*. I was so arrested by nostalgia I stood reading it front to back on the spot though, I'm ashamed to say, did not buy it, when L finally found and collected me. Will return and buy as soon as possible! Promise.

I loved it. Loved. It. This was a cut above, and not because I read in it a virtual echo of my own life from 1992 until 1999 but because it was written with such wry sensitivity, not the usual desire to shock with freakiness or jump through cutesy-gay-characters hoops. It read as real in a way that, I hope, even people who did not see themselves somewhere on those pages would recognise.

It's made me feel all wistful and sad, which is horrible. I hate feeling sentimental. I despise the idea of people under eighty being nostalgic for a time gone by, but couldn't help it. It reminded me of the straight boyfriend I brought to a sex party and whose lovely round bum I had to hustle out of there before he was attacked/died of fright (we went outside and had sex watching through the window instead – everyone loved that); of the day I stopped counting how many people I'd slept with, because once it's divisible by twenty-three there's no point keeping track; of the first time I bought toothed nipple clamps; of the first time I sold some; of the man who taught me how to use a bull-whip on his boyfriend; of the lover who dressed like Grayson Perry in little-girl mode and had seemingly infinite anal capacity; of the dungeon in Bloomsbury; of arguing with friends about what the minimum attendance should be before something can be classified a 'gang-bang' (we settled on six). Good times all.

And yes, I feel bad about leaving that life behind. Not for the endless boredom in between social engagements, nor the Machiavellian internal politics, nor the seemingly bottomless self-pity I had then but for the adventures. I'd love to meet someone now who wants to explore these things – but it's not a place you'd take a tourist.

And I wouldn't know where to start. I'll smile at a

particularly well turned-out trannie on the street and forget that I don't have the sartorial semiotics anymore to deserve more than her sneer. After the initial embarrassment passes, it irks me. I don't like the idea of identity being about outward appearance. All groups have it. You can't like indie music, for instance, unless you have elbows like sharpened points and a pair of trendy glasses. Or the rare times I went camping and, by not having either dreads and sandals or the latest high-tech kit, I was viewed as a bit of a dabbler by some, even though . . . well, I don't feel I should have to present my bushcraft credentials for approval. I am whatever I am (points to head) in here. Not (gestures to rather bland clothes) out here.

Still, maybe I'll buy myself the book as a gift. A travel brochure, if you will.

lundi, le 16 janvier

I was planning to tell you about this excellent gig I was at the other night with N and A4 but a girl has to have some secrets! At the very least, I can say I was dressed in an absolutely fierce pair of skinny jeans, open-toe metallic wedges, a broderie-anglaise shirt with a pink silk tie round the waist . . . with my fave cropped leather jacket on top. I looked great (pity no one noticed, ho hum).

Contrast this with today, when Giles broke off in the middle of a work meeting to ask, 'Sorry, but are you wearing gardening clogs?'

Yes. Yes I am. Wanna, as BA Baracus would no doubt ask, make somethin' of it?

mardi, le 17 janvier

Maybe it's genetic. Maybe it's because of where I was raised. Nature? Nurture? You decide: As the weather grows colder, my skirts get shorter.

mercredi, le 18 janvier

The wonderful thing about being a homeowner is the satisfaction of knowing that everything in the place where you live belongs to you and you alone. No more worry about lease agreements and rent hikes. You can have whatever pets you like and as many as you like. If someone drops a splash of red wine on the carpet, you don't automatically deduct from the running-security-deposit total in your head.

When the weather is fine, you open the windows and let the sun stream in, enjoying the feeling of pride that comes with home ownership. You fill your house with flowers, light, and laughter. When the weather's rotten and damp you can turn the heating up, curl up on the sofa under a wool blanket and enjoy the simple comforts with a brew. You're an adult when you have your own place, positively contributing to the economy, giving a good example to all the renters on the rung of the ladder beneath yours. It's an indescribably good feeling: warm and full. They say an Englishman's home is his castle, but it's so much more than that. It isn't where the heart is. It is the heart.

Though I'd give it all up in a minute for someone else to deal with the plumbing.

jeudi, le 19 janvier

'Blech,' A1 said, pulling a face. 'Not very nice in here.'

'I know, I know,' I said. 'Guess in the past I always imagined cat owners were immune to the smell. Now I know they're just resigned to it.' As the saying goes, if you want boxes of shit in your house, get a cat.

'I know I said I was going to have a look at that dripping shower, but . . . uh . . .'

'Want to go out for a drink first to steel yourself?'

'Please. I reckon it's a two-pint, if not a three-pint stink at least.'

vendredi, le 20 janvier

The box was dropped unceremoniously on the floor. 'Is that all of it?' N asked.

'Everything.'

'Do I have to check anything past you?'

'I trust you.' I rethought the comment. 'But yes, check with me first.'

N's hands dove into my total collection of pants and bras and associated items of lingerie. 'First things first, lose these and everything like these,' he said, holding up a greying pair of M&S's finest.

'Ye gods, yes. I don't even know when I bought those.'

We had set ourselves the task of reorganising my wardrobe, the first step of which was filtering the wheat from the chaff in my underthings. Some underwear is gorgeous and only meant to be worn for the few minutes it takes a man until he rips it off you; some are beautiful but also functional; some are an abomination unto womankind. It was that last category I was seeking to lose.

'You've probably got enough thongs in here to supply the entirety of Brazil,' he laughed.

I nodded. The Boy had liked thongs and, while I found them neither attractive nor good value given the ratio of price to fabric, I'd been buying them to please him for years.

Thongs, in my opinion, are inherently not sexy. Sure, you can make them out of lace, and you can stick bows here there and everywhere – in fact, most manufacturers of the damned things seem unable to stop themselves doing so, making it a distinct possibility that you may end up in casualty with a badly-placed-ribbon injury of the worst possible sort. But there's nothing left to the imagination no matter how you cut it. And I have never held much truck with the VPL-avoidance argument for buying them; surely part of looking sexy is to make someone think about what underwear you might have on under there?

'Actually, some of these are pretty cute,' N said, holding up a blue net g-string. 'Can I keep?'

'They go,' I said with conviction. If for no other reason than the associated memories. And so they did, apart from the leopard one which I never got around to wearing at all. 'Because it's cute,' he insisted.

'I won't wear it.'

'Save it anyway. If we ever do it again you can wear them.'

'Deal.'

As for brassieres, I was obliged to hold on to one designed specifically for the gym – I like high impact in my sporting life as much as in my sex life – and a single flesh-coloured seam-free bra for the occasional white t-shirt. Otherwise, if it was boring or if there was a single pop in the elastic or tear in the lace, it was binned.

'Sure you wouldn't like to check the fit as well?' N asked. 'I could give some objective feedback.'

'You wish. I'll do that on my own later.'

By the time we'd finished, I had in the yes pile a much smaller collection of frillies than I'd started with – but one that had passed all of my (and N's) stringent requirements. And more importantly, I wouldn't be segregating my work knickers from my home knickers any longer. It was time to ditch the schizophrenia in my sartorial life.

dimanche, le 22 janvier

Surprise text this evening:

Just wanted to let you know I still consider you a friend. Mx

Magnus is the Boy's younger brother. He'd visited me a few times in London and was always considerate enough to extend a reciprocal invite; I finally decided to take him up on it and nipped up to Edinburgh for the weekend.

Was introduced to the Aladdin's Cave that is the Canny Man's and, really, while I can think of few events in life that warrant buying a Nebuchadnezzar of bubbly, the mere fact of finding a pub that sells it will – almost – do. Unfortunately our cash reserves had been rather depleted by that point, so guzzling a person-sized bottle of champers would have to wait until next time. Pity.

I like my boyfriend's brothers a little too much. I like Magnus especially; I've known him since he was a teenager and have watched him blossom over the years into a smart, attractive – if far too young for me – man. Not that I would ever . . . no, I learned that by unfortunate experience years ago. You don't. You simply don't. (I don't have brothers; how could I have been expected to know? Sisters poach each other's castoffs all the time.) Magnus was like the Polyfilla in our relationship. I liked him and all the other brothers, I liked seeing how my boyfriend would have been if he were more bookish, more sporty, fair-haired. Seeing how he fits in to a large family helped me understand why he is like he is. And possibly refrain from throttling him.

And the one reservation I had about chucking the Boy on his well-padded arse was the prospect of losing his family.

'See, the problem with the girl who plays Hermione is that she's hot, but she so knows it,' I said.

'God, yes,' Magnus said. 'But I'd still do her.'

'I would, but I wouldn't call her afterwards.'

'Oh, I would.' A well-brought-up boy to the last.

Magnus likes the sort of music I like; we discussed fine spirits and religion and hit the rare whiskies (my ex-boyfriend would have chosen cocktails – yes, cocktails). At least one of them will join me for a serious drink. I slept on the floor of his flat in Morningside and in the a.m. took him to my fave place for breakfast. Afterwards, we wandered back to his, looking in shop windows and talking about computer games, films, dissertations. I really could do with some brothers, even if they're someone else's.

lundi, le 23 janvier

Giles has up to this point taken a rather laissez-faire attitude to his duties. But he must have picked up on something in my smug smile because suddenly he's asking about the progress of a project that's meant to finish in February. And I don't know how to say that I haven't done anything yet. So I proposed that we have a meeting in midweek to go over it, figuring that this would give me just enough time to make it look like I haven't been slacking off instead of toiling away behind the computer all winter.

He emailed this morning: Bit long to wait. Why don't you write a summary of how it's going and what you're planning to do in the next month?

Fuck fuck fuck. How best to say that I was so wrapped up in other things that I didn't even notice until yesterday he hadn't sent me all of the initial data for the project, without looking like a complete twat?

mardi, le 24 janvier

Dropped in to see my sister and nephew though, honestly, happy domesticity ain't my style. That said it's looking like it's not hers either, with a squalling infant and a late-arriving husband very much making the experience less cosy family and more dreaded family chore.

Still, I did manage to nick a few nappies on the way out. I'm sure with a sharp pair of scissors and some lateral thinking I could make them suitable for the cat.

mercredi, le 25 janvier

'What you need is to blow off a little steam,' N said, his large hands digging into the knots in my shoulders. 'Get laid, have some fun.'

'What I need – just to the left, there, you've got it – is to avoid getting physical with anyone until I'm sure of where it's going.'

'And that's exactly where friends come in.'

'You know, I do appreciate being able to talk to you about this,' I said. 'I'm glad we can be so open with each other after all that's happened.'

'Well, as we're being honest . . .'

'Yeah?' The tension was draining from my neck. N really did have magic fingers.

'How about it? You and me.'

'Are you talking about sex?'

'I'm always talking about sex.'

'I don't know what to say.'

'We always had a good time together. We're both single. Neither of us is in danger of falling for the other; we've already been through all that. We know there's friendship after sex if either of us meets someone else. And it would be a shame for that body of yours to go to waste. You're looking especially foxy these days. The other day, when you had on that blue dress after work . . .' His hands went slack as he was lost in a reverie.

Men, eh? Even when they shouldn't be thinking about sex, they're thinking about sex. Although when I stopped to think about it, that was one of the things that most endeared them to me. The abstract enjoyment without the need to overanalyse. I couldn't say yes. But I couldn't immediately say no, either. Maybe a little abstract enjoyment would do me the world of good.

jeudi, le 26 janvier

The most recent eligible bachelor . . .

. . . works one floor down from me at work (but crucially, not with me)

. . . is freaking adorable

. . . as well as being excruciatingly fuckable, is also whip-smart

. . . asked me out for drinks

. . . turned up drunk and swiftly proceeded to get even more smashed on my tab

. . . so I made my excuses circa half-ten. I didn't ring after. Neither did he.

Analysis:

Boyfriend material? 2/10 – I earn a reasonable salary, but not quite enough to support two lushes. Sorry, babes, but I gots to have a man who buys me G&Ts, not the other way round.

Fuckable? pick 'em – Would most likely pass out sometime before the bedroom. Apart from that, great! Or is it? This is someone so petrified of interaction with me that he lubes himself up with liquor in order to have a conversation, and not even a conversation that involved negotiating the use of sterile instruments, a drop sheet and a police baton. So 9/10 for straight-up, one-time sex; 3/10 for anything kinky. And I bet he considers going down to be kinky.

Client material? 6/10 – The sweetly earnest sort who would request GFE, insist on a lot of awkward conversation first, down half a bottle of white and fall asleep while you were blowing him. If he sobered up enough before you left to feel bad about this, would tip well.

Would date again? 4/10 – Would be a 7/10 if he dropped by my office and asked for a second try – but he hasn't yet.

Final comments? – His desk is between my office and the ladies loo. Am just going to have to hold it in for now.

Watch this space . . .

vendredi, le 27 janvier

This morning a DJ saved my life.

Or if not saved, at least improved significantly; that is,

after all, what I assume the song is about. No one's life was ever really saved by a DJ, was it? If you were having a heart attack in a club, for instance, what are the chances a DJ would strip off his headphones, jump down to the dance floor and administer the kiss of life? Slim-to-none is my guess. And how many people can say that a DJ gave them the kidney they needed to survive, or a bone marrow donation? Very few, if any at all.

Anyway. I've been a bit down lately. Various reasons. Work is tedious. Not just normal tedious, but actual watching-paint-dry-would-be-better-than-this, full-on, brain-meltingly unbearable. My friends are all away on holiday. And my life is distinctly lacking someone who turns up three times a day to service my needs. So this morning I was sitting in the office feeling a mite sorry for myself.

But then a DJ saved my life (figuratively, as discussed earlier). It started with Bauhaus – 'Bela Lugosi's Dead'. Followed by Blondie – 'Rip Her to Shreds'. And then, when I was already perking up considerably, the icing on the cake: Sultans of Ping FC – 'Where's Me Jumper?'

If you don't know this song, all I can say is, I'm sorry. And if you do know it, and it doesn't make your day to hear it, you're probably beyond saving.

It was at this point I started pogoing around the room, much to the amusement of . . . well, no one actually. My door was closed and unlike in the movies, no one walked by at a particularly embarrassing moment. It cheered me up no end and made everything that's been bothering me lately seem just that bit less important. It was followed by some French a cappella beatbox-y thing (that was when I went to the toilet). Music loves you, baby. Music will get you through. Yes, I thought. I can handle things. Life isn't so bad. I should count my blessings, &c.

Doesn't mean I'm not half-looking out for a new lover,

though. Happily I have two dates this weekend, so who knows? Might even get lucky.

samedi, le 28 janvier

'So, you just moved to London. Interesting. What sort of work do you do?'

'I write for the *Daily Mirror*.'

Think I set a new land-speed record getting out of there.

dimanche, le 29 janvier

We were three hours in to a *Battlestar-Galactica* marathon when the subject came up.

'You know you want to . . .'

'Never. I would consider it a betrayal of all I stand for.'

'You stand for neat shots and chocolate for breakfast, which is not much of a moral high ground as far as I know,' A2 said. 'Anyway, you can't say no, I've already booked us.'

Speed dating? For realz? 'Such a stupid idea.'

'I'm single. You're single. Tell me one reason why it's stupid.'

'What do we do when we get to each other?'

'We compare notes, dur. You tell me what the other women say about me, and I tell you what the other men are really like. You need the help. Your taste in men is terrible.'

I scowled. I had spent the better part of the evening rehashing those terrible two dates, it's true. But still, did he have to be so mean? 'I chose you once, remember?'

'Even a blind dog finds a bone sometimes,' he said.

I sigh. Today, I'm feeling very 'I Am a Rock, I Am an Island'. No one worth remembering was ever remembered strictly for being part of a couple, right? Napoleon sans Josephine would still have been Emperor. *The Sunday Times* bestseller list does not note marital status. Oh, to be a Cylon. On the other hand there are certain realities that cannot be denied, and one of them is that I hate staying in of a Friday night and am too young yet to go back on the game at MILF-level. So I (reluctantly) agree.

lundi, le 30 janvier

Blech – what I said about the chap who works a floor down from me and any associated possibilities? Scratch that. We are fundamentally incompatible in unspeakable ways.

And we hadn't even got to talking about sex yet.

We met for lunch and, seeing nothing in particular I fancied, I ordered a cheese plate. 'Wow, bit heavy for lunchtime,' he said over his salad.

I grinned. 'I love everything about cheese . . . in fact, if given the opportunity to live solely off cheese and chocolate, I probably would.' I sipped a glass of red wine; he took gulps of mineral water.

'Huh. Well I guess that's okay, if you're looking to get gout,' he said.

'It's only cheese,' I shrugged. 'Besides, I eat veg from time to time.'

'Really? I've not seen any yet.'

'Cheers, Mum,' I said. 'Bit of a generalisation considering we've met exactly twice.' And you were drinking like a champ the first time, I thought.

'No but you get a good idea of someone's health habits straight away,' he said.

I bristled. I go to the gym several times a week and when I was younger, loved sport – still do. In fact, put against most of the Diet Coke-guzzling, chip-packed women my own age, I thought I was holding up rather well. 'Tell you what, darling. The day you go from being a glorified temp to being my GP, you can criticise my diet. Until then, I'd appreciate if you did the gentlemanly thing and shut the fuck up about things you know nothing about.'

No, don't think we'll be seeing him again.

mardi, le 31 janvier

The hotel was mid-level, central, anonymous. I knew it well. Favoured by business travellers and the occasional tourist who booked without knowing where anything was in the city. I walked in confidently – place like this, no one would even look twice, much less stop me.

A large figure hovered into my view and I turned sharply. The man's eyes narrowed, then softened in recognition. 'Sorry, I thought you were coming later,' he said.

'Have you checked in?'

'We're good to go. Would you like a drink from the bar first?'

'No, I'm fine.'

'Let's head up to the room then.'

The elevator pinged as it rose past each floor. It was tense with anticipation, and we avoided each others' eyes in the mirror. Such moments were make-or-break in these situations, so I smiled to try to put him at ease. Still, I wondered if each second in the elevator felt like ten to him, as well. 'You look nice,' I said. His shirt was well-tailored, I noticed, emphasising the breadth of his shoulders.

'Cheers. You're looking particularly sexy,' N said and wrapped his arm around my waist as the elevator doors opened on the sixth floor.

We fell on the bed together laughing. It had been years since I'd seen N naked, but he was just like I remembered. His long, heavy limbs wrapped around me as he struggled with the bra clasp. 'Now those are quality tits,' he said, grasping them.

'Careful how hard you're going there,' I said.

'Sorry, did you want harder?' He dug his fingers in, so deep I squealed. This was the N I'd known and loved, the one who couldn't help but find my sexual boundaries and push them. I wondered what had kept us apart for so long.

It was a great night – we didn't do anything new together, just revisited all the old favourites. He had brought a whip and flogged my arse till it was studded with pink welts that were hot to the touch. I sucked his large cock while he pulled my head back and forth by the hair. I begged him to pull and pinch my nipples as we watched me masturbate myself to an epic, shuddering orgasm, and when I was done he came on my face.

And then, for the first time in a long time, I slept over in a hotel. There had been plenty of times I'd been paid to as a call girl, though of course even on an overnight assignment you're never really off the job. The men normally crash out, but I was often too wound up to truly rest. But in this anonymous bed, in this anonymous hotel with the man who was the closest thing to a best friend I'd ever had, I slept like the dead.

When the first light came through the window he rolled over, pressing his erection between my thighs. 'Morning, glory,' he said. 'How about you suck me off and we go see what this place has in the way of breakfast?'

Ten men to avoid in dating:

1 The Yes Man: what does he want to do? Whatever you want to do. What are his interests? Wow, identical, who would have guessed! Like gardens? Funny you should mention it; he's setting up motion-sensitive cameras in yours as we speak!

2 The Me-Me-Me: because let's be honest, I don't care-care-care. Not quite yet, anyway.

3 The Sad Dad: divorced and looking for someone to fulfil the coveted role of stepmother. Let's be honest, gents, if you feel it necessary to point out that you're not bitter about how it ended with your ex-wife, you're bitter.

4 Roman Abramovich.

5 Anyone you've ever seen on *Crimewatch*. I feel on some level this shouldn't need to be said, but occurrence of prison marriages is far too high for the point to be moot.

6 Your father, or anyone remotely resembling.

7 Anyone whose mother remotely resembles you.

8 A man who feels the need to mention Jeremy Clarkson at any point or in any context on a first date.

9 The Fake Londoner: admit it, we've all met him – born in St Albans, but throws down mockney like the bastard son of an unholy union between Jamie Oliver and Lily Allen. Can often be found holding forth on the demise of jellied eel. Has largely cribbed his chat-up technique (and indeed life philosophy) from episodes of *Only Fools and Horses*.

10 The Untouched Heart: anyone who says he's never been in love by this age is, frankly, either a sociopath or lying.

Fevrier

mercredi, le 01 fevrier

Text from me to N: My nipples are still aching. Cut your nails, man! Hell getting a bra on this morning.

Text back from N: Careful what you tell me, or I'll have to come round and administer some more punishment.

jeudi, le 02 fevrier

Who knew? Speed dating always happens midweek. Presumably so you have a decent shot of actually being able to hear what anyone's saying in the bar, I suppose.

'More like so you don't have to lie to your friends about why you won't be joining them on a Saturday,' A2 said. Get the cynic. He came by mine because, really, men don't need time to prepare.

'I can't believe I let you talk me into this,' I griped from the bathroom, where I was applying makeup.

The secret to perfect eyelashes, I learned a long time ago, is to have them dyed black. That way you never have to worry about touch-ups, clumps or makeup running in the rain, but I hadn't made time for an appointment beforehand and can never quite manage to wield the home kits without spreading the stuff all over my cheeks. No, it was going to be a mascara job. I was trying to get just enough to hint at a sexy, smoky look but was probably going to end up looking more women's shelter than supermodel.

'I can't believe you're so impressionable,' A2 said, holding the cat.

'Careful, you'll get his fluff all over your shirt. Wouldn't want the ladies to think your clothes have more hair than you do.'

'At least my house doesn't smell of shit in a box,' A2 said. But he did let the cat down.

More than a few times on the way over I caught myself wishing the Tube would break down and we'd be stuck in a tunnel all night, but no such luck. The event itself ended early (school night, dontcha know) and, left to our own devices, A2 and I drifted back together at the bar to compare notes.

'Why are you so smiley and happy? Meet anyone nice?'

'Just amused by the absurdity of it all,' I said. 'Also pleased that I got the number six.'

'You are not Number Six. Kara Thrace, more like. Number Three at a stretch. But you have about as much in common with Number Six as I have with . . . uhh . . .'

'A sensitive, attractive man worth getting to know for longer than three minutes?'

'Piss off. Anyway, who did you tick?'

The night started off well: my first three-minute 'date' was with a good-looking chap I found easy to talk to. Unfortunately, it was all downhill from there.

'You ticked him?' A2 said, checking over my card. 'Bit simple, don't you think?'

'You're just jealous cos he's fit,' I said. 'Who'd you tick?'

'His housemate, for starters.'

'Ugh, you ticked her? Bit too much cleavage on show for a weeknight.'

'You're just jealous cos more men are ticking her than you.'

'Fucking hell. Really?'

'Yeah, the ones I saw, anyway.'

'Shit. Well, at least I can be confident my first date didn't tick her as they already live together, and . . . um, what happens if they both tick us?'

'Then the game is on, bitch,' A2 smiled.

vendredi, le 03 fevrier

I went on to the speed-dating website to make my selections. There were five men I'd marked as definitely yes; the others, I'd written a few notes on, in order to decide later.

Oops. I'm sure John, thirty-one, from Manchester, is probably a very nice person, but all I wrote on the sheet was 'works for Procter and Gamble'. I don't know what to think about that. Was this a note to my future self of a liaison worth pursuing? ('Works for Procter and Gamble? Therefore has a job! Yes!') Or some coded warning for my future self? ('Works for Procter and Gamble? Therefore is a satanist! Only a maybe!' or even 'Works for Procter and Gamble? In three minutes, that's the best he could come up with? No!')

To be honest, most of my time since then hasn't been spent considering the relative merits of this man vs. that man. It's been spent trying to imagine the logistics of a bisexual speed-dating event, or one for lesbians. *Manhunt* and *Gaydar* are like speed dating for gay men, so they're already covered.

In the end, I stuck with the five that were marked as definitely yes. It seemed a small figure, given the number of available men. And I could always log on and add more later. But who knows if they'd even choose me?

Within minutes, my phone started going . . .

samedi, le 04 fevrier

. . . and in under an hour, I'd learned that the five chaps I'd chosen had also chosen me. Does anyone know a good place to learn circus skills? I foresee some juggling in my future.

lundi, le 06 fevrier

Oh fark. I am *so* found out at work. I haven't done anything productive, at least not from Giles's point of view, for the last six weeks.

On the other hand it wasn't as bad as I expected. A gentle email telling-off and a reminder of deadlines, nothing drastic. This could be down to one of a few reasons:

- I'm so shit hot I can do anything and get away with it.
  Likelihood rating: 2 stars.
- I'm so shit hot he fancies me and is maybe a little scared of being humiliated by a pretty woman.
  Likelihood rating: 3 stars.
- I'm so premenstrual he is maybe a little scared of what I might do if confronted.
  Likelihood rating: 4 stars.
- It's not really that important a project anyway; who cares?
  Likelihood rating: 3 stars.
- He's passive-aggressively criticising me behind my back instead of to my face.
  Likelihood rating: 4 stars.

- Everyone does this and I'm only just catching on.
  Likelihood rating: 5 stars.

Shirking work is not usually a part of my ethos. Coming in late with an obviously new pair of shoes on, yes; calling in sick any day with more than four minutes continuous sunshine, yes; going off for two-hour lunches without telling anyone, yes; reading the Internet incessantly (well, who doesn't?), yes. But I'm always on time with hand-ins and always to spec, if not above. I am of the opinion that if your work can't be carried out well within the confines of the working day, something is wrong. Whatever else my parents gave me, their genes for last-minute flashes of inspiration have been a godsend.

But I don't know where my head is these days. It's not the Boy – or is it? Not the lack of sex – but I can't be sure, can I? The late arrival of spring? Festering resentment about voluntarily choosing a lower paid job for more hours?

I'm torn. I don't know whether a telling-off from Giles is a good development or not – whether it will inspire me to work harder or to take yet longer lunches. Should maybe work on option number two just to have all my bases covered.

mardi, le 07 février

'You, my office, now,' Giles said.
    'Phone conference, my office, go away,' I snapped.
    Giles looked sheepish. 'Oh, sorry. Fifteen minutes then?' he said.
    I nodded briskly and turned away as he closed the door. What could he want? True, my mind hadn't exactly been on my work lately, but I'd at least been making an attempt to

get to the office early – a lame attempt to get my mind off my empty house. Empty, that is, apart from the damned cat.

'Okay, boss man, what's up?' I said, sitting in the brown leather chair opposite his desk.

'It's about Alex,' Giles said. 'I'm concerned . . . about her motivations for being in this company.'

I shrugged. That, as the saying goes, is not my dog. Attractive, rich older man shields her from any trouble at work, and she quite sensibly takes full advantage? Cry me a river, mate. 'What do you want me to do about it?'

'Make friends with her. Get to know her. Find out what's going on.'

Make friends with your piece of fluff? No thanky-thanky, mister. If I know women – and I don't know women, only well enough to know that in general, I don't want to know women – she'll stab me in the back given the slightest opportunity. 'I don't think welcome wagon was exactly on my to-do list for the week,' I said. 'Why not ask the secretaries? They're like the paparazzi of office gossip, only crueller.'

'Because I need someone who can talk to her on her level,' Giles said. 'And if I'm not mistaken, I'm at least nominally still the boss around here.'

'Fine. I'll take her out to coffee. But don't expect miracles.'

mercredi, le 08 février

Speed Date Bachelor No. 1 (or, How to Lose a Guy in Ten Minutes).

I arrived a few minutes early and went to the bar to get a drink. The barman smiled. 'So, what would you two like?'

'I'm not drinking tonight,' I said. 'But the pumpkin will have a pint of Deuchar's.'

'The pumpkin has good taste,' the barman said, drawing the pint and setting it on the bar next to the white pumpkin.

'Thank you. But a handled glass? The pumpkin is a lady,' I said. The barman laughed.

I'd passed a farmer's market on the way to the date and got chatting to a chap behind the veg stand. He sold me a white pumpkin. In my defence I can say it seemed like a good idea at the time. I texted my date: Am here already, sitting near the back, with a white pumpkin.

He arrived a few minutes later. 'Wow.'

'Yeah, it's a pumpkin. Sort of like how men on blind dates used to wear white carnations, I guess.'

'This isn't a blind date.'

'No, but it's as near as.'

And that, friends, was the sum total of conversation. That was it. He went to the bar, came back to the table, sat down with his pint, and sipped it slowly – very slowly – looking from me to the pumpkin and back again. At first I thought it was his schtick – no talk, let me start the conversation, put me on the back foot, whatever. But as the clock ticked through five minutes, then ten, and he was still looking at me silently, and hadn't taken his jacket off, I began to feel awkward. Very awkward.

'So, how did you find the speed dating?'

Silence.

'Did you have many matches?' This was starting to get beyond desperate. Please, say something, say anything, so I don't start dialling nine-nine-nine surreptitiously under the table. I had a bad feeling about this guy. As in, this man is a freak and has my number. It's been years since I felt that way. 'There were a lot of nice girls there on the night.'

Silence.

'Wow, is that the time. No, thank you, don't get up, I have an early morning tomorrow and must get home now. Good night!' And I grabbed the pumpkin and left.

On the upside, the cute fellow at the veg stand did get my number. Maybe it won't be a total loss after all. And I do have a pumpkin.

Analysis:

Boyfriend material? 1/10 – No, no, no, no, no. There's being a good listener, but this was something else entirely.

Fuckable? 4/10 – Somewhat resembles A2. A2 is fuckable. It does not necessarily follow that all people who resemble him are therefore fuckable, but I'll give this guy the benefit of the doubt (though not the chance to up his rating).

Client material? 4/10 — He'd do it once then never again. Or, he'd turn into one of those working-girl obsessives who 'collects' girls like some people collect comics, and given the fug of creepiness that emanated from this dude like stink off a Stilton, I'm guessing the latter.

Would date again? 0/10 – Please let him lose my number. Please, please, please let him lose my number.

Final comments? – I told the taxi driver to get out of there like he was trying to lose someone, and keep an eye on the mirror for any cars that might be following.

jeudi, le 09 février

'Cheers for inviting me out,' Alex said, gathering up her bags. She put on her coat – nice, an Aquascutum. Vintage. She might be annoying but her eye for style was improving.

When she buttoned up I caught the faintest whiff of perfume. Unusual for midweek. And her hair was looking very sleek, as if she'd just come from the salon.

I nodded. 'It's good to see people outside the context of work, isn't it?'

I hadn't quite meant to imply anything, but she blinked in an eerie, slow way that let me know she'd taken in every possible implication of what I'd said. 'Yes,' she said. 'It's good. Doesn't happen nearly often enough though.'

'You back at work this afternoon?' Now that I noticed it, she was wearing a higher heel than usual, and her nails looked as if they'd recently seen the business end of an orange stick.

'Dentist's appointment,' she said briskly. 'I'd better jet, I'm already late.'

I nodded. And when I got back to the office, as she must have known I would do, I checked the online appointment system. Yes, there it was: dentist appointment. No contact details. No follow-up.

On a hunch I clicked onto Giles's schedule. GP appointment, same slot. Well, it didn't tell me anything I didn't already know. But why was he pushing so hard for me to befriend her when things were clearly going well between them? Unless he'd told her the same, in order to spy on me?

vendredi, le 10 fevrier

Is it wrong that whenever I see a Leon Uris book I think of Cletus from *The Simpsons*? *'Pour casser une carapace de tortue, y'a pas mieux que Leon Uris.'*

Is it wrong to have made no plans for Valentine's Day, and be happy with that?

Is it wrong to place a wager with a co-worker on how long before Smug Married Colleague and Smug Giggly Intern hook-up?

Is it wrong to spend five quid on twelve biscuits, thereby getting ever deeper into the twisted game of Friday-Coffee-Break one-upmanship?

Is it wrong to save someone's number on your mobile under 'MBP' where MBP stands for Mouth-Breathing Pikey?

Is it wrong to blow an afternoon shopping on the Web and then completely forget what you've bought until a package comes to the door?

Is it more wrong if it's a package of knickers in the wrong size?

samedi, le 11 fevrier

Speed Date Bachelor No. 2 (or Tim, Tim, Nice but Under-motivated).

As it turned out, the hot girl with mile-long cleavage did not tick A2. But the good-looking guy she lives with did tick me.

'In your face, Smuggy McTwat!'

'I bet he wears a nice shirt and talks about his nice school,' A2 grumbled. 'I bet you die of boredom before they even bring the starters and run off with the waiter.'

'Jealous much?'

A2 looked me over. I was wearing a slinky red mini-dress, brown woollen over-the-knee socks, and red patent shoes. 'Nah, I been there already.'

Bachelor No. 2 had suggested a trendy bar near his house. Asian theme, secluded tables, good music on not too loud. Nice.

Drinks: Belgian beer for him; whisky for me.

I thought he'd suggest going on for a meal, but he didn't; we went to another bar instead.

Drinks: Stella for him; another whisky for me.

Then a pub.

Drinks: Pint of bitter for him; same for me.

Then some music venue. Then another bar. I'd half hoped the night might end up being a session, I just hadn't thought it would be of the pub-crawling sort.

The chatting, such as it was, was okay. I talked a lot about nothing in particular. He made encouraging noises and stood closer and closer to me. We flopped on a squidgy leather sofa and I nattered on, hoping he'd have been sufficiently lubricated with drink to bust out the mad conversational skillz. No such luck.

Maybe it was because I'd had nothing to eat, and the drinks were going to my head. Maybe it's because after the last disastrous date I was determined to kill any awkward conversational silences dead. Maybe it's because he just kept nodding and smiling, and putting his hand on my knee. But I got progressively more drunk and he just kept nodding and, finally, I got to the point where I was either going to have to eat something, go to the ladies' and be sick or take him home with me.

My guess? He was angling for choice three. Well, it could have happened. It might have happened. But while he did seem to be rubbing up against me not-so-subtly at any opportunity, he never went in for the kill.

Sometimes, I can be bold. No – most times. But we'd met at speed dating, so I assumed he at least wanted to get to know me first. Given my own preferences I would have said something to him along the lines of: 'Look, I enjoy this flirting/hugging/touching business, but I have better things to do with my time than to waste it guessing whether you wanna fuck. So do you wanna fuck? If not, ring me a taxi and enjoy the rest of your pint. But if you do, meet me in the men's loo in five minutes and bring a map because we are going to have a motherfucking adventure.'

But what I actually said was: 'Can you ring me a taxi? I think I'm going to be sick.'

The next morning I cleaned out my handbag and found the phone number (!) of some other man I didn't remember meeting (!!) who, in my handwriting apparently, is an 'accordion player' (!!!). So not running off with the waiter, exactly . . .

Note to self, have a sandwich before going out next time.

Analysis:

Boyfriend material? 4/10 – Meh. Wasn't feeling it.

Fuckable? 6/10 – Problematic. On the one hand, a nicely put together figure of a man. On the other, so pretty he probably hasn't had to ever try very hard in bed. Possibly good, possibly yawn.

Client material? 3/10 – Apart from a stag-do jaunt, most likely the sort of fellow who wouldn't even go there.

Would date again? 6/10 – Guardedly optimistic but, as my dad says, hope for the best, expect the worst.

Final comments? – A flurry of texts in the morning, then nothing. I reckon he's cycling through his other dates by now.

The phone rang insistently. I was not in bed, but about four feet from it, having decided the toilet was just that bit too far away to walk. But crawling also proving a difficulty, I simply gave up somewhere in the vicinity of the laundry basket. 'Gahhhh . . .'

'Good morning, sunshine, good one last night then?'

'Uh. Yeah, you could say that,' I croaked. My muscles felt shredded, as if someone had stuck me in a slow-cooker for the night. I rolled towards the door, then gave up and settled for panting on the carpet.

'Is he there?

'No, I thank god I managed to ruin the night before the late-night vomiting started in earnest.' I squinted against the bright sun streaming through the window. 'For some reason men don't make passes at girls who spend an hour yodelling into the rhododendrons.'

'You don't say,' N purred. 'If it was me, I'd find that rather a sexy addition to the total package.'

'Hmm. Well, it's just foam and bile since four a.m. so you're out of luck. But if you don't mind coming round to service a half-conscious invalid, then by all means, get yourself on over here.'

'Great. Mind if I bring my own porn? There's this amazing magazine I just picked up.'

'What's in it?'

'Only your favourite third-trimester-pregnancy-porn model, with the full watersports and anal-fisting scenario.'

I'd seen a few photo sets with that particular woman, always in full headgear so you couldn't even see her hair, much less her face. And the shots were always appalling and stunning in equal measure. She was, not to put too fine a point on it, my hero. 'Go on then, hit me.'

'I will. Believe me, you won't have to ask twice.'

lundi, le 13 fevrier

Email from Alex: Fancy lunch today? The nice sandwich place? Axx

Eurgh, I've always hated that. Women who sign their names with kisses, as if you're sisters, or even friends. But we're not friends, we're workmates at best.

Fab! Meet you by the fountain at one? B

I thought it through. Whatever the game was that was being played, I still had a chance to take control of it, to turn things to my advantage. I revised the message before sending: Meet you by the fountain at half one . . . Bxx

mardi, le 14 fevrier

Truth is Stranger than Fiction, part no. 3,425,679,008,743:

Joan Jett.

Carmen Electra.

Joan. Jett.

Carmen-motherfucking-Electra.

Joan JETT!

AND!

CARMEN ELECTRA!!!

The idea that these two may have ever gotten together is a little gossip titbit that will keep me going for ages. I don't care if it's true or not. I want it to be true, which in the world of masturbatory fantasies, is as true as anything ever needs to be.

mercredi, le 15 fevrier

'Jewish? Really? That's fantastic, because Larry David is my hero.'

'No. You don't say?'

'I love that show. It's like he's writing about my life . . .'

Sigh. Readers, meet Speed Dating Bachelor no. 3.

Chaps, keep your pound coin – this clue is free. You don't open with the Larry David comparison. You just don't. Especially if you're a twenty-something fellow with a BMW, all your own hair, a wardrobe stuffed with designer labels and expensive shoes and if you're as English as the day is long.

Why not? Because unless you bear an actual physical resemblance to Mr David, I'm now going to spend the entirety of the date trying to figure out precisely what you meant by that comment.

'Blah blah then I did this . . . then I moved here . . . Then there was the time I went to . . .'

Aah, it's finally hit me. You're like Larry David not because of any shared heritage, not because of an as-yet-undetectable sense of humour but because you're self-obsessed to the point of absurdity. Sorry, there's room for only one monstrous ego in a relationship and I'm not prepared to give up that for just anyone.

So right after coming home I Googled around and learned that Larry David also drives a BMW. German car?

Yougottabekiddingme. Maybe this guy has more in common with Larry than I initially credited him, and not in a good way.

Analysis:

Boyfriend material? 1/10 – I'm certain Larry David's a wonderful guy. No offence, but I wouldn't date him, nor anyone who claims to be like him. (Also: German car? Sorry to dwell, but it gives me gooseflesh.)

Fuckable? 5/10 – Fit enough, no question, though I would be tempted to gag him first. If he was cool with the gag, 7/10.

Client material? 9/10 – Strong marks here for being wealthy, on time and more likely to talk about himself for a full hour than ask me potentially awkward personal questions. Misses the top ranking for being the sort who probably doesn't tip.

Would date again? 2/10 – Maybe after a little cultural re-education my mother would like him as a toyboy. But not for me.

jeudi, le 16 février

'So how's it going?'

'Fine, Giles. We're like sisters now. In fact, I'm going to be her maid of honour.'

'You? Brittle old maid, more like.'

I couldn't help but smile. I like a man with a sense of humour, particularly one who's brave enough to take the piss. Not going to help him one bit with getting me into bed, but that doesn't seem to be high on his priority list at the moment. 'I wish I had some gossip to give you, dear,' I said. 'But she's straight.'

'Seriously?'

'Unmarried. No apparent smack habit or crack babies hidden away anywhere. Reasonable degree, though of course not as good as mine. Her bona fides check out. Strange habit of scheduling dentist appointments for mid-afternoon . . .' I looked right at Giles, but his face betrayed nothing. 'Otherwise, fine. Just your run-of-the-mill ambitious office girl . . .' sleeping her way to the top. 'What is it you're so worried about, anyway?'

'Uh. Nothing, really. I – I mean.' He stammered.

I can't take a stammer. I know it's not always under the person's control, but I will always associate it with the Boy – when he stammered, he was lying. Of course such a glorious verbal tic was very useful, if a bit heartbreaking because his lies were so regular they put Senokot to shame. But a stammer did not mean Giles was lying, only nervous. In which case, nervous about what?

'Of course it's none of my business,' I said. They're playing it cooler than they were, anyway, and I'm relieved for Giles's sake. On Valentine's Day there were no gossip-making deliveries of flowers for Alex, nor did she act as if she'd been expecting any. Of course that does not count out something being sent to her home. 'Whatever passes between the two of you is . . . your business entirely.'

'Um, yes,' Giles said. 'Yes, it is.'

vendredi, le 17 fevrier

'He's so fit . . . and kind, and I know you'd love him . . .'

No, not another potential date. Mum. Gushing about her new man.

'And he's so sexy . . .'

'Mum!'

'And great in—'

'MUM!'

'I'm sorry, honey. If it's any consolation, your father was also—'

'STOP IT! It's not a consolation!'

She went very, very quiet. I gulped.

'For years,' she said, finally, softly, 'for years I wondered what it would be like to live the sort of life young women live now. Things weren't like that for me as a girl, they simply weren't.'

'But you've told me the stories. The swinging sixties. You lived through it all.'

'I lived through it all, all right,' she said. 'Men who thought they were changing the world and women who were offering free love just for the chance to be where the excitement was. But even in the seventies, we never had any real power. Maybe this isn't power as such, but it feels good to finally be at a point where I don't care what other people think about me. So what if I'm shacked up with a man, and he's younger? That doesn't—'

'Wait, what? What did you say?'

'I don't know, what did I say?'

'You said you were shacked up with a younger man.'

'Ah. Yes. I – I probably thought your sister would have told you.'

Like fuck. She never tells me anything. That would mean giving up her role as the person in the family who has something on everyone. 'No, it hasn't come up.'

'Well. He's moved in.'

What was I supposed to say? That this man, whoever he was, was clearly after her for the money, for status? For an easy life? Except that would have offended her, and my mother is still an attractive woman, and he probably made her feel that way like no one had for a long time. And isn't that, on some level, what my job in the sex trade had been about? Making people feel good, even if the glow stopped right at the hotel room door? 'Congratulations are in order, I guess.'

samedi, le 18 février

Speed Date Bachelor No. 4 (In Which Belle is Feeling Rather World Weary).

I was on time, he was late. As in, half-an-hour late. I'm not the sort of girl who usually stands around waiting so long, only a nice-ish fellow with curly-blonde hair was chatting me up, otherwise I'd have zilch date-wise to report here. We exchanged emails. If nothing else, I came away with that. I think you can predict how the rest of this is going to go . . .

My date turned up, no apologies for the time. The bachelor in question is a well-regarded* young** man with good prospects*** and much to recommend him****. We join yours truly, trying to keep the conversation light, if a little surreal. GSOH and all that being ever so important: '. . . As Kanye left the bar to rejoin his parents, he turned around and told the two, "And nobody ever got poor pretending to be robots."' I paused to sip my drink. 'To this day, Kanye West receives a ten per cent royalty check from Daft Punk, as well as a VIP Reception whenever he's on French soil.'

'So when are you going to stop this jabberwocky?' Date

* in his own mind
** says 30. Looks 45
*** considering giving it all up for a year of hostel-hopping. Is either Steve Jobs or lying about his career
**** timeliness isn't one of them

said, bursting at the seams to tell me how well-travelled, indie-fabulous and bone-crushingly cool he was. Ugh. The only way I've found to tolerate such people is to consider my half of the conversation as an impromptu tribute to Ivor Cutler, complete with Weegie accent. This amuses me, but rarely meets with approval: men who require admiration don't do humour. Like, could you picture Vlad Putin at an Andy Dick gig?***** Exactly.

I sighed. Best get this over with, then. 'What would you like to know about me,' I said, looking him straight in the eyes. 'My useless degree, my boring job or the details of my mortgage? Will that make you feel sufficiently un-conventional? There are no doubt countless other girls happy to fawn and flutter and agree it's a great idea to travel the world with a ferret called Jammin. Why not go find one?'

His (distilled) response: 'Fuck off, Miss Morose. If you think you're the cleverest thing out there you're wrong.'******

Unfortunately, this all went down halfway through round two, and both of us being loath to leave half a cocktail and face the cold night with not even a sturdy buzz on, a good five minutes of SMS-checking and stony silence ensued. There are few times I am thankful the average volume of music in a bar is too high to hold a sensible conversation, but this was one of them.

Analysis:

Boyfriend material? 0/10 – This chap lost his rag at not being able to drone on about Patagonia or whatever and can't do banter like vegans can't do steak tartare? Buh-bye.

***** even factoring in the homoerotic shirtless holiday snaps?
****** oh, undoubtedly. But I'd wager folding money on being cleverer than he is, at least

Fuckable? 2/10 – Joke 'em if they can't take a fuck, I say.

Client material? 5/10 – The sort you would make pay £30 for your taxis, then pocket the cash and take the Tube instead. Also, no candidate for overspill time. A one-off at best.

Would date again? 1/10 – Didn't even get through the first one!

Final comments? – Andy Dick, call me anytime.

dimanche, le 19 février

'You didn't.'

'I did.'

'Good on you, girl. And you didn't get caught?' N laughed. He was about the only person I could tell who wouldn't judge – I'd logged on to the departmental server as an administrator and had a look through Alex's shared files, which included – much to my horrified delight – her CV.

'So what's the craic?'

'Apart from the fact that she's clearly under-qualified?' I said. 'I was damned impressed. She manages to make almost no relevant experience sound like the most well feathered cap in the world.'

'Buzzword-tastic?' I nodded. N got out of the City young, but has long held a fascinated disdain for all its twists and turns – and lexicon. 'Go on, hit me,' he said.

'Let's see if I can remember any . . . okay, she described herself as a – brace yourself – inspired and articulate communicator.'

N mimed vomiting into his pint, but was also laughing. 'More! More!'

'She is "passionate" about her "vocation", and delighted to work with people who are – not exaggerating – "similarly impassioned".'

'Fuck me sideways. Is "impassioned" even a word?'

'God knows,' I shrugged. 'It sounds like a brand of cheap perfume. But the jewel in the crown was the paragraph about her key skills.'

'Don't leave me hanging, what was it?'

'Customer experience, innovation, discovery, proposition development, creative commercial solutions, facilitation.'

'Fucking priceless!' N doubled over, almost crying with laughter. He finally sat back up and wiped the tears from under his eyes. 'So what did you do?'

'Are you kidding? I ripped off all that shite for my own CV,' I said, sipping my drink. 'Like they say, talent imitates, genius steals.'

lundi, le 20 février

'Any news on the dating front?'

'Nothing to report, apart from all men being inconceivably idiotic.'

'Pity your brother-in-law only has sisters . . . L's done so well, nabbing that one.'

It's one thing to be bucking for promotion in your workplace and quite another to feel like you have to do the same with your family. Not that we're a naturally competitive lot – for a Jewish family, that is. My mother seems to have taken it with good grace that I neither am, nor am married to, a doctor. Just as she eventually got over the disappointment that, apart from A1, I have never been particularly interested in dating a fellow member of the tribe.

So when she rings me up to wax lyrical about my sister,

well, it grates. 'And did I mention the surprise holiday he planned for their anniversary? Honey, I said, they shouldn't have broken the mould when they made that one. God knows you could use a real man like that to straighten things out.'

'Mum, please. Whatever happened to you just want to see all of your children happy?'

'Oh, that's just the crap you say at weddings and birthdays.'

I sighed. Not that I don't love L; I love her with all my heart. The parts that aren't devoted to holding a grudge for her pulling a boy I fancied when she was fourteen and doing it wearing one of my dresses to boot. But spare me the marriage-and-baby spiel. I wouldn't marry a man like her husband if you paid me. I'd say he puts the fun in frum, only there is no fun in frum.

mardi, le 21 février

Alex smiles and half-nods as we pass in the office now. Not sure what the office wags will make of that, whether this puts us in league with each other, whether they rip me apart like they do her – correction, I know they do, because all of them, especially Jane, stare at my tits whenever I'm talking.

She's just back from another late lunch carrying a small shopping bag I don't recognise. I've noticed a general improvement in her clothes lately. Less on-a-budget, less try-hard. She's easing into a style – perhaps one encouraged by a certain suitor? In particular her footwear has come on by leaps and bounds – fewer *New Look*-secretary-specials, more hand-tooled, Italian-leather jobbies. 'Nice day out?'

'Lovely, ta.'

The bag she's carrying this time is too small for shoes . . .

lingerie? Jewellery? A trinket from Giles? I smile back, and we disappear into out respective offices.

As a matter of curiosity I log into the online diary. Alex, my dear . . . dentist appointment again? You'd better start mixing it up, girl, or people will notice. Giles . . . wait, nothing in for Giles.

I pop out and scramble over to his office. Knock lightly on the door and swing my head in. He looks up from his desk, half-eaten sandwich and all.

'Hey . . . just . . . checking you're here.'

'Working over those quarterly reports,' he said. 'Can't say I've not been here for some time.'

'Ah. Okay, I'll leave you to it then.'

Went back to my office. So it wasn't Giles she was out with this time. But if not him, then who? And was my spy detail intended to go as far as where she spent her lunch hours? I decided not to say anything to him, for now.

jeudi, le 23 février

I'm coming back from the toilet when Alex and I pass on the stairs. 'You all right?' I say, but she looks up at me, surprised, and scuttles on down to the exit, as if trying to avoid someone. She's clutching her bag, coat on – going to meet someone, clearly. And she looks as if she might have been crying.

Note to self, watch this one more closely.

samedi, le 25 février

My brother-in-law, bless his soul, is a sweetly naïve young man. I take every opportunity when he's in town to turn him to the dark side. Not for nothing does L always insist he stays elsewhere. But she needn't worry, my intentions aren't serious – I wouldn't touch him with someone else's pussy. But a little flirtatious sex talk is usually on the menu. For one thing, it saves me chewing off my own hands out of boredom. For another, it may save him too.

'Hold on. You're saying there are two different kinds of wet?'

'It's like a mouth. You know, it's moist all the time, but when you see something you like, you salivate.'

'I can't believe it. So we can't trust you already because you never say what you mean, but now I learn when you're wet you're not even necessarily wet?'

'What I can't believe is you've managed to have a child without knowing the difference.'

dimanche, le 26 fevrier

Speed Date Bachelor No. 5 (or, Oh, Shite, His Parents Live Near Mine).

Went back up to pay respects to the parents, not that they notice, what with their having far more interesting single lives than I am. So when SD5 texted to ask about meeting for a meal and drinks, I had to regretfully reply I was otherwise disposed in the Northern Counties.

No worries, I'll be up visiting my parents this week. Anthony's tomorrow?

As Starbuck would say, frak.

I hadn't packed much for the two-day visit and would have to rely on what was at hand if I didn't want to go shopping. The only outfit in the house that was suitable for a date that did not a) belong to someone of pensionable age or b) until recently do duty as wedding wear for a pregnant sibling was precisely what I'd worn to the speed dating. Well, at least he would recognise me. We arranged to meet at a local landmark. He said he'd like to browse the bookstores before they closed. I was precisely on time, half-five.

Quarter-to-six passed. Then the hour. A number of other women who'd clearly also been waiting to meet people had already paired off and been replaced by new halves of couples. And the few people who had been sitting in the vicinity all along, who noticed I'd been waiting for half an hour dressed rather slinkily for so early in the evening, were looking at me like I was some sort of hooker.

Well, okay, fair dues. But I'm not just any hooker.

A man in a linen suit (at this time of year?) came up to me. 'Hi, how long have you been waiting?' he asked.

It was my date. And nice though he seemed, I genuinely didn't recognise the fellow.

'Um, half an hour. I was about to go, actually . . .'

'I texted to say I was in the shop over the road? Had to pick up the new *Discworld* novel.'

Aha. My phone had been on silent. Probably just as well, since I am violently allergic to the sight and smell of Pratchett. As Dredd would say, drokk. He put out his arm for mine and we walked to the restaurant.

'You look nice,' he said, and ordered drinks. Sazerac double on ice, no water for me; some trendy weirdy beer for him. I silently counted down from ten in my head. I try not to judge people on their bad taste in alcohol these days. Not often, in any case.

And there were a few other hiccups. Conversations that went a little like:

He: 'What sort of films do you like?'

Me: 'I used to be obsessed with Fritz Lang, but will watch almost anything these days. I like Hal Hartley, and Zhang

Yimou's a favourite. Not seen the Ian Curtis biopic yet so looking forward to that. You?'

'Oh, I like sports films.'

'Sports . . . films?'

'Yeah.'

'You mean like movies about . . .'

'Yeah, sport.'

'Like, uh . . . *The Longest Yard*?'

'Yeah, that was great!'

I know, I know, I'm a spoilt snob. Sosueme. But for the most part it was a lovely date; he's a genuinely nice chap. I steered the conversation well clear of politics, sex, work, and books by Terry Pratchett, and we had a good time. Oh, and he does yoga, apparently. Yoga. He even paid for the meal, which (I'm swiftly learning in the world of non-call girl sex) marks him as something of a gentleman in the old mould these days.

Analysis:

Boyfriend material? 5/10 – Definite potential here. Then again, we didn't talk about anything real. Must start vetting possible mates by asking how they fold their socks and whether they agree Jeremy Clarkson (or at least his irritating habit of squatting at the top of the bestseller lists) is evil personified, thereby gaining some accurate judgment of how all the important arguments will go.

Fuckable? 8/10 – Nice body, well maintained. No bloody clue if he knows what to do with it, but that's okay cos I do.

Client material? 10/10 – Dream client, hands down. Pays for things. Holds doors. Easy easy easy to talk to.

Would date again? 7/10 – Yes, okay, obviously worried

about his opinions re Clarkson, socks and any possible social connection between our families, but otherwise yes.

Final comments? – So far, the front runner in a very tired race.

mardi, le 28 fevrier

'I can't go another day like this,' I whined. 'What are you doing right now? Get in your car and come see me.'

N laughed. 'And possibly die of thirst before you get around to offering me a cup of tea? I'm sure whatever drama you're having now we can sort it out over the phone.'

'No, I'm talking about you coming over here and fucking me silly,' I said. 'Remember the last time, when we—'

'There's something I've been meaning to tell you,' he said.

And in that moment, I knew exactly what it was. 'You're seeing someone,' I said flatly.

'Yeah.'

I took a deep breath. He's not your boyfriend, silly. He's your friend. Be happy damnit. 'Anyone we know?'

'Nah,' he said. 'Friend of a workmate.'

'Is she . . .'

'Nice?'

'I was going to say good in bed, actually,' I said. 'But is she nice as well?'

N laughed. 'Since you ask, both,' he said.

I gulped. I totally did not need to hear that.

When N and I met, the attraction had been immediate and overwhelming. We went from a pub to a comedy club straight back to mine. He sensed somehow that I liked it rough; I figured he was just the man to give it me and he certainly didn't disappoint. It was N who first pulled my hair, who first tried to fist me. He was the sort of man who spanked a girl without caution, never asking if he'd gone too far. 'You can talk, if you want me to stop, I'll stop,' he said. And even though the romantic side of our relationship quickly foundered, I never did want him to stop.

'I'm happy for you,' I said through clenched teeth.

'You know the brilliant thing about you?' N said.

'What's that?'

'Your lies are so transparent. But thank you anyway.'

Ten secrets of being alluring on a date:

1 Be in the right frame of mind before leaving the house. For me, this involves playing Van Halen's 'Panama', on repeat, at full volume while looking in the mirror and saying, 'God damn it, I'm Belle de fucking Jour', though your results may vary.

2 Lip gloss – just say no. Sure, it looks great. But would you fancy kissing a half-melted, Vaseline-flavoured lolly? Didn't think so.

3 No one should ever be ashamed to own a cat, just don't mention the fact to a man you're trying to impress. Ever. And for fuck's sake put those kitten photos away.

4 Look over his shoulder. Having a man think he might lose your attention has never been a bad strategy. And staring deep into someone's eyes as they hold forth on the mystical magical world of working in HR is wrong, wrong, wrong.

5 Perfect the walk. It's a little bit leading from the hips, a little bit loose at the top of the thigh. They say Marilyn Monroe would cut the bottom centimetre off her heels to get it. However it's done, you'll know when you've nailed it.

6 Fake tan, hair extensions, Lycra content in your outer clothing? Hello, Essex hooker look. Avoid.

7 Laugh. But not at the lines he thinks are funny.

8 Eat normally. Don't push the salad round your plate, but don't fake a ravenous hunger for Argentinean steaks so rare they're still mooing, either. It's just food, so shut up and eat like a normal person already.

9 Turn off your damned phone. You can be uncontactable for two hours.

10 Smile at other women, especially the attractive ones. Never be the scowling jealous type (until you're behind closed doors talking to your most trusted friends, of course).

Mars

mercredi, le 01 mars

Whether it was because of N's news, I don't know. But SD5 rang right after I'd hung up the phone. It was such a nice time of year, he said, how about we go for a walk in the country at the weekend? And because I had nothing better to do – no fuck buddy coming around to lighten my mood, anyway – I said yes.

And texted N to tell him about my hot date. Take that, Jerky McJerkerson.

jeudi, le 02 mars

Transport in London is truly broken when it takes the same amount of time to walk to work as it does to catch either the bus or Tube.

Not that I would make a habit of walking to work, mind.

vendredi, le 03 mars

'Hello gorgeous, what are you doing in . . . say, three week-ends' time?'

Lamenting the loss of my youth, beauty, and all that's good in my life. 'Very little, Giles. Why do you ask?'

'Nothing, just planning something. Checking everyone's availability.'

Oh dear, probably a drinks do with an important client. At least those were the types of events where I could shine. After being a call girl to the moneyed and influential – or at least the polite and middle-management – I liked to think I had the art of formal grooming and delightful patter sorted.

'Pencil me in, dear,' I said. 'As long as it's something I can justify buying new shoes for.'

'Gotcha. Talk soon.'

samedi, le 04 mars

When I was working, there were only two types of men: Average Client and Grin and Bear It. Because for the most part, while there were nice men, sweet men, boring men and arsehole men and all varieties of man under the sun to be found, it all came down to a single bottom line: I wasn't going to be dating any of these people, even if I was single, which I wasn't.

Which was fine, because these were dates with a guaranteed expiry time. Didn't like his breath? Avoid kissing, and watch the clock. Real dates, I'm finding, are a whole other story.

Now I have to steel myself well in advance of a meeting – will he be nice? If not, how soon can I get out of there? Will he be boring? If so, how much can I put up with? And is it really true what my mother says, that first dates count for nothing, and you should never make a decision until the second, or even third?

Heaven help me, I still stupidly believe that if there isn't a spark of chemistry straight away, it's not going to happen. Maybe my ideas about love are adolescent, maybe the physical matters too much to me. But I know that's not true – I've been desperately physically attracted to men most women would find plain or even ugly. I can't quantify what they have to have but they definitely have to have it.

And the men I've met lately, they definitely don't have it. But is this a recipe for ending up lonely? Every rom-com, every agony aunt column, every advice forum seems to boil down to two messages: Chemistry's Not Important and Accept His Faults. Which I was once perfectly prepared to do – to the tune of three hundred quid plus travel and tip. So I doggedly grin and bear my way through the second date and maybe the third, and try to weigh up which is more horrifying: dying alone in a flat full of cats who will chew my lips off long before my body is discovered, or being bored to death by someone I never really felt anything for in the first place.

I know, I'm childish when it comes to lovers. So sue me.

dimanche, le 05 mars

'How was your hot date?' N asked.

'Freezing,' I said. Literally as well as figuratively. SD5 said to prepare for a bracing walk in the out-of-doors, followed by a pub lunch somewhere cosy. Okay, I can do outdoors. And cosy, well, that is practically my middle name. But by the time he came to pick me up, it was cold, it was windy, it was raining, and he didn't have a backup plan.

'Well, if you waited for the weather to improve in order to do things, you'd never do anything!' he said.

This is something that has definitely changed since I was last on the market: people apparently don't care to put up any pretence of being on best behaviour anymore.

Me, I love best behaviour. Because of my former

occupation getting involved in a serious relationship involves a level of auditioning that most people reserve only for their gynaecologists and best mates; I want – no, absolutely require – a long settling-in period.

I forced a cheery smile and trudged for four hours along an exposed coastline, every step reinforcing my belief that outings like this be reserved for Year Five, the year in which the resentment creeps in and you stop speaking to each other. Not, like, the second date?

'You're fucking kidding,' N said.

'I wish,' I said. 'Then there was the matter of the feet.'

'Uh-oh,' N said. He could see it coming, because I have this foot thing: I believe men's feet should be clean, nicely shaped and free of toenail dirt, strangely-shaped nails and, as far as possible, lint. Don't get me wrong – I like feet, but they have to be nice feet. N thinks it's part of my control freakery; I think it's basic hygiene.

So, somewhere between the pub (not as cosy as I'd hoped) and returning to the car, SD5 suggested a sit-down at a spot with a nice view. And then he proceeded to take. Off. His. Shoes.

And socks.

And then, after offering me a baby wipe (!), which I refused, proceeded to floss his rather unkempt toes with said wipe. Again, speed dating aside, this is date two for fuck's sake. I pretended to be very, very interested in the father and son off to my left enjoying a fishing outing but in fact I was trying not to vomit. Then, just in case my stomach hadn't turned enough already, he offered me a piece of chocolate with the same hand that had just been cleaning his feet. Out of concern for my lower digestive tract and the potential risk of athlete's foot, I refused.

'Suit yourself,' SD5 said jauntily. 'But you're a woman,

and once you see someone enjoying chocolate you know you'll have to have some.'

This offended me on so many levels I didn't even know where to begin. 'No, I'm sure I'll manage not to, somehow.' I'm more of a savoury person anyway.

N guffawed.

'It gets worse,' I said. Turns out SD5's a fraud investigator, and while I'm not committing any fraud as such, I certainly felt under the microscope for most of the afternoon. Slyly disguised as caring about what I said, he managed to get rather a lot out of me in a very little time. Such as what my father does for a living (something surprisingly odd) and where my mother was born (somewhere surprisingly . . . er, surprising). In doing so, he rapidly hit what N calls my brick wall – the things I won't talk about. And that usually doesn't happen until somewhere around month six.

Worse still, he invented an excuse to come in my house – next time I'll claim there isn't actually a loo and guests are required to bury their shit in the back garden – and then wouldn't leave for ages. In spite of the fact that I'd put on a load of laundry, begun washing up and had Radio 4 on at full volume. Every time something caught his attention I cringed. 'Where's this from? What does this do?' He patted the cat and leafed through a recipe book. His eyes rested, blessedly briefly, on a notebook that I realised with horror contained a few notes and scribblings from early on in my previous career. Honestly, he was all but taking inventory.

Against my better judgment, I rang N. Deep down I knew I'd only continued accepting dates with this man to make myself feel better that N was no longer available to entertain me, but that didn't negate the fact that he was still my closest friend. Especially when the subject was dating and mating. And I couldn't face whatever L might have to say even if she hadn't been away on holiday. 'I feel bad about it,'

I whinged. 'He's a nice guy, but . . . yeurrrgh.' When he moved to kiss me on the cheek at the end of the date, I actually jumped away. And yet he still sent a text to say he'd had a great time and asking when we could meet again. Wtf?

'Feel bad? What the hell do you have to feel bad for? Chalk it up as a fail and cut him dead.'

'Serious?'

'Serious. What happened to your edge, woman?'

'The rules are different when it's real dating,' I said. 'The last date went pretty well, maybe this is just a one-off disaster.'

'Like fuck. You've not been on real dates in so long you've forgotten what the rules are.'

lundi, le 06 mars

Giles has called me in for a meeting. I'm wracked with nerves. But it turns out okay – far from criticising my recent performance he says he's 'pleased' I'm 'finally settling down' with 'fewer overachiever tendencies' and giving 'more considered effort' to the work I've been doing. Er, yeah. If that's the way he wants to frame it, who am I to argue?

'So, three-sixty me,' he says. I always hate when people say that, a three-sixty gets you right back where you started, but a work meeting with the boss is probably not the time to discuss degrees, radians and the unit circle.

'It's all good,' I say. 'But about that other little project you have me on . . .'

Giles stops chewing the end of his pen. 'Alex?'

'There's definitely something going on,' I said. 'I'm going to keep watching her, but Giles, I'm warning you now . . . I don't know what it is, but she's very erratic, and you might not like what I find.'

He nodded, slowly, as if considering what to say and how to say it. 'It's up to you,' Giles said. 'Confidentially speaking, she's in consideration for a transfer to our other site. I'm . . . I've much less reason to be concerned about her at the moment.'

I nodded. 'Let it go, you mean?' Giles nodded. I smiled. But I wasn't about to let it go, now that I had the scent.

mercredi, le 08 mars

Things my mind fails to comprehend:

Monthly breast size fluctuation: why has no one invented a bra yet that can cope? I'm growing a neat crop of quadro-boob bulge above the cup here, but know it'll be gone by the end of the week.

The statistical impossibility that you will ever, and I do mean ever, turn up at the bus stop exactly on time for the bus, rather than waiting twenty minutes in a giant queue or watching it just pull away as you get there.

How it is that the air, this time of year, can smell like a cesspool from one direction or a clean Scottish forest post-rainfall from the other.

If when I was in various relationships I was having sex in semi-public places such as pub toilets and in parks all the time – not particularly exhibitionist, more very impatient – yet I never seem to stumble across anyone else at it? Not that I'm particularly looking, mind . . .

What it was the women who populate coffee houses all day

with their yoga partners and prams did with their days before they got knocked up.

How the construction in and around Kings Cross can have been going on for the last, ooh, fifteen billion years and still not be finished.

Why when I clean out my handbag there are six pens (four working, two not), but when I need one at my desk, I can never find one?

jeudi, le 09 mars

According to the online organiser, Alex is at a second site meeting today from two to three. Only our second site is in Leeds and she's still at her desk so, unless she's planning to teleport there and back, it's a ruse. Today's definitely the day.

At half-one I spot her on the way from the loo – she's freshened her makeup, run a brush through her hair. Hmm.

Fifteen minutes later she's gathering up her coat. The way out takes her past my office door. I put my head down and pretend to be so engrossed in work that I don't notice her exit. But five minutes later, I too am out the door.

Wherever she's going, she's walking. Thank god – I wouldn't want to have to follow a taxi, or worse, get onto the Tube with her. Her heels clickety-clack through the late lunchtime crowds. She turns onto a street of shops and I drop back to stay just out of sight.

Two minutes later I'm coming round the corner, hair down, sunglasses on pretending to be a window shopper. A flash in a shop door catches my eye – it's her, and she's turning back to someone, talking and laughing. This is it, I think, and I pretend to be interested in a shop that seems to specialise in vile shoes.

Vile wedding shoes, that is. When I sneak a look back at Alex, it's not a man she's walked out onto the streets with, it's a middle aged lady beaming at . . . her daughter?

I look up – it's a bridal shop. Oh dear god, Alex is getting married? But if she's engaged, why has she never worn a ring? Unless . . .

. . . Giles?

vendredi, le 10 mars

'Cherie,' L said, kissing both cheeks.

'How was Gay Paree?' She stepped aside to let me in the door.

'Same as always. Crowded, filthy, disappointing,' L said. 'Utterly wonderful. Wine?'

'Ooh, you brought some back?'

'No, darling, Tesco's finest,' she said. 'So what's your news?'

'Nothing much,' I said. 'Usual work, usual dating. Get up to anything naughty?'

'Apart from shopping? No,' L said. 'Oh, I found this fabric shop, they supply to all the couture houses. I saw this amazing silk satin I would definitely use for my wedding dress.'

'But you're not even seeing anyone!' Not for the first time, I was in awe of how different L and I were.

'Like the scouts say, Be Prepared,' L said. 'Anyway, your dates. Dish!'

I gave her the complete rundown, gory details included, from the toe flossing to . . . actually, she made me stop after the toe flossing part.

'First impressions are everything,' L said. 'Like, what did you think of your ex when you met him?'

'That he was a loudmouth idiot and I wanted to fuck him,' I said. Her flat really did have amazing views this time of year. The lights of the city flickered and wobbled on the river. Boats and barges floated down going dead slow. L poured another glass.

'And when you split up?'

'I thought he was a loudmouth idiot.'

'And when you met A4?'

'That he was far too reserved, and that I wanted to fuck him.'

'. . . when you split?'

'That he was far too reserved,' I said. 'Yeah, I see where you're going with this.'

'Basically,' L said, topping up her glass, 'you can't make yourself want to like someone. It's only downhill from the first glance, so if there's no chemistry to start with, why prop up the corpse?'

'I get that, I totally do,' I said. 'But it's horrible being alone, and I don't want an endless string of one night stands.' Lying a little there. I wouldn't actually mind a string of one-night stands, so long as the sex was good, but I wasn't about to admit that to L.

'It's only going to get worse if you string this one along,' she said. 'And god help you both if you sleep with him. You have to cut him off, the sooner the better. Do it.'

I smiled as she poured the remnants of the bottle into my glass. 'Just how did you get so good at this advice lark?'

'It's the glossy magazines, hon,' she said. 'I'm just repeating what they say every month. Maybe I should get you a subscription and cut out the middleman.'

'Unless they can have me round and get me drunk as well, no dice,' I said.

'We should buy a joint gift for Mum's birthday this year,' my sister said. We were in her kitchen, which is light and yellow, without actually being light yellow. It seemed to me only last week my sister was living in filthy shared student digs with two men and another woman, arguing over who used the last of the milk. She never said anything, but I suspected she had exactly zero equity in the house. And with the baby, now. It would have scared me rigid to be in her position.

'And we'd better do it soon.' She was juggling the baby on one hip. I'm not sure if this is actually serving a purpose, or something mothers do because they've seen every other mother in the history of the world do it. Is it meant to keep the baby quiet, or what? If so, it's not working.

And forget what I said about breast size fluctuation – she's going from Hoover Dam to Lake Chad in a matter of minutes these days.

'Oooookayyyyy.' Call me crazy, but I've never known exactly when Mum's birthday is. Seriously. When we were little, Dad would just chuck a gift and card at me and tell me to wrap and sign them. When I moved away, I'd post a card in the first week of July and figure that was close enough. 'Still, I had a general idea when it might be going down. 'Isn't it a little early for that?' I said.

'Thing is I was wondering about getting her to go on a cruise,' my sister said. 'With her boyfriend.'

'Oh no. No. Uh-uh. I'm not paying for him to have a dirty week away.'

'What? It's not like he's some gigolo, you know. I think it's serious, the way she talks about him, and the way he . . .'

I stood up. 'You know what? I don't want to hear about this. I don't want to hear how well Mum's getting on without Dad. I don't want to hear about this lovely young man who's sleeping in the bed that used to belong to our mother and, in case you've forgotten, father. I don't really care, to be honest, except for the part that the family I thought I had is not the family I have and this seems to be just okay with everyone.'

My sister narrowed her eyes, still bouncing the baby on her hip. 'Don't be such a child. Being Daddy's Little Girl does not entitle you to disapprove of everything Mum does now. It's not as if you're as pure as the driven snow, either . . .'

'Oh? Are you saying something?' I squared up to her, my nose almost touching hers. 'Is there something you think you want to say?' My head was pounding, my blood boiling. I would have laid her out, then and there, fuck the baby.

She looked surprised, blinked, and backed away. 'No . . . no, I just mean . . .'

'Mean what? That because I'm not married like you that I'm less than you? That your life experience is worth more than mine? That your opinions are worth more because you stuck on a white dress and squeezed out a baby? That I can't have an opinion on Mum's boyfriend because I happen to have slept with more men than you did before you looked around, decided that was the best you were ever going to get and settled?'

She sat down. Her face was pink and white, which used to happen when we were little and someone at school teased her. I knew it was the colour of shame, also of suppressed rage. Back then, when she looked like that, it was me who stood up for her.

'That's not what I'm saying,' she said. 'I'm not saying anything. Forget it came up.'

But I was already halfway to the door, and not about to turn around.

dimanche, le 12 mars

There was no call from my sister when I got home, nor that night, nor the next morning. I don't know what I was expecting. When I went back over what had happened, and how quickly, it was just like those times as teenagers when we'd get on each other's nerves, have a giant bust up then be giggling and laughing together within the hour. I just expected that she would phone me, say something to smooth it over, and she didn't.

lundi, le 13 mars

There are few concepts more likely to strike fear in the heart of a woman like me than . . .

'Team . . . building?'

What the hell? Team building is what evangelising Christian teenagers do. What multibillionaire moguls call their expensive group jaunts to Mustique. Not anything an actual office has ever actually done in actually real life. Actually.

But apparently Giles had an epiphany over Christmas and is now bleating the office-as-family line, convinced it will work to the benefit of our bottom line.

All I can say to that is: bottom.

'Come on, what's the harm?' A1 said. 'Some of the activities can be a lot of fun.'

'The harm? Oh, no harm. And did I mention he's going to select the activity from suggestions we make, as well?' Thing is, it all seemed a bit suspicious to me. Like maybe he was trying to butter us up . . . perhaps before he and Alex told the office about the engagement?

'Well that's even better then,' A1 said. 'You can twist it whatever way you want it to go. Do something you like.'

'Soz, but what part of this seems like a good idea? If any of the numerous the co-workers with whom you have no common social interests suggested team-building, you would be creeped out.' I swapped my pint glass for A1's, because he drinks faster, and because I didn't really fancy mine much. 'Oh, I know – strip club. We should definitely hit a strip club.'

A1 laughed. 'You crack me up,' he said. 'Not that there's anything wrong with a strip club, you're creeped out by the suggestion of team-building with your co-workers, then suggest something that can be marginally creepy?'

'That was the point. Make them face up to the creepy by suggesting something creepy, and hopefully they will back off.'

'Ahh, good point. It's like a game of chicken. Someone starts with the creepy, you up the ante of the creepy then hope someone doesn't take it a step farther and actually say okay. It could even carry on to lap-dances, champagne room, and so on.'

'None of them would have the balls to call my bluff.'

mardi, le 14 mars

You can tell a lot about someone by what he says about himself – though not always what he'd intended. It's a bit like deciphering sex workers' websites, where voluptuous inevitably means surgically enhanced, twenty-one means twenty-five if you're lucky and adventurous means watch your wallet. And when it comes to dating, there's a whole other language I'm just now starting to decipher. This is what I've learned so far in the interpretation game:

He says: 'I'm essentially a happy person.'
He means: 'I am frequently depressive with mysterious bouts of manic aggression.'

He says: 'I'm friends with all of my exes.'
He means: 'I send my exes creepy texts when drunk that they never reply to.'

He says: 'It's been a long time since I've met a woman like you.'
He means: 'It's been a long time since I've met a woman.'

He says: 'I'm a successful professional.'
He means: 'I've managed to convert a temp position into full-time wage slavery.'

He says: 'I'd love to travel all over the world.'
He means: 'I'd love to see all-inclusive resorts all over the world.'

He says: 'You have beautiful eyes.'
He means: 'Please have sex with me tonight. Please.'

He says: 'I like to think of myself as an old-fashioned romantic.'
He means: 'No, seriously, sex now.'

mercredi, le 15 mars

'How to Let Him Down Easy'

'Men: How to Date the Ones You Want and Avoid the Ones You Don't'

'Ditch the Loser! A Good Girl's Guide to Breakups'

Sometimes I wonder if the glossy magazines L leaves in her toilet are selected to give me not-so-secret messages. Then again, they probably have identical articles every month. I maintain that you could just recycle the June 1988 issue of *Cosmo* with a different cover every month and no one would be the wiser.

jeudi, le 16 mars

Coffee with Giles while we discussed the tax situation but, instead of traipsing out to the nearest chain, I brought two cups back to his office. Chai latte for me, triple shot skinny cappuccino for him. They say you can tell a lot about a man by what he drinks, which in this case indicated someone vain. Also overworked. Due to planning a secret wedding, perhaps?

'Guess you must be very busy of late,' I said.

'Great Jupiter's beard, yes,' he said. 'Never-ending.'

'Must be absolute loads to do,' I said. 'The invitation lists, choosing the food . . .'

'Huh? No, I think the team building day will stay fairly simple. Some sort of planned activity, maybe drinks after.'

'Oh, that,' I said. 'I meant the other thing.'

'What other thing? My birthday? That's ages yet. Why, are you thinking of organising a party? That would be lovely, but really, I haven't the time these days.'

'No, I imagine not.' So he was going to play dumb, was he? Maybe it was time to go straight to the horse's mouth.

vendredi, le 17 mars

SD5 and I met again. I wimped and instead of doing it cleanly, over the phone, I agreed to go to dinner. Probably sending mixed messages but I am a sucker for a man who picks up the bill. Yeah, yeah, bitch all you want about me letting the side down, rubbish feminist &c. but come on, I was a hooker – I get off on the man paying. It's how I'm wired.

Incidentally, because he is too damn good at getting information out of me, he managed to extricate the chocolate truffles recipe. Not that's it's a state secret exactly (after all, I found it on the web) but I do tend to big it up among my friends. It's good to know there's at least one thing you can make, and make well.

Anyway, as far as SD5 was concerned, this was the all-important, third date – what I understand to be known in civilian circles as 'the one with the kiss'. Probably he was expecting rather a different outcome to the evening. I let him down sometime between the main course and the coffee.

'Is it the yoga?' he asked.

'No, of course not; it's not the yoga.' I think yoga is generally undertaken by wispy lack-brains with a deep-seated need to convince themselves they are better than everyone else and to sound interesting.

'I could understand if you thought the yoga made me seem a little . . . effeminate.'

Whoah, he's giving me a get-out-of-jail-free card here. Grab it and run! 'No, I don't think that at all.' D'oh! 'You're a nice guy, just not for me.'

'What is it? Is it the way I look? Is it because of where I'm from?'

I sighed. In spite of what everyone tells you, there is

actually no way to dash someone's romantic hopes elegantly. I heartily believe in the zipless fuck, but there is no such thing as the zipless date. 'No, you look fine. Also, I don't care about background.' I have that option; I'm middle class. 'I just . . . think . . . you're not for me.'

'Is it the car? No? The suit? My job?'

Dear Christ-on-a-chicken-stick, if he didn't watch it, he was going to annoy me into saying something I'd regret. Breathe, Belle, breathe. What would the Dalai Lama do? 'No,' I gritted my teeth. 'None of that. I simply think we'd work. Better. As. Friends.' Preferably the kind of friend you neither see nor speak to again.

'Be honest, were you ever romantically interested in me?'

Oof. The guilt manoeuvre. Don't take the bait. 'You are very nice, and interesting, and it's just . . . bad timing.' Shit. The bad-timing ploy. I can't believe I've sunk this low.

'You're seeing someone else?'

'I've kind of started talking to my ex again,' I said. Oh, horror, what a terrible lie. For one thing I'd sooner date the entirety of the Inland Revenue than talk to my ex again. It's a chicken-shit move, and I know it. 'We're sort of . . . trying to make it work.'

He nodded. 'Bad timing.'

'Yeah.'

'Well, if you ever . . .'

'Of course, of course.'

The waiter, who I noticed out of the corner of my eye had been hanging back, swept past. 'Anything else for you two?' the waiter murmured.

'Just the bill,' SD5 said. The waiter nodded and went away.

'Please, let me,' I said.

He waved his hand. 'No, of course not.'

Sigh. A gentleman to the last. A gentleman who flosses his

toes with a baby wipe, perhaps, but still. You can't buy class like that.

samedi, le 18 mars

They say London is a lonely place. A city where isolation is endemic, where you can pass innumerable days flicking in and out of public transport with the swipe of an Oyster card, grunting at the shop assistants and not speaking to anyone at all.

What they don't say is how keenly all of this is driven home when you realise the only person you've spoken to in the last twenty-four hours is your damned cat.

lundi, le 20 mars

So it's settled: unless I can manage to convincingly fake my own suicide before the weekend, I will in the not-too-distant future be joining my esteemed colleagues for a spot of team-building through line dancing.

Alex, Paul, Jane and all the rest of the office smiled around the break room, but they looked distinctly like rictus grins to me. Our leader had officially gone mad, and we were powerless to stop him.

'It was you who gave me the idea with that crack about buying new shoes,' Giles nodded to me. 'I thought to myself, what kind of shoes are you unlikely to already own? Cowboy boots, of course!' He looked so proud of his reasoning I think I vomited in my mouth a little.

If only I'd still been with the agency, then at least I would have had a reason not to go – albeit one I couldn't explain. But while I can easily lie to cover another lie, making lies out of thin air is very difficult. And the horror of this – oh, the horror! – is beyond contemplation. Fat women in high-waisted jeans and cowboy boots. Men with dodgy facial hair. Country music hits of yesterday and today as sung by, no doubt, a bunch of forty-somethings from Suffolk.

There are few things that irritate me as much as ersatz Americana.

Correction – there are plenty of things that irritate me more than that but I presume you don't care what I think about the parking on my street or the fact that while probably less than two per cent of humans will ever have need for an 'extra large' condom, about a third of men buy them.

I don't understand this fascination with all things beer and steer. Fuck's sake, we're going line dancing. In Fulham. You don't see Californian surfers going round dressed as Morris dancers, do you? No cutting-edge New York rock band ever got together, out of their skulls on smack, and decided that a gratuitous bagpipe solo was the way forward. (Well, maybe they did, but they passed out before it ever became reality.) And, weirdly, there seems to be a positive correlation between the presence of banjos in British music and the level of vehemence against the US president. What message are we trying to send? Really, this is not at all ironic – it's poor. When an activity makes you embarrassed to be in the same room that's not a good thing.

Don't misunderstand, I've nothing against country music as such. In fact I have an admiration for Dolly Parton that is at least as robust as her cup size. But by and large, the vast majority of such things should be left to the continent where they originated. Especially Shania Twain. Please, stay there. Please.

Speaking of extra-large condoms, none of the American clients I had used them. Now before you go and make the inevitable joke about everything being bigger in Texas – it was a refreshing change from the considerable subset of British men who unveil their cocks as if they expect a band to play fanfare as the glans emerges: ta-daaaaa! Really, boys, it's just a penis. If it were that special it would be me who'd be paying you, yeah?

mercredi, le 22 mars

There was a missed call from SD5 (aka toe-flosser) so I phoned back.

'Hallo,' he said, forcibly jaunty. 'Thanks for ringing. I was just trying to make the truffle recipe you gave me . . . I was wondering, where you wrote about adding grated orange peel, is that like orange zest?'

I thought he'd said he was a good cook? Even I know how to grate and/or zest and orange. 'Yes, more or less. The outside. Really small.'

'Thanks! So how are you?'

'Um, really busy right now.'

'Oh. Okay. Bye.'

. . . four hours later . . .

'Hi, sorry, so I'm in the shop buying ingredients.'

'Okay.' Just to bring everyone up-to-speed, apart from optional additions like orange zest or brandy, this recipe has, like, three ingredients total. It's not rocket science, in fact, it's almost exactly orthogonal to rocket science. I managed to make what is already a basic recipe still easier this year by melting the truffle mix in the microwave. Children could make this. Monkeys could make this. Hell, even I can make this. Incidentally, this does not detract from the fact that the truffles are impressive. And delicious.

'Should I get salted or unsalted butter?'

'I don't know. I don't think it matters.'

'I'll get salted then.'

'Great. Good luck with that. Listen, I have to go. Bye.'

jeudi, le 23 mars

'I've always wanted to try this place,' Alex said to me in a conspiratorial whisper, leaning across the table. 'So thank you.'

The bare brick walls and zinc tables felt modern but cosy, the scrubbed raw floors earthy and reliable. I ordered an ox-tongue salad with poached eggs. Alex – to her credit – opted for black pudding and candied figs. I admire appetite in a woman and could imagine just a bit of what Giles must see in her, past the terrible eighties hair and too-tight wardrobe.

'No worries,' I said. I couldn't say that I liked her any more than I had at the start, but was starting to admire the way she carried on this engagement with Giles without anyone being the wiser. In my opinion honesty is overrated; a woman's ability to keep a secret is in direct proportion with her value as a lady.

The sommelier came over with the bottle I'd requested. 'Wine? At lunch?' Alex said, and giggled.

'I phoned ahead,' I said. 'You deserve a treat after all the planning you must have been doing.'

Alex looked at me. 'Planning? What do you mean?'

I tasted the wine, nodded, and we were poured two glasses of an especially respected Sicilian chardonnay. 'Oh, come on dear, I'm not blind. The so-called dentist's appointments, the secret lunches . . . I saw you and your mum coming out of a bridal shop. And by the way, congratulations. You must both be so thrilled.'

Alex looked shocked, but recovered herself quickly. I guess it must come as a surprise to find out that someone has figured out their little game. 'I . . . well, thank you. It's been in the works for a long time, actually, before I even started working here.'

'Oh, I hadn't realised you already knew each other,' I said. But it certainly did explain a lot. 'And don't worry, I'm not upset you haven't invited me. I can understand if the two of you want to keep it small.'

'Sorry, now I'm confused. Are you friends with Richard or something?'

'Who's Richard?'

'My fiancé. We're marrying in July.'

Ah. 'I . . . oh, dear. I thought you and Giles . . . I'm sorry, because, you know, that time I walked into his office . . .'

Alex's face darkened and she looked away. 'Yeah, that. Giles. I mean . . . I don't know.'

Oh god, now she was crying. What had I done? What do I say? I'd never had enough close female friends to know what to do when a woman cries. This must be how men feel pretty much all of the time. 'Is it . . . he. Does he know?'

'He knows,' she said, wiping a tear from her cheek. 'Of course he knows. He wasn't interested in me at all until he found out I was engaged; maybe that's his thing.' I thought about how the flirting from Giles had more or less come to a halt in the weeks after the Boy and I split up; maybe Alex was right. I'd attributed it, wrongly, to his becoming more involved with her. 'And I know what you think of me. What the entire office think of me. But he's lovely. And I'll have you know, we never even had sex. There was a weekend Richard was away, and Giles said he'd booked a hotel, and we went to dinner, and I told him . . .' Alex dabbed her eyes with a linen napkin. 'I told him . . . that I was in love with him, and that I was going to leave Richard as soon as he came back.'

'What did he say?'

'He looked very angry and then he went to the cloakroom and came back and said you'd just rung his mobile and there was a work emergency and he had to go straight away. And that was that.'

I bit my lip. 'I never rang him,' I said.

'I know. I knew he was lying. After that, I started looking for other jobs, and then just recently Giles came and said he thought I should transfer to the Leeds office as soon as possible.'

'Leeds is nice,' I said weakly.

'Yeah,' she said. 'I guess. Richard wants to be closer to his family in York, so what else can I do?' She was properly crying now. 'The thing is . . . I really . . . I care so deeply about Richard . . . I would never leave him now . . . but I really do love Giles, you know?'

I nodded, 'Yes, of course,' but, actually, I didn't know. About love or any of it. The waiter came with our orders, and Alex pulled herself together, and we did eat rather a lot of food and drain that bottle of wine plus two more. It wasn't the start of a friendship, exactly, but more an alliance.

On the way back I played what she'd said over and over in my head. Love? Really? That's . . . well, if that's the case, then I must admit defeat, I really do not understand the interior workings of every other female in existence, and can see why I am considered an aberration. But falling in love? That's what 'normal' women do after having unsuccessful sex once with a co-worker? Really?

No wonder relationships are so fucked up.

A missed text from Toe Flosser: Can you ring me when you wake up? I have a question about the truffles.

He'd sent the message at half-five. I waited until lunchtime. 'How's it going?'

'Hi, B, thanks for ringing back!' He sounded jaunty. Really, really chipper. The sort of manic brightness that means the caller is watching you from behind a pillar box whilst stroking a voodoo doll. 'I had a question about the recipe . . .'

'Yes, you said. What is it?'

'You know where you wrote a note about seventy per cent or higher cocoa being better – does that mean you add seventy per cent of the weight of the chocolate in extra cocoa powder?'

What planet was this guy from? 'No, it means buy a chocolate that already contains a high percentage of cocoa solids. They say on the label. In really big numbers.'

'Right. I'll go back and have a look today. So if I just bought cocoa powder, I can't use that?'

I shut my eyes and took a deep breath. Sitting about ten feet from my open door was P, who always eats lunch at his desk, and is always eavesdropping on my business. 'I'm happy to help you with this, but I'm not really comfortable with you calling me so often.'

Toe Flosser was silent. Now, let's freeze the moment and drop out Matrix-stylee for a quick analysis: Toe Flosser is an active yoga practitioner. If there's one thing I've learned about men who practise yoga, it's that they come in two types: Passive-Aggressive Hippie or Barely Suppressed Rage. On the surface, these appear much the same until you do something they don't like. At which point Passive-Aggressive

Hippie will withdraw, telling you 'that's your trip, man,' preferably while doing something to fuck up your life on the way out, like leaving your house keys at a homeless shelter. Barely Suppressed Rage, on the other hand, will snap à la the *Titanic* just before it sank but is usually rendered incapable of doing any actual harm as a result. Let us drop back in and see which one Toe Flosser is.

'Okay, like, you know, I just thought I was being FRIENDLY,' he said at such volume I'm certain my work mate P could hear. Surprise, surprise, he's a Barely Suppressed Rage.

'There's friendly, and there's friendly,' I said, in as low and calm a voice as I could manage. 'If you had a genuine question about what is really a very simple recipe, I'm sure you wouldn't have to ring me all the time to ask it.'

'Maybe you don't have many MALE FRIENDS,' Toe Flosser shouted down the phone. 'Maybe you don't know what FRIENDS ARE.'

'Actually I have a lot of male friends. And you know what they all have in common with each other, but not you? They don't freak me the fuck out.'

I could hear him stomping around wherever he was, and quickly looked outside – to confirm that he was not, in fact, standing under my office window. 'FINE,' he snorted. 'WHATEVER. SO I'LL NEVER RING YOU AGAIN.'

Result! 'Thanks, hope so. Bye!'

samedi, le 25 mars

I took in the washing, the slippery silken knickers N and I had sorted through together, the unreliable flimsy skirts and barely-there blouses, and sighed. The cat sniffed at the air, his ears and whiskers twitching one way, then the next, as he caught scent of one thing and another. The whiff of breeze was warmer than I had reason to expect and I knew it would be gone as soon as the sun left the sky, which was very soon.

I was gathering the limp-fabric leaves of some other life, someone else's dreams. I was living in a house where I was a stranger, a city where no one would care if I were to disappear tomorrow.

And I felt a pang, the sort of pang I sometimes felt in the anonymous meetings in desperately samey hotel rooms. The forced jollity of the opening door, the smiles exchanged between hooker and client as a silent agreement passed between them: we will never mention each other's loneliness. Another step into the room, a welcoming gesture from the man and then all of that disappeared back under the surface. But for a moment it was acknowledged in the basest possible way that solitude is the base state of human life: you arrive alone; you leave alone and soul mates and all that crap be damned. Inside your head you live alone.

For all my protestations at my sister's marriage – for all the snide comments I gave N about his new relationship – I know why people do it. With someone else there, even if you don't love them or particularly like them, it feels less lonely. Even if they're a stranger.

And if I'd been a man that would probably be the point at which I rang an escort agency. As it was, I went back inside, made a cup of tea and listened to *The Archers* while the sun took the last of its meagre heat away.

dimanche, le 26 mars

I had six missed calls on my mobile from a blocked number. I never pick up the phone if the number doesn't come up;

having been a call girl for so long . . . well, you just never know. You hear things about people, five, ten years out of the business, then all of a sudden one day the past comes crashing into their real lives.

But I knew it wasn't that. It was SD5.

Why do men do this? If you believed the television, the men's magazines, you'd think it was girls who went all bunny-boiler when they were rejected. But in my experience, women are far too pragmatic for that. In fact they probably thought he'd never ring back in the first place, so are unsurprised when it ends. But men, their egos are fragile little things, and hit them the wrong way . . . presto. You got yourself a stalker.

As far as I knew, he didn't know quite enough about me to go that far. But anyone motivated enough – no, I didn't want to start thinking that way, not yet. Just wait and see.

'You okay?' A1 looked at me as I set the phone to silent. His wife was in the kitchen, washing up from Sunday lunch.

'Yeah, there's just this idiot who keeps ringing. Can't take no for an answer.'

'Sugar, if I were him, I wouldn't.'

'Since when did I ever say no to you?' A1 smiled at me warmly. He's such a bear of a man and as sweet as they come, and I often wonder what my life would have turned out to be if we were still together. But I was too young then, and the wrong time is the same thing as the wrong person in my eyes. 'But it's been like five times today, he's just not getting the hint.'

'Five times?' A1 looked concerned. 'Do you have the number?'

'Honey, don't. You're not going to beat up some random just because he's got phone-itis. Anyway, the number is blocked.'

Aɪ nodded, but I could tell he wasn't convinced. 'You should know, if you ever need—'

'I know.'

'Just ask, okay?'

'Okay.'

'Promise?'

'I promise.' He frowned. 'Don't worry, I can handle myself! And if I can't of course I'll always call you first.'

'I'll have my phone on all night, just in case. Even of you just want to talk.'

lundi, le 27 mars

'I just got off the phone with HR,' Giles said. 'Don't tell me you haven't sent down a CV.'

'Whatever for?'

'For the position, daft woman,' he said.

Oh. That. 'Really? You mean that wasn't simply a ruse to get extra work out of me on no additional pay?'

'Well . . . uh, not entirely,' he said, fumbling the words. 'What I mean is . . . oh, just apply for it.'

I raised one shoulder listlessly. 'What's the point? I'll never get it. I don't have the background. I don't have the connections.'

Giles raised an eyebrow. 'You know, dear, just because things aren't tickety-boo at home doesn't mean the world is over,' he said. I looked up, and saw genuine concern in his face. And then it occurred to me, what if the fling with Alex had affected him more than he cared to show? Could he really be suffering from a broken heart?

'Besides, I can't flirt with you if you're always underneath me, and serious carrying-on is right out,' he continued. 'For one thing I always pegged you as a woman-on-top type in bed.'

I rolled my eyes. Yeah, broken heart, that's it. Men.

mercredi, le 29 mars

The phone rang. No number again. I decided to put an end to it once and for all.

'Hey.' It was a quiet voice, and not the one I was expecting.

'Sorry about—'

'No, don't apologise. I'm a judgmental idiot.'

'Runs in the family I guess.' A pause. 'So . . .'

'The cruise.'

'You pick it out, I don't know anything about cruises. Just tell me how much it is.'

'Okay.' She put the phone down, so softly I didn't notice she'd rung off.

It wasn't a victory, moral or otherwise. There's no such thing when it comes to family.

vendredi, le 31 mars

Things I learned, courtesy of line-dancing:

- There's a fine line between arch and trashy, and country music has left it well and truly behind.
- Fake-American accents are worse than real ones. But only just.
- It's possible, in under three hours, to have Rugby old boys talking about Dollywood as if they'd built the place.
- Cowboy boots are really just high heels for men.

- There's no figure that can't be improved with the addition of high, tight jeans and a fringed satin shirt. And possibly a straw hat, but never a sparkly one, those are for amateurs.
- Given the opportunity, I would go again in a heartbeat.

Ten things about being an adult that are nothing like you could have imagined:

1 Alcohol, in its pure state, is not sweet; nor is it meant to be.

2 Men, in their pure state, are very sweet; though they will go to extraordinary lengths to hide this.

3 All those models who looked so womanly and grown-up in the magazines when you were a child were in fact drug-addicted teenagers who grew up to bear Rod Stewart's children, so quit idolising them already.

4 All that grumbling your parents made every month about the pay packet and the taxes? Must be genetically inherited.

5 The coolest party is the one that wasn't planned, and the coolest people are the ones who leave earliest, knowing that nothing good ever happened after two a.m.

6 An appreciation for classical music will not, in fact, overtake any childhood punk leanings.

7 There's a lot of down time in being a grown-up. That's why alcohol and television were invented.

8 Your parents will treat you as if you're fifteen forever.

9 Sex is nowhere near as gentle, romantic or perfect as you thought it would be. It's far better than that.

10 No one else knows what they're doing, either.

Avril

samedi, le 01 avril

April in London is invariably foul. Either wet and cold – 'April showers bring May showers,' says N, grimly – or unseasonably hot, so much so that you are forced to confront far too early in the year the cruel reality of an entire city's windows being hermetically sealed by five generations' worth of magnolia paint. Either way, you'll spend a surprising number of hours sheltering in the nearest available Tesco Metro.

How did anyone cope, in fact, in the millennia before this de facto public space existed, helpfully staffed by people too poorly paid to care that you've been lingering, slightly damp, in the ready-meal section for twenty minutes? How did Londoners of centuries past get by in this cruellest of months? Probably tucked into the nearest available gin house, I imagine. Or else decamping to a muddy country estate to stomp around all Austenesque and tubercular.

Whatever good may happen in spring, the underlying awfulness of London in April cannot be avoided. If it were a person, it would be that fat ginger housemate you had at uni: pointless, unbearable and utterly convinced of its own importance. Only unlike that housemate, you can't just give notice and decamp to the other side of the river while the getting's good. You're stuck in a thirty-day lease for which there is no appeal. And just when you're thanking fuck it's over, you remember in eleven months' time it will be starting all over again. Yes, April, herpes and Cliff Richard: like it or no, they always find a way back.

dimanche, le 02 avril

'You look like someone weed in your cornflakes, sugar. What's up?' A1 asked.

I threw my now-useless umbrella to the ground. 'That's the last time I spend upwards of thirty quid on a collapsible brolly just because the Queen supposedly carries the same one. She doesn't know umbrellas, she's probably always had people to hold hers.'

'Hey, calm down. It's just rain. Skin's waterproof.'

'Yeah? So's Mustique. I hate this city, I need a fucking holiday.'

A1 smiled indulgently. 'Sit down, sugar. Here, I'll get you a coffee,' he said, gesturing at a hovering waiter. 'What's eating you?'

'Nothing,' I said. 'Everything. I hate being alone but I can't imagine spending another moment with the people I meet. I'm good at my job but I'm not certain I actually like it. I haven't had a whiff of proper sunshine in months. And my friends all seem so happy, so sorted.'

'Okay then, let's hit those one at a time.' I sigh and roll my eyes – ever the scientist, A1. Ever the man. 'Everyone goes through life alone, I met my wife just when I'd given up – you're still young, and still cute, and I wouldn't worry about it so much.'

'Thanks, Mum.'

'Second, it's just a job. There's going to be something you don't like about anywhere you work, so why not stick this one out a bit longer? Isn't it better than being out of work?'

'I guess,' I said.

'And, you know, maybe it's Seasonal Affective Disorder. My wife goes through it too, and it's always worse after the New Year because it seems like the sun will never be back. She goes to a tanning bed once a week – not enough to change the colour of her skin, but enough to lift her mood. It might be a placebo effect, but it seems to work. Have you considered that?'

'Ugh, no. I might catch chav.'

'Well how about a change of scene in the city? Join some new activities, start going out to different places.'

I shrugged. I guessed I could try that.

'Now, perhaps the time has come to pass on the one piece of advice my father gave me, why, when I was about your age. I had my first professional job and was walking to work every day in the rain, from Finsbury Park all the way into the City every day and getting sick of it pretty damned quick, I can tell you.'

I exhaled. A1's father had been, if nothing else, a font of timeless Jewish wisdom. 'Go on then. What did he recommend? Deep breaths? Counting down from ten backwards? Always look on the bright side of life?'

'No, he said to me . . . he said, "Son, life is shit and you're gonna step in it more times than not. So always carry dry socks."'

lundi, le 03 avril

Leafing through the papers this morning. Budget scandal, sex scandal . . . yet another politician embroiled in an affair. Will they never learn? Apparently not.

Turn the page again and, alongside pictures of the girl involved snapped on what could euphemistically be called a bad hair week, are photos of the politician in question giving an official statement. With his wife positioned close by for maximal impact.

They all look the same at these moments, as well. Ashen skin, serious makeup, understated dresses. I wonder if they have stylists to hand for just such an occasion? 'Mary, John's cheated again. I need a look that says dignified pain.'

I suppose we have Hillary Clinton to blame. By staying with her husband, she made it de rigueur for shell-shocked wives of shamed politicians to appear with their men in public after the scandal breaks. Goodness only knows what deals go on behind closed door: 'Stay with me now, darling, and the presidency of the United States will someday be yours.' Or, 'Don't leave me, you'll get the home in Surrey and we'll only appear in public together twice a year.'

And why-oh-why do politicians always have such depressingly predictable taste in feminine charms? The big, blowsy, sexy-for-idiots Sloanes like Petronella Wyatt? The endless perm-and-blow-dry brigade that followed Bill Clinton around? When here's so much power to be wielded, why can they never be counted on to exercise a little – dare I say it – taste?

Of course, whoever the other woman is, she'll be eviscerated. That goes without saying. Sleep with a football star and you'll be offered a lucrative career in reality television. Sleep with a politician and you'll be ridiculed for life. Instead of weighing up offers from Endemol and ITV, you'll be spending your days working the till at Tesco. Unless you're Edwina Currie but, even then, I wouldn't rule it out for the future.

So in this corner, we have the wives, with their expensive educations, charity fundraisers and all the benefits old-school feminism can buy. And in the other corner, the younger women in their ill-advised black nylons and knee-high boots for whom the glass ceiling well and truly just came crashing down. Because in case you hadn't noticed, there's no such thing as sisterhood when you're embroiled in a sex scandal, baby.

That, more than anything else, is the most offensive part of the whole distasteful circus. That when the chips are down, older women enjoying the benefits of marriage to rich, successful men will never rock the boat. Whatever feminist claptrap they may spout at dinner parties obviously comes second to their husbands' careers.

Now back to your regularly scheduled programming . . .

I spent a wholly obscene amount of money today on silk underwear. Even more unforgivable considering there's no one apart from me who'll see it.

That is all.

mardi, le 04 avril

In the past, when I said I've not been with someone in so long I fear I'm going to seal up, it's always been a joke. As of this month I'm starting to fear it isn't.

Under normal circumstances I can't take the idea of vibrators, they seem so . . . mechanical and useless, but now I'm looking at them with new eyes, as if a ten-inch realistic jelly dong with rotating beads at the base may be the only thing standing between me and retroactive virginity.

mercredi, le 05 avril

There's something to be said for keeping your true feelings under wraps and my time in the sex biz made me a past master of that particular art.

It can be a fantastic advantage, as when I'm on the seemingly never-ending rollercoaster of terrible dates. All I have to do is remember that since he's not paying, I can go home at the end of this drink, and hey presto! A smile magically appears on my face.

'Another terrible one,' I trilled to N before I was even out the pub door. 'I think I'm setting new records in meeting idiots.'

But there are definitely drawbacks. I've become so used to not sharing the good as well as the bad that it's become ingrained in my personality. Everything good that happens comes off as a bit of an anti-climax. And I am beginning to wonder if this has seriously affected how I view achievement or life in general.

Such as, at work, if something goes very well, the first instinct of my colleagues is to piss off to the pub for the rest of the day, go screaming the news up and down the corridor, fill the office with air-kisses and mutual admiration and so on. At the very least someone comes round to shower us all with treats and congratulations. I don't. Something that is moderately successful is 'okay'. Something that is world-beating legendary is 'hey, not bad'. The experience of having to keep everything under wraps has dampened my enthusiasm to the point where a global cataclysm would probably be met with 'well, okay then'.

Like, last week. Giles, who has been holding the possibility of promotion over me almost since the minute I got here, has finally advertised the job. I'd finally sent in my CV – and later that day, passing in the hall, he gave my shoulder a squeeze.

'Great application,' he said. 'I have no doubt you're going forward.'

Anyone else would have given him a hug, or at least a thousand-watt smile. Or proclaimed the news Excellent,

Cool, Awesome, or any of a thousand hyperbolic phrasings. I just nodded. 'Okay.'

I'd never been like that before. I have, in the past, been extremely demonstrative of my feelings both at home and in general. People whom I like, know I like them. And the other way round too. My appreciation for good things has until recently been generous, if not a little vocal (ask the neighbours). In short, I'm a lover, baby.

Not any longer. On the other hand, having to keep the bad things under wraps can't be entirely wrong, can it? I roll with the punches a little better now. So what's a girl to do? Well, I do have a lot of great friends. But, you know, they have their own lives too. Ditto family. And, apart from the fact that I think Jungian analysis &c. has about as much relevance to Planet Earth as Scientology does, I suppose I could look into getting a therapist – after all, isn't that what everyone does? But unloading to a stranger would just be weird. And everyone, but everyone, has a price. I know what I'm worth, and the hourly rates for the talking-cure, and they don't add up to much in the way of peace of mind. Yeah, so I'm paranoid. Issue one, day one. Again, this realisation does not exactly send my pitch rolling anymore.

A long time ago, I had this friend, who was known in the online world as 'Anhedonia'. And now I think I know what he means.

vendredi, le 07 avril

L and I were comparing laminated lists. Mine – the male one, anyway – goes something like:

1 Bill Murray. Proof, if proof were needed, that personality goes a long, long way. This is a choice that people either

get, or don't, and if they don't, I cease any and all communication with them. Bill Murray is, in a word, godlike. So much so that A2 and I had a standing agreement that I would be permitted to cheat on him with the actor who made *Stripes* the single funniest film of the last century.

2 Clive Owen. Brooding, tall, dark and handsome, though not too handsome, more dangerous-looking. And you don't get the feeling he takes himself that seriously. Just quirky enough to be irresistible. Yum.

3 Matt Dawson. There has to be a sport star on every girl's list somewhere, and he is mine. I always thought he was fit but, when he started appearing on *A Question of Sport*, he went stratospheric. I love his laugh, his look, everything. In one episode of *QoS* there was a round where Matt had to get up and act out various sports. I noticed Sue Barker was checking him out, too. Good girl.

4 Shahrukh Khan. Bollywood actor of considerable reputation, already possessed of a finely muscled frame, who recently underwent a full-body overhaul (three-hours' training a day) for a film role. It paid off and then some: SRK has abs you could shred cheese on, plus is not too proud to cry in his films. Simply put, he is perfect.

5 James Callis from *Battlestar Galactica* . . . I think I may have covered this one already? In short, he's fit. And he's evil. Nuff said.

L was going to disqualify the last two because she's never heard of them. Some quick Googling assured her they were in fact famous, so she reluctantly allowed the list to stand.

'Go one then, let's have yours,' I said.

'Robbie Williams five times,' she said.

I laughed. 'You can't do that! Besides – Robbie Williams? I know you fancy him and all, but that man's such a tightly wound ball of neuroses, I doubt he'd be very good in bed. As if he's ever had sex with the same person five times, anyway.'

L frowned. 'Attraction's not always about sexual prowess, you know,' she said.

'No, but it's a hell of a lot of it. And we are talking about your laminated list for sex, not meeting for coffee and a pastry.' I had to admit that probably the last two years with the Boy were powered on sex alone and when that fizzled out the relationship was doomed. 'I mean, great sex is great, what else do you need?'

'But the whole point is, sex isn't always great,' L said. 'This is just a fantasy. Real life sex isn't like that.'

'Bull,' I said. 'Sex is all about what you put into it. I've had great sex, because I've pursued it. If you show willing, that's ninety per cent of the job done. If people are having bad sex then I'm sorry, but I tend to feel it's their own fault.'

L pursed her lips. 'Well as it happens I wouldn't say I've had great sex with anyone, actually,' she said tightly.

'Are you joking?' I said. 'Of the seven men . . .'

'Not a one's made me come. And even leaving that aside the sex is . . . well, I'm not sure what people get so worked up about. I think you need love to see you through.'

'Oh, I'm not arguing, love's important in the long run. But what about the first few months together, the passion, when you can't get enough of each other, when you want to do anything and everything with that person in bed?'

'Can't say I know what you're talking about,' L said, looking away. 'I guess I'm the sort of girl who looks for something deeper than that.'

I sighed. Again, we were going to have to agree to . . . no, fuck that. I'd work on her. There's only one reason a woman should agree to sub-standard sex, and that's when she's getting paid.

There's this thing. A small, valuable object that has been at the back of my mind for some time. It stayed in my bedroom. Under a pile of jumpers you'd find it, still in its box, the box still in a carrier bag.

I like watches, always have done. The most expensive thing I ever bought myself, apart from the house, was a watch. I spent more on that watch than most people spend on cars and would have paid twice as much. When that watch went in for much-needed repairs earlier this year, I couldn't bear to wear something cheap and nasty in the meantime and so bought an even more expensive watch. I don't know why I like them so – just do. I'm not a girl who fancies jewels or cars much but I love a great watch. Preferably handmade. Preferably Swiss. Something understated that drapes in a whisper over the wrist, something whose bling is hidden, sensual, secret.

It's been a useful sort of knowledge to use on rich clients – I always notice the watch, the shoes. People might wonder what sort of conversation you could possibly have with a stranger when you're about to have sex with him, to which I say, watches.

So this thing that's in a box in a bag in my room, it's a watch. The watch was meant for him, the Boy, one birthday of his. I never felt comfortable giving it to him – he got a meal out at a very nice restaurant instead, that year. He was a little puzzled, because I'd mentioned a gorgeous gift I planned, and on the day it's just a night out? But for one reason and another (one reason's name being Tracey and another's name being Sue) I couldn't bring myself to hand it over.

Cruel some would say. When you give a gift it should just be given, not held on to like ransom for good behaviour. In my defence, I'm not the sort of woman who withholds sexual favours when angry. Even in the middle of stressful, antagonising relationships I am always up for the sex. I can't hold back on the sex, it's too much of a punishment to myself. I can hold back on pressies.

The thing about watches is, they're like little mechanical hearts. They mark your time and mostly go unnoticed and sometimes they stop, sometimes forever. The price of a watch has little to do with its reliability, and we should all have one. Different things make them tick: some run on batteries, others run on sunlight. I've always preferred ones that wind themselves – kinetic, I think some people call it now, though I've always known it as automatic.

So the thing in the box in the bag in my room, the watch, it was a little heart I was saving to give away to someone someday. But the day never came and, eventually, the some-one went away, too.

Only just today I took the watch back to the shop. They were very understanding; I'm a good customer. They com-miserated – it's fairly obvious what the story is when a woman returns a man's watch, unworn – and they gave me a full refund. The money will provide a nice birthday pressie meal for A4, for being such a solid friend, for never asking me for anything at all even when I know he knows I make three times what he does. Some of it is being donated to a charity; some will buy a much needed new computer for home. Some is going to buy a bottle of spirits, to still my aching heart.

lundi, le 10 avril

If Napoleon were alive today, he would no doubt opine that England is a nation of people wandering aimlessly around air-conditioned boxes built on former wetlands. But whoever turned to a short French despot for advice about buying new laptops? So I went to the closest Compu-MegaWarehouse, or whatever, and I took the single geekiest person I know – a close run contest among my acquaintances if ever there was one – A2.

Only, we had a serious divergence on the matter of just what flavour of shiny techno toy I should be investing in. 'You're buying an Apple?' A2 said incredulously.

'What are you, my accountant?' I snapped. 'I haven't had to clear my spending habits with you since 1999.'

'Well, I can see why you'd like one. They are cute and everything. But they don't really say grownup, now do they?'

'This from the man who still sneaks references to *Doctor Who* into his work reports,' I said.

'Oof, fire with fire,' he said. 'But consider this, the Doctor wouldn't use a Mac. He's a PC man, you just know it.'

'Get fucked,' I said. 'He does not.'

'Oh no?'

'Oh no, my friend. Because Doctor Who would not use a PC. Doctor Who would not soil his fingers on a Silicon Graphics. He would not give the time of day to Sun, Amiga, Next, Cray, Xerox Alto, Datapoint 2200 or indeed any other box you care to come up with.' I took a deep breath through the spittle collecting in the corners of my mouth. 'Doctor Who uses a quantum computer, fool. And don't even ask about operating system, because he manipulates the qubits directly with his mind.'

A2 was quiet for a minute. He knows when he's been beat. 'So, uh, you going for one of the 13-inch screens or something larger?'

'Small as I can get with the most memory and storage I can afford. Pimp my Tardis, baby.'

'That's it, I've had it,' L cried.

'What?'

'I'm tired of hearing about your abysmal love life. Fuck, I've gone without sex for longer than you could possibly comprehend. I can't believe I come around and listen to you whinge about sex when you've had more than most people get in ten lifetimes. Do you know what your problem is? The problem is not that you don't meet enough people,' L said, shaking her head. 'It's that you only ever meet people with an eye to bedding them.'

'What do you mean?'

'I mean, what exactly is it you do apart from work and sit around drinking with all your ex-lovers?'

'Hey, I've done a lot in my life, I'll have you know. We can't all be law graduates and part-time actresses.'

'I know you've done lots. You talk about it all the damn time for a start. But what are you doing now? Bod all apart from desperately seeking to get laid on a continual basis.'

'And this is wrong why exactly?'

L gave me one of her patented Dear-God-Are-You-Really-That-Daft? looks, which to the best of my recollection she has been using on and off since the age of eight. 'You're an open book as far as your inner life is concerned,' she said.

I snorted. If she only knew.

'Seriously, I know what you're thinking, it's written on your face. When you look at a man, you have an agenda. They know it, they can see it.'

'So? It's not as if my agenda includes buying in the Home Counties and natural childbirth. All men want sex, surely.'

'Oh, I wouldn't disagree,' L said. 'But they are hard-wired

to be hunters. They see sex as the inevitable reward to a chase. And we, my dear, are the quarry.' I rolled my eyes. 'See, there you go again . . .'

'I'm sorry but this is bull. You expect me to believe I can't find a regular man to be with because he evolved to track antelope across the savannah while I stay at home decorating the hut?'

'You've tried it your way,' L said firmly. 'Now consider trying a different tack for once. Just because someone else might have a point doesn't ipso facto make you wrong.'

Ah, she was a good little lawyer, my L. 'Right. So?'

'Join some activities. Ones that don't involve hurling yourself at twenty strangers a night. Leave the internet dating alone for a while. Get back into a sports club, join an activity, and just see where it goes . . .'

'. . . because that's where the fit men are?'

'No, idiot. Because you might see there's more to spare time than planning the next shag. Try volleyball for a while. Or reading to the blind. Or singing.'

Singing?

mercredi, le 12 avril

Quote of the Week:

I won't go about to argue the point with you – 'tis so – and I am persuaded of it, madam, as much as can be, 'that both man and woman bear pain or sorrow (and, for aught I know, pleasure too) best in a horizontal position.' – Laurence Sterne

vendredi, le 14 avril

'Is there something caught in your eye?' I said to Giles as he passed me in the corridor.

'No, you numpty, I'm winking at you.'

'Oh. Uh, why?'

'Because I've seen the short list,' he hissed, leaning in towards me.

'Is that supposed to be good?'

'What planet are you from? It's great. Don't you want your future here to be assured?'

I smiled and returned to my office, but couldn't answer the question exactly. Had I taken this job because of what my ex wanted? Because I was afraid of what my parents would think? Or had I done it for myself? And as far as I could tell, I had never particularly known what I wanted to do – just treated every crap student job and part-time disappointment as an object lesson in what I didn't want to end up doing. Sex work had paid well, and suited me, but that wasn't the same as being in love with my work. I was in love with the lifestyle, yes. And I was in love with the freedom. But the work? It was fine; I could take or leave it. And in the end I'd decided, almost on a whim, to leave it. What, I wondered, would make this career path any different?

samedi, le 15 avril

So, keeping in mind what L said when she gave me that (entirely figurative) furious tongue lashing, I decided to get back into singing.

From time to time, I've found myself involved in music – not that I have any special talent for singing, mind; nor am I possessed of anything even approaching perfect pitch – but as I don't embarrass easily, being on a stage fully clothed making a tit of myself does not faze me in the slightest. Doing the same with clothes off wouldn't particularly, either.

Most people would never do in public things they enjoy in private – double penetration for a paying audience, anyone? No? No takers? – I'm finding the opposite to be true. So I found an ad in the back of a local paper and rang. One-on-one to start with, in a tiny office in the corner of an old building. And to sweeten the deal the lady academic turns out to be something of a looker.

Holy smokes – I thought that having mastered the art of stripping off and fucking strangers was the height of difficulty. Not so. As soon as this (very cute, very hard-bodied) young lady went to the piano, all flirtatious moves were off. She played a note and demanded a scale. And then another, higher. And another. And so on until I was (literally) cracking under the strain.

'Good,' she said. 'Now we can begin.'

Clearly, in my line of work I was just playing at domination games. Others are born to it.

lundi, le 17 avril

I was at home, doing not much of anything, when A4 rang. 'Fancy going to a gig?' he asked.

'Of course, who and when?'

'Half Man Half Biscuit, tomorrow night in Cambridge . . . oh, and it will just be you and A3.' A3 had bought two tickets, one for him and one for A2 (who was away at a conference) and A4 couldn't go. Well, at least I'm third choice.

[Quick background: I met A3 while on holiday with A2 some years ago; we fooled around a bit until I found out about his girlfriend; we hang out a few times a year and there's always a little tension. If by 'little' you mean 'metric tonnes of'. Oh, and he still has the girlfriend. And he works for A2. And is A4's boss.]

'Great.' I checked train times; I could probably just make the last train back afterwards, especially as HMHB date from the Pliocene and are thus usually finished before eleven p.m.

I arrived in Cambridge and found the venue, only getting lost once or twice on the way (a record for me – but then I did see Yo La Tengo there some years ago). Also, there was a thick stream of fans in gold and garnet Dukla Prague away shirts to follow.

No one was waiting for me outside. I ventured in – no sign of A3. I amused myself with a pint and reading the backs of people's shirts. Also noticed there seemed to be a slight discrepancy in Dukla kit; some people going for the 1960s burgundy sleeve/gold shirt scheme with others opting for the somewhat more flattering but certainly inaccurate home kit (colours reversed). And I'm certain I saw a goal-keeper.

The support band was rather good but, really, who comes to these things to hear the support? I figured the probability of my being the only person in the room who had never seen HMHB live before at about one.

There was a tap on my shoulder. 'You're looking very clean and nice tonight.' It was A3.

'I didn't have time to think about dressing the part,' I said.

'I thought I was the most conservative-looking person in here until you turned up.' A very large Goth woman of a certain age bounced by, facial piercings all a-jangle, waving her Joy Division oven gloves madly.

The music, incidentally, was very good. It's always a pleasure to be somewhere where people are actually interested in the music rather than chain-smoking and screaming dull conversation at their duller friends; at other gigs I have been tempted to buy the shirt I spotted once that said SHUT THE FUCK UP – THE BAND IS PLAYING (on the back as well as the front), but that night there would have been no need for it.

Did we enjoy it? Yes, undoubtedly. I was aware of A3's proximity to me, especially as we edged towards the mosh pit and then halfway through, when his hands rested gently on my shoulders, then my waist, then my hips and I was certain he was sniffing my hair but I wasn't going to move, because to do so would certainly have made him stop.

A2 has always accused me of not-so-secretly holding a torch for A3. (And his point is . . . ?) He's right, of course, I probably would drop everything if someday A3 rang to say he and his girlfriend had split. But I equally expect that will never happen – both the ringing and the splitting – so have to live with the inevitable disappointment every time we do meet alone.

We sang along to most of the songs and I slowly inched back towards A3, tilting my head to his chest, feeling the warmth of his body. We've kissed only a few times and that was, what, two World Cups ago? Eventually I did have to peel away, to get down the front for the encore, and then we made a quick escape from the club and ran all the way to the train station.

I laughed, panting, we had made it with a few minutes to spare. A3 patted the seat next to him. We sat on the platform, trying to remember which songs the band had played, and in what order (as were more than a few others fresh from HMHB). 'So, what time's your train?' I asked.

'Tomorrow morning,' he said. 'I've booked a room in town.'

'Oh, you should have said.' He gave me a look. I hate the look. You know it – the look of someone who likes playing the come-here-go-away game, but is mortally offended when you call his bluff. 'I mean, I could have booked a room myself. We might have gone for a few more drinks or something. Or you could have come back and stayed at mine . . .' Careful, woman! Remember, he has that girl-friend in Spain! '. . . in the spare room of course.'

He ruffled my hair as the train came in. 'On your way,' he said.

'Good night.'

'It was; it certainly was.'

mardi, le 18 avril

I came in to a missed call from my father, so I rang back. 'Daddy, hello?'

'Uh, no,' a woman's voice said. She sounded slow and throaty, as if she'd just woken up, even though it was six in the evening. Just woken up, or . . . no, I didn't like to think about it. I know Dad had always had strange female friends but he'd always insisted they were just friends, that he was just trying to help people he saw in trouble. Of course now that he and Mum were split there was nothing to stop him . . . stop, don't go there. 'Who you looking for?'

I told her my name and that I was returning my father's call. 'Oh, right,' she said. 'I didn't know he had a daughter. How old are you, sweetie?'

'Old enough,' I snapped. 'Is he there? Put him on.'

'No, he just went to the pub,' she said.

'Tell him I called,' I barked. 'And what did you say your name was?' But she'd already hung up, whoever she was.

mercredi, le 19 avril

I went around the corner quickly and just caught Giles and Alex jumping away from each other in the hall, looking guilty. He turned on his heel and disappeared down the hall, but Alex stood glued to the spot.

'You all right?' I said, trying to sound casual.

'Yeah. Good,' she said. Voice wavering slightly. 'I just . . . there was this position I'd been aiming for, and Giles had said . . . well, anyway it doesn't matter. I guess I'd been counting on things to work out a certain way and they didn't.' Her eyes reluctantly met mine, and I could see real disappointment there. 'Apparently I don't have the experience . . . nor the aptitude . . . and Richard and I . . .' she sighed. 'Anyway, it's nothing. Forget I mentioned it,' she said, and walked in the opposite direction to where Giles had gone.

I wanted to run after her, to tell her . . . I don't know what. I don't know any better than anyone else what women want to hear. I wanted her to go, to get away from this office and from Giles, in a sort of possessive way that made me uncomfortable, and not just because I wanted the job too. But I felt for her dilemma, and guess in some way she was my friend. Still, a very small part of me was secretly glad that it looked as if she couldn't sleep her way to success, after all.

Yes, I know I'm a fucking hypocrite.

jeudi, le 20 avril

Have been in again to see the lady music professor. I feel much more comfortable with her now, due in no small part to the fact that during the last lesson, she let me touch her up in the name of a breathing exercise.

'Hokay,' she said in her breathy voice. 'Do you mind if I put my hands on you now?'

Dear god, it was the stuff of a thousand soft porn films. 'No, but I feel it only fair to warn you I'm a little bit sweaty having just come up the hill.'

'I don't mind.' Cue porn music intro. Ba-dowwww. Oh I wish.

And then went on to describe how someone instructing her in the vocal arts once suggested that she 'sing up from the anus'.

I'm not certain she realises the suggestive nature of her methods, but it seems to help, as the dreaded scales are far from dreaded anymore. In fact, I have been considering taking up music more regularly and feel far more confident in my range than I have at any point in the last decade. Perhaps it's too early to ask if anyone out there needs someone to front a band, but . . . a girl can dream.

After the lesson she held me back for a few minutes chatting. 'There's something I've been wanting to ask you,' she said. 'Of course, you don't have to say yes . . .'

'What is it?'

'There's a musical theatre group I work with. Teenagers, mostly. I need a few extra hands for our next production. It's a little ambitious, something one of the g
we can always use a few extra adults around
run errands, maybe get some experience of c

'Really? What makes you think I'd be goo

She smiled and tilted her head. 'I don't know, I simply have this gut feeling that you don't mind interacting with strangers. Someone who can put the kids and their parents at their ease is always useful to have around.'

I considered the point. If nothing else, this would certainly broaden the type of people I was meeting, and all without any expectation of sex whatsoever. 'Count me in, then. What do I have to do?'

'We're having a little garden party at mine next week,' she said. 'The theme is blue – it ties into the new play. I even think I heard that some of the girls will come dressed as Smurfs. You could just wear jeans if you feel like it.'

vendredi, le 21 avril

The backlash has started, I know it. I can tell by the way Audrey and Jane at work exchange conspiratorial looks whenever I pass them, the way they stop talking as soon as I enter a room. I can only imagine what invented infraction of office politics I'm supposed to have committed. But now that Alex is clearly (and openly) into full-on wedding prep and therefore untouchable, I suppose it was only a matter of time before the harpies turned on me.

Ho hum. I can deal. I've had career hookers trying to write fake bad reviews about me, a manager who took a third of my income attempting to undermine me and younger, more pneumatic girls who tried to stab me in the back, thinking they were entitled to the clientele it had taken skill and patience for me to acquire.

I walked back through the office to make a cup of tea. Jane and Audrey fell silent, Jane slightly giggling. I stood in front of her, hot tea in hand, until she finally stopped, looked up, and met my eyes.

With careful deliberation I mouthed a single sentence – Bring it on, bitch – turned, and stalked back to my office.

Let them try. Just let them fucking try. I've run with the hardest of the hard and no Dorothy Perkins-clad office gossip is going to intimidate me.

samedi, le 22 avril

'Hey, sport, what's up?' N never rings in the middle of the day.

'Nothing, just seeing how you are,' he said, but I knew he was lying. I let him go on for twenty minutes chatting about the usual things (the usual things = the decline and fall of the Conservative party and women on TV with great tits. He's not called N the Tory by A1 for nothing).

'So what's really going on?' I asked. 'Everything okay with your lass?'

N sighed. 'Everything's good at the moment. Stagnant, but . . . good. She's moved back to Surbiton to save some money, then we're talking about selling my house and buying in Kingston or thereabouts . . .'

'Wow, congratulations. I had no idea it was so serious.'

'Yeah, well, that's the thing. Between her schedule and mine we're only hooking up once a fortnight at the most and I had a message the other day that M is leaving for Australia next month . . .'

M is a woman with amazing – and I do mean amazing, they put Keeley to shame – breasts and whom N and I bedded a few years back. Obvs, who wouldn't want another go?

'And your girl is okay with . . .'

'No, she definitely isn't.'

Ah. The horns of a dilemma. N is nothing if not

completely honest, sometimes to the point of hurtfulness – I know from experience. He doesn't mean to be so, of course, it's just that raised on a diet of boys who will smile and flirt and still never call you back, the novelty of being with someone who never hides anything, ever, can be a very odd experience.

'Thing is, you know me.'

'Yeah.' For the fact that N has bedded almost as many women as I have men, he's never cheated on a girlfriend, and when he's had multiple partners they always know. Always. 'And you're sure she'd never . . . ?'

'No. We've talked about it. Never.'

'Huh.' It struck me as strange that someone as into hard-core pain and torture as N's current girl could possibly draw the line at threesomes, but I guess we all have our limits, and that is hers.

'If she and I move in together, then this is it. This is really it. And . . . I'd love to see you again too.'

'Last fling and all that.'

'Mmm.'

'You know I'm up for it; I'd love another go at M. Tell her if she wants to hook up with me before she leaves, she has my number. But I can't tell you what to do. You know if it was me I'd do it,' I said, and let that hang in the air. He'd been the one who rejected me, so let him squirm. It was only fair. '. . . but I'm not you, and that's just not what you do, is it?'

But if N noticed me twisting the knife a little, he certainly didn't show it. 'Thing is, even if I decided to do something, I'd probably get all the way to the hotel room with you two, and then bottle out.'

'Well if that happened I'd be cool. But you have to decide what to do yourself. Go have a think about it, and let me know.'

'Yeah. Okay. Um, well, how are things with you?'
'Oh, you know, the usual.'

dimanche, le 23 avril

In my father's opinion, no day is wasted if you have learned something.

Yesterday I learned that a group of seventeen-year-old girls drinking Pimm's in the garden and painting each other's bodies blue isn't remotely as sexy as it sounds.

lundi, le 24 avril

Out of curiosity, I log back on to the departmental server as an administrator. (Note to admins: don't make the password so darned easy to figure out. Okay, so it took me three attempts with l33t-ware, one of which turned out to be a virus that, had it not been detected, would have sunk our IT department for a week minimum, but still. Try harder next time.)

Ooh, looks as if Alex has updated her CV . . . hmm, interesting, she's taken Giles off her referees list. I wonder why? Surely embarrassment about the whole affair gone wrong would guarantee her good letters of recommendation until well into the next decade. Oh, and she's updated her Mission Statement or Statement of Intent or Career Focus or what-the-hell-ever it is. Let's have a shufty shall we?

'Management potential'? 'Career momentum'? 'Analytical evolution'?

Holy ass shitewipes, she's going for that job after all. The same one I've been holding out for all these months, which I thought she'd finally given up on in favour of Leeds. And she's bypassing Giles completely. The brazen bitch.

mardi, le 25 avril

Guilty admission: I've been reading those crap glossy magazines L left behind.

But it's not all bad, as in doing so I've discovered a new girl-crush: Liz Jones, former editor of Marie Claire.

My admiration for her is sky-high. I read her pieces in the magazines because I vaguely remembered a piece she wrote about her wedding some time back. I was shocked, disgusted, and certain it was a wind-up. No woman could possibly be so successful on the back of a personality so riddled with self-hatred.

And yet, here she was in the glossies, and no, it's not a windup. Week after week, year after year, Liz Jones has offered up the full and complete truth about what she thinks of herself. And that's when I realised, whoah, she's telling it like it is. Not the do-me bravado of, er, me and people like me, nor the giggle-cuteness, gosh-I'm-so-inept Love-Me! of Bridget Jones. Liz Jones lets fly those real, disturbing inner voices, the ones that creep up on you just as the lights go out and make you recount stupid things you did at the age of twelve, in real time, in harrowing detail. You can't tell me every woman – hell, every human – doesn't experience this at least once in their lives (if not once a day).

She's like a stripper, except what she strips off is any pretence of self-confidence. It's so horrifying, yet you can't look away. Because she doesn't do it on an anonymous blog or with the disclaimer that she really, actually, thinks the world of herself. Her self-deprecation is not false, it's not forced; it's right out there for all to see. I want to gather her up and bring her to my house and feed her (skinny, sugar-free) hot chocolate until she's well again. I hope whatever else, that her writing is therapy to her.

So, that's how I went from Liz-sceptic to Liz-fan. And why I bought my own glossies for the first time as of this week. Liz is the tell-all Queen. Long may she reign.

jeudi, le 27 avril

Is there some vital lesson I've missed, a course I failed to take or some coded message that goes out at regular intervals to the females of the species that I, for some reason, lack the necessary equipment to detect and interpret?

Is there some reason why all the women in the office are still, in this day and age, buying – not to mention wearing – kitten heels? Hell. If it's an issue of comfort, I'd sooner give up entirely and go shod in clogs than wear the vile things.

I mean really, what gives?

samedi, le 29 avril

'Hey, how are you? Didn't hear back from you last weekend.'

'Last weekend?' Dad said. 'Was I meant to see you?'

'No, I just rang . . . a woman answered it. She said she'd pass the message on. When you didn't call back I was very worried.' Let it never be said I inherited nothing from the maternal line of my family; a talent for dishing out passive-aggressive guilt grows stronger every year.

'Sorry honey, I just didn't get that message. Is everything okay?'

'Yeah, it's fine, usual stuff going on. But I've not seen you in ages, how are things? Are you . . . seeing someone new?'

'What? No, just some girl I'm helping out.'

I pursed my lips. I knew what that meant. Another case of Dad playing father figure. It drove my mother crazy, but he's a soft touch and in the end that must have been just one of the things that drove a wedge between them. Now he was free to do as he liked – and 'help' whomever he wanted. This girl was probably giving him sex in return for a place to stay and, who knows, maybe ripping him off on the side. I mean, there are whores and then there are whores.

'Please at least say she's not younger than me. And not a mother. And maybe even is looking for a job.'

But of course, I didn't say these things out loud. I couldn't. Not to him. But I still burned with hatred for the women who could use my father for any little crisis when I never, ever would have taken advantage; for my father, who was too blind to see when his daughter needed him most. Who rated company, even with wildly inappropriate girls with habits, above being dignified and alone.

'Great. Well, I'd love to see you,' I said hopefully.

'Sure, I'll call you next week,' he said. But I knew if this girl had her way – and she would – that he probably wouldn't.

dimanche, le 30 avril

Apparently the kids took to me – I've been invited out on a three-legged pub crawl with the cast of the musical.

I dressed carefully. Sure, there would be single men, but single men something like ten years younger than me. Say what you will about looking for sex, but cougar just ain't my style. At the same time I didn't want to look too mumsy so I dressed in a pair of designer jeans and a cute polka dot blouse. I think I got the balance just about right.

On turning up and realising I'm the oldest person by a decade all round, the penny finally drops. Some of these kids must only have been allowed out on the promise there would be adult supervision and I'm the nominal adult. Call me a hypocrite, but if I were a parent, I wouldn't send my sixteen-year-old daughter into town of an evening with only me as chaperone.

The turnout was approximately, as the song puts it, two girls for every boy. And, no, I was not exempt from participating. Which is how I found myself one slice of bread in a freckled eighteen-year-old boy's sandwich. He certainly looked well pleased with himself.

Being, as I was, gaffa-taped to two teenagers for the better part of a night, you might have thought it was a more interesting night than it turned out to be. And perhaps that would have been true had I been a) drunk or b) a teenager and drunk. We wiggled around for a bit and several dance floors, trying to make the best of a bad situation and then around midnight (having run out of all other possible conversation either of them could muster) came the inevitable question:

'Just how old are you, exactly?'

Sigh.

Ten signs that your peer group has outgrown you:

1 Your younger sister invites you round to see her house, dog and baby.

2 Someone describes your ex-boyfriend as 'a little bit ADHD' and less than a minute later wonders why you're not still together, as you were such a suited couple.

3 Barbecues aren't bring-your-own-food anymore . . .

4 . . . and the bangers are organic, hand-stuffed gourmet Cumberlands.

5 The homeowners have exactly as many chairs in the garden as guests.

6 The women agree – you're lucky you can still get away with wearing that . . .

7 . . . and as soon as you leave they'll say what they're really thinking.

8 If someone says 'conveyancing' one more time, you will have to kill them, even if it might be you who says it.

9 It's ten o'clock, half the party have gone home, everyone over the age of two is fully conscious and no one's vomited in the rhododendrons yet.

10 You have more in common with the children playing flip-swing on the hammock than anyone else.

Mai

lundi, le 01 mai

This weekend, in a fit of boredom, I shaved my pussy.

You might be asking what could possibly be so boring that denuding your mount of all follicular growth seems a good alternative way to spend time and the answer is, the prospect of driving n-hundred miles to sit in my sister L's back garden at the Most Domesticated Barbecue Ever. And, damn it, if I had to spend my weekend surrounded by people talking about *Masterchef* and babies, then I was going to do it with less pubic hair.

Let's get this straight, the razor has never been a friend of mine and less so since coming off the game. Trusty Gillette in hand, I did the deed. And, damn, but it feels good. I'd forgotten how nice it is. How a few square inches of smooth skin can make such a difference to your boyfriend's enthusiasm for cunnilingus.

There are always the drawbacks – the possibility of in-grown hair, the daily maintenance, the fact that you can suddenly feel the difference between cheap lacy knickers and the silk-and-satin heart-stoppingly expensive variety (if you're wondering, it's to do with texture and quality of gusset stitchery). Also, is it just me, or do you seem to spatter the toilet a little more when you wee after a shave? No? Forget I mentioned it then (*ahem* discreetly wiping the underside of the seat).

But all in all, I'm pleased. I can't imagine why I let myself go for so long. And if nothing else it's dampened the desire to get a radical haircut-and-dye for, ooh, a good couple of months I should think.

mardi, le 02 mai

With still no word about where my application has disappeared to, and not even a breath of a hint about possible interview arrangements, Giles has gone on the management warpath again. At the morning meeting he asks each of us to come up with a phrase to describe ourselves. Brainstorming for some kind of company restrategising in advance of going global, whatever that means. So of course going round the table everyone's on best behaviour, not least Alex, who comes up with the vomit-inducing 'team players'. I look at her pointedly but she ignores me. 'Now, no one's exempt,' Giles said, looking at me. 'Hit me with your best shot.'

Boy, would I love to. For so many reasons. But being acutely embarrassed in public would do for starters – spontaneity is my worst nightmare. I live by routines, rituals, schedules. There's nothing worse than being put on the spot. Especially in a context where people go to great lengths to emphasise there are no wrong answers. Just like how women who say penis size doesn't matter are invariably the worst sort of size queens, you should instantly distrust anyone who says there are no wrong answers. What they really mean is there are no right ones.

You know what? Fuck 'em. Fuck the people who think the world should be recast in sitcom episodes, tidy little lessons and management speak. Might as well go for shock value. 'Perezoso y despiadado,' I say. If nothing else, at least my old friend Tomás – whose valiant efforts to teach me even the simplest Spanish vocabulary were exceeded only by my pigheaded inability to learn it – would be proud.

'Spanish, is it?' Giles looks puzzled. 'What's it mean?' Alex and Jane ask in unison.

'Lazy and ruthless,' I say, wondering why I bother to care anymore.

Alex's jaw drops. Giles laughs, a big, bounding, retriever-dog-yelp. 'I knew I could count on you to come up with something brilliant!' he crows.

mercredi, le 03 mai

Went salsa dancing in Islington with some of the kids and had a time, as they say. Is always a tonic to have strangers' hands all over your arse, especially if they are fit and Latin. Less enjoyable was making certain straying teenage hands wandered no further south than my waist and as the token adult, turning a blind eye to all but the most blatant of sneaky San Miguels. Would have met up with lady L after, but dear me, she begged off because of a drinks date! Being as I am largely unschooled in the ways of normal women, I shudder to think what this means. Possibly betrothal?

jeudi, le 04 mai

Expect a call soon, the text read. Impromptu phone interview. I didn't recognise the number, so I rang it back – only to meet a recorded message saying it was a number reserved by a privacy company. So someone was tipping me off about the job situation, but wanting to stay incognito? Hmm. Not too many someones that could be . . .

vendredi, le 05 mai

At home for the next few nights. Shoulders hurting from dragging an overstuffed suitcase around the stations and terminals that comprise a frighteningly large part of my environment these days and looking forward to something nice to eat, or at the very least a smile from my mum. I've packed jeans, T-shirts, a few skirts, trainers and a ridiculous pair of heels that should never see the light of city streets, much less suburban ones. A cashmere jumper or two and a new jacket that treads, I think, the fine line between practical and cute. A new handbag. An effing huge pair of sunglasses. The obligatory late-spring brolly.

It occurs to me that the last year has passed in no time at all – I know, I know, everyone always says that, and yes, typing the words does make me feel old, thankyouverymuch – but just the same, I really think about this time last year as if it were last week.

samedi, le 06 mai

'So I take it from the sneaky phone conversations and general air of subterfuge that you and your sister are plotting something for my birthday,' Mum said, leaning against the door of my room – sorry, I mean the guest room.

'Whatever gave you that idea? I don't even know when your birthday is.' In my long and storied career using avoidance tactics, I've found disguising the truth as a lie to be a particularly fruitful stratagem.

Mum smiled. 'You don't fool me one bit,' she said. 'Just give us a hint – does it involve Artie?'

I pulled a face. 'You know I can't bear to think of you

306

having sexual relations under the family roof,' I said. 'Leave the fornicator out of it.' Of course one drawback of the strategy is you can sometimes go too far, and make your real feelings even more clear than if you'd just said it in the first place.

'Oh, honey,' Mum said, resting a hand softly on my shoulder. 'I know you're upset about how things happened between me and your Dad. For what it's worth it's not because we ever lost the romance. In fact, the last time we had sex—'

'Ack, no, stop it!' I stuck my fingers in my ears. 'I'm not listening to you! Get out!'

Something about going home always makes me feel young all over again. Not in the good way. 'Be careful,' Mum said, turning back to look at me. 'Hold that face long enough and it'll stick.'

lundi, le 08 mai

Running late and sweating like a very sweaty thing. Luckily I'd stashed a few hotel toiletries in my desk from my past life, so took them along to the theatre with me. I came back into the women's changing room from the shower, dripping wet. My clothes were on the bench. I put on pants and wrapped the towel round my hair, turban-style. Looked for a bra. No bra.

Ran to the cupboard. Went through my knickers and socks. No bra, no bra. Where the hell could it have gone?

Oh, right. Of course. I put on a baggy top and padded to the green room, where seventeen-year-old star of the play, K, was sitting, surrounded by men (i.e. her native habitat). 'K, darling, I have to ask you something . . .' I said, trying to indicate the hallway, where we could speak privately.

'Sure,' she said, giving me a look that said she wasn't about to leave the room, and possibly forfeit being the centre of attention on Man Island.

Fine then, she asked for it. 'Are you wearing my bra?' The boys gasped.

'Are you two actually the same size?'

'I want to see! Tits out!'

'We'd better check her!' Whereupon the squealing K was pinned to the table as I pulled up the back of her shirt. Black lace, stretch leopard print – yep, she'd nicked me bra. Cow. The boys turned to me, but their faces fell – it must have been quite clear, from my stormy expression, that there was no way in hell they'd be doing the same to me.

'Come on, you can't do all that and not at least let us watch you trade them back,' a tall, freckly one said.

'Fat chance,' K snarled, and dragged me back to the changing room.

mercredi, le 10 mai

Irony is the hallmark of the postmodern age. Another hallmark of the age is people using words impressively, even when they don't know the correct use. Such as 'whom' when 'who' is called for. 'Presently' instead of 'at present'. And of course no one manages to pinpoint what exactly constitutes real irony, just making a few random and unfortunate connections seems to do.

Let me tell you about irony. Irony is a phone interview for a job you've wanted for the last six months coming the very morning you've decided you don't want it anymore.

'So I says to her, only if you give us a blowie . . .'

Backstage fell dead as I walked in. The freckled boy who just moments ago had been holding court in a group of his friends went a deep crimson. 'Now, if you must talk about girls that way, keep it for later when you're not in mixed company,' I said and frowned. 'I'm sure you don't know the new blocking yet, why don't you chaps get to practising that?' The boys shuffled towards the stage silently, one or two looking back at me.

I wondered if they talked like this in front of their parents. Granted, there's more than the average ration of slap and tickle – or piss and whipping, to be strictly accurate – in my past. But I wouldn't have dreamed of letting my family in on anything like the full extent of it, even if I had never been a sex worker. My parents were liberal in their attitudes but firm in enforcing behaviour and, damn it, there are just some lines that mustn't be crossed. Letting your children talk like *Penthouse Forum* editors is one of them.

Not because teenagers shouldn't experiment. Far from it. No, I believe that it's part of the privilege of youth to have something – anything – to hide from grown-ups. For some kids that's smoking, for others bunking off school. For me it was sex. Even then I didn't get started until sixteen. I get the feeling now parents all but provide a bowl of condoms outside their fourteen-year-olds' doors.

When everything is permitted, how will they ever appreciate the thrill of the illicit?

vendredi, le 12 mai

It's official: I really must stop listening to Radio 4 in the morning.

As far as history goes, I've always been an avid listener, but think the current obsession really took off round about the time England last won the Ashes. A4's mum had an old long wave that was going unloved so we bought new batteries for it, hauled it into the sunny garden and enjoyed what was the most English of victories: the wobbly sneak into the history books as opposed to the showboating tour-de-force.

Anyway, since then, I'd kept the radio upstairs and listened to it in the mornings when showering and brushing my teeth. As it tends to crackle out of reception whenever the knobs are touched (hmm, there's a dodgy analogy to men to be had there, but can I bother?), I've left it on Radio 4 long wave. Which means that several times a year I am treated to the cricket from, say, New Zealand on my waking; the rest of the year it's the *Today* programme with John Humphrys and his cronies.

What is it with John Humphrys? I can put up with a lot in my just-awakened, pre-caffeinated state, but sub-Jeremy Paxman haranguing of minor shadow ministers is not one of them. I like confrontation; nay, I live for it. But like taking your daily tot of rum it really should be reserved for when the sun is well and truly over the yardarm. On average I find I must switch off the radio in disgust three out of any five weekday mornings. And that just is not right.

Also, I have never had particular occasion to imagine Mr Humphrys in his pants. There, I've said it. I'd do Paxo in a minute. I'd make him bellow 'hurry up' like I was Somerville struggling with any question not pertaining to fashion or gossip. Make of that what you will (a deep-seated obsession with authoritarian men, perhaps. Though I draw the line at Gordon Ramsay).

This morning the guests were arguing two sides – for, this being the mainstream media, there are only ever two positions allowed – of prostitution. Needless to say the hypocrisy burns me up. The butter-wouldn't-melt, middle-class women who go on and on about the 'debasement' and 'humiliation' of streetwalking – this out of the mouths of people who have never had cause to be hungry, homeless or desperate in their lives. When you are an addict, when you are living on the streets, you come tell me how debasing poverty is, and whether you still think the stigma of selling sex outweighs that. But not before. Of course – as Jarvis Cocker so eloquently put it – you'll never get it right . . . if you called your dad, he could stop it all.

Then there will always be a man they trot out to parrot much the same thing, about what an 'abomination' the 'degrading' work of prostitution is. Sir, if you yourself have not enjoyed the services of a working-girl at some point – or indeed within the last fortnight – I will eat my fucking shoes. And you can even choose the pair.

Once, in my non-call girl life, I had occasion to meet a middle-class, professional man who admitted he was a frequenter of sex workers. He preferred kerb crawling to meeting call girls in hotel rooms. The admission fascinated me; I couldn't stop asking him questions about it. He said he never picks up a girl who hesitates to get in the car, because she's probably an undercover policewoman. He didn't want to be caught paying for sex any more than a girl wants to be seen taking money for it.

The girls don't argue with this logic. Vetting a customer puts you more at risk of being seen by a police officer than getting into a stranger's car without asking questions.

As it happens, he worked in radio. So I listened just closely enough to the morning diatribe to discern that it wasn't him being interviewed, then switched the offensive thing off.

lundi, le 15 mai

I nodded at Alex as we stepped into the elevator and the doors closed. Once it started moving, she turned to me excitedly.

'You'll never believe . . .' she said in a hoarse whisper.

'What's that, dear?' There's very little I wouldn't believe.

'I got it after all?'

What, herpes? 'What's that?'

'The job I mentioned! They said no one else was suitable, so . . . I'm in!'

My heart dropped. She definitely hadn't known, then, that I was going for the same position. I wonder what it was about the phone interview that took me out of the running? But one look at her face, so bright and eager. It's not that I couldn't be angry – but I couldn't be angry straight away. Even if it did mean she was going to soon be, for all intents and purposes, my boss.

'But . . . what about Richard, and moving to the Leeds office?' I said. 'I thought . . . that day when I saw you and Giles, you were definitely moving.'

Her face went hard and she suddenly looked ten years older. There was real toughness there, something I hadn't noticed in her before. God, would she have made a world-class call girl. 'Richard doesn't understand about my career. He said either the job went, or he did,' she said. 'He made his choice.'

No, I thought, you made your choice. When you slept with Giles, you made your choice.

'It does mean a lot more hours, but it's a lot more pay, too!' she said, swinging back to bright and chirpy. 'I'm really looking forward to the challenge . . .'

So that was it, why I had been found wanting in comparison. She could not only talk the talk, but she was a True Believer. Someone for whom concepts like Three-Sixty Turnaround and Total Involvement Management had actual meaning, rather than being bad punchlines. Someone for whom small matters like sleeping with the boss then going behind his back when it went wrong were but minor blips in the overall picture.

And if nothing else, it meant that she hadn't been making as much as me until this point. A small victory, but perhaps just enough to keep me from tearing Giles's head – no, fuck it, he tried to stop her, any suit will do – straight from his body in the next three minutes.

'Well done, darling,' I said. 'I've no doubt you've done everything to deserve it.'

mardi, le 16 mai

After rehearsals, the crew and some of the parents usually retire for drinks at a pub. One of the fathers of the teenage boys had offered me a lift the week before and refused to take any money for petrol – so I buy his drink. We pick up our pints and retire to a corner table with the others.

The conversation turns, as it often does, to pairing off. The father works with a fellow who's just popped the question six months after meeting a girl. Me and one of the stage managers scoff, and say in near-unison: 'Six months? Pah – six years, then maybe.'

The father smiles at me. 'But, Belle,' he says (and he didn't call me Belle, but for the sake of reporting dialogue, imagine he did.) 'But, Belle, even if you meet someone now, in six years' time . . .'

'I know, egg quality declines after thirty-four. I'm not worried. I don't plan to have children.'

'Really?' The father, I think, is rather a sweet fellow, and I certainly like the look of him: silvering hair; sharp, blue eyes; gorgeous, Northern accent; nice tan from a recent holiday in Mauritius. 'You can't imagine a bunch of cute little Belles running around? From what I hear you're rather popular with the kids.'

Eek! Clearly, someone here can imagine plenty of cute little Belles, and it's not the one with the ovaries. 'It's not a concern. I'm not so broody that I would rather have children than marry the right person. My parents were together over twenty-five years – I'd aim to do at least as well if I did it at all.'

'Well, you should think about it,' the father said, thoughtfully. A little too thoughtfully. 'I think you'd make a great mother.'

Analysis:

Boyfriend material? 4/10 – He's already imagining my offspring? Something tells me I should keep a taser to hand just in case.

Fuckable? 7/10 – Mild back-hair issues – nothing that can't be solved with a discreet trip to an aesthetician. Otherwise fit in a Captain of Industry way. I love me some silver fox.

Client material? 8/10 – I'm seeing a mid-level hotel, somewhat central, and him in a slightly wrinkled suit, post-meeting. He's seeing me in frillies, proffering a bottle of lotion, and saying 'Shall I leave my shoes on?' He'll almost-but-not-quite mention his ex-wife. I'll convince him to ring the agency and book me again before I leave.

Would date again? 10/10 – As this wasn't a date then, yes, I'd like to see him in some other context, if only to convince him that I am definitely not the sort of woman who should be responsible for the welfare of children.

Final comments? – He all but offered a vial of his sperm, and I'm actually considering this a possible suitor? Wow, them pickings really have got mighty sparse here in Desperadoville.

mercredi, le 17 mai

Giles is avoiding me. I can tell because it's been a good forty-eight hours since anyone tried to pinch my bottom in the stationery closet. Not that we actually have a stationery closet as such – we're a Paperless Office, dontchaknow, which means that such antiquated concepts have been removed from the floor plan while actually everyone prints out their emails and relies on Jane and Audrey to keep us in sticky notepads and staples.

But, he's shown neither hide nor hair in my office, and isn't hanging around when I take lunch. No unnecessary emails are finding their way to my inbox and no flirty inter-office messaging is happening.

I don't know whether I'm upset or not. Disappointed? Yes, undoubtedly. But still unable to decide if this is what I really wanted. So feeling far from gutted. More like semi-gutted. Only partially eviscerated.

'Hey, how goes it?' Alex greets me jauntily in the lobby, and runs to catch the same elevator. She's on a real high now, and sees me as an ally. If only she knew.

No, the real problem is whether I can deal with being supervised by someone who is my junior, who less than eight months ago was an intern . . . and who has slept with the boss, a line I refused to cross. Would the situation be completely different now if I had?

Is that a question I seriously want the answer to?

jeudi, le 18 mai

Apropos of nothing, L rang up and invited herself over. I said I'd meet her after going to the gym. When I got to the flat she was standing outside, a bottle in one hand, phone in the other.

'Hey, gorgeous,' I smiled and unlocked the door. 'No dates this week?'

'No dates, like, ever,' she moaned, flopping onto the sofa and waving the bottle in the air. I fetched a cork-screw.

'Glasses, too, or are you going to swig straight from the bottle?'

'Glasses, duh,' she rolled her eyes. 'Je suis une lady.' She looked around the room frantically. 'Don't you have any music you can put on? Some Cowboy Junkies or something like that?'

'Careful, there, hon, that's pure Colombian Grade-A melancholy you're requesting,' I said. 'So what happened to your hot date from a few weeks ago – fizzled out?'

'Worse than that,' she said, and poured a half glass for me and a rather more generous serving for herself. 'Chemistry, we had tonnes. We flirted. We made a second date – dinner this time. That went well too. He walked me home. We snogged. I even . . . well, I didn't invite him obviously, but think it was clear I wouldn't mind seeing him again. So you'd think he'd ring, right?'

Actually, as far as I had experienced the last few years, men rang your manager, who made all the necessary arrangements. But whatever. This was the straight-dating world; there were rules and apparently one of them had been broken in this instance. 'Um, I guess.'

'Well that's where you don't know thing one!' she said. 'Boys don't ring.'

'If that's so,' I said, 'a toast. That next time you might step up from boys to men. Or indeed,' I said, dropping an old skool CD into the stereo, 'Boyz II Men.'

Never let it be said there's a situation so bad the judicious application of hip-pop can't make it better. 'Amen to that, sister.'

vendredi, le 19 mai

It really has got bad when I'm primping in anticipation that maybe Silver Fox will be out this evening and maybe I can invite him for drinks *a deux* afterward.

'Whatever else you do,' I pleaded with the girl at American Nail Bar (or whatever it was, that being approximately what they're all called), 'please make it subtle. I just want to look clean and nice.'

That'll be the three-inch iridescent French talons with diamante accent, then.

samedi, le 20 mai

Where there's life there's hope, or so they say. But even so there are things that simply must never happen on a first date, for instance:

1 You mention any long-standing eating disorders/ psychotic episodes/ history of opium addiction, complete with detailed analysis of your therapy and/or recovery.
2 Your glass eye falls into your date's drink.
3 The last man who pissed on you in a sexual context (not that it happens in many other contexts, mind) walks into the bar just as your date finally takes the plunge and lets his thigh brush yours.

So guess which one went down while SF and I were sharing an intimate drink? N, to his credit, must have sussed the situation and quickly vacated the premises with his lady friend, but it didn't half put me off my stride.

Apart from that, I think the evening was a success. I giggled more than strictly necessary. SF touched my arm, then my knee and, reader, I quite literally gushed.

'I can't figure it out,' he said, as I polished off another pint. 'It's like you're the perfect woman, so . . .' and his voice trailed off.

'Sorry, I missed that, what did you say?'

'Nothing,' he said, and coughed slightly. 'Nothing.'

dimanche, le 21 mai

So this is spring, eh? Flowers. Birdsong. Lambs and suchlike. Except in London the flowers are cut orchids flown in from third-world countries, the birdsong is largely confined to the flock of escaped parakeets that terrorises Hampstead Heath, and lamb's on no menu I can think of, even in the stodgier clubs.

lundi, le 22 mai

'Saw you the other night down the pub, but you were on the way out,' I said. 'Why didn't you come and chat?' My, I can be insincere.

'You seemed otherwise engaged, I didn't like to interrupt,' N said. 'Watched you guys for a while, you seemed happy and chatty, anyway.'

'Mmm,' I said. N smiled suggestively at me.

'Going well?'

'A bit too well, actually,' I said. 'He's a lovely man. And before you ask, no, we haven't slept together yet. But I get the feeling he wants something . . . more . . . from me.'

'Something more? As in money? Drugs? Amateur porn photos?'

'As in a relationship.'

'Man of Certain age and considerable means in looking to settle down shocker,' N said. 'So what's wrong?'

'I just haven't thought through how I'd ever tell someone . . . you know, about the sex for money thing.' That wasn't entirely true, I'd thought about it often. If you told someone too early, and it didn't work out, they might get their revenge . . . well, in any number of unpalatable ways. But then if you left it until the point where you completely trusted that person, they might lose trust in you, wondering what other secrets might be in store. Neither solution was any more palatable than the other, and as no one since the

Boy had really seemed boyfriend material, I'd never puzzled out a way to deal with the problem.

'Oh, because your ex knew.'

'Exactly. And it's not something you'd tell a one-night stand. But someone who might – shudder – want to be your boyfriend, well, that's a different story altogether.'

'You could spend your time worrying that he'll run screaming because of your past,' N said gently. He picked up my hands and looked deep into my eyes. 'Or you could spend your time worrying that he'll run screaming because you're an insane fucking harpy who will make his life not worth living.'

I pushed his hands away and scowled. 'It's good to know my friends are so supportive. So, all other things aside, what did you think of him?'

'I think he looks like a decent guy. I think there's something to be said for keeping an open mind. I think you should take things as they come and stop worrying so damn much.'

mardi, le 23 mai

Pet-peeve list v. 2.0.4:

1 The cause of feminism being invoked so someone (namely, Jane in the office) can ditch work whenever the hell she likes for some to-ing and fro-ing of her offspring. Lame. Get a fucking driver already.

2 Actual email sent by Giles: To fully own this challenge, we need to be goal-orientated and results-driven. I want to be sure we're on the same page about this, so let's open a dialogue whereby we can each keep an eye on the other's status.

Uh, sure, whatever. Tell it to Alex.

3 Citrus fruits which are not easy to peel, in spite of having been labelled Easy-Peel. People with Range Rovers and organic boxes wonder why the earth is being desecrated with plastic containers for ready-cut foods that we could just as easily prepare ourselves? Because yellow manicures are so 1987, dur.

jeudi, le 25 mai

'What flavour of tuneless crap is this?' N said, grimacing as he shed his jacket on the sofa.

'That's the genius Rufus Wainwright, I'll have you know.' I was in the kitchen making tea. His: NATO, the international notation for milk two sugars (because apparently that's the standard drink international forces serve on duty). Mine: Julie Andrews, the international notation for white none.

'The man sounds like his balls are being twisted,' N said. 'And not in a good way.'

We rarely agreed on music. N's mother, sister and estranged father had all been musicians – classical pianists, in fact. When I asked N how it could be that he came from such a family and couldn't play a single chord, he explained that by the time he was born his sister was already on Grade VIII. When he was old enough to reach the keyboard, he couldn't comprehend why his childish hands made such a racket on the instrument when everyone else in the family played so well. Unwilling or unable to put up with the embarrassment, he flat refused to learn.

'I think you'll find that Rufus Wainwright's musical

pedigree is at least as good as your own,' I said, bringing the mugs through. 'A sister and father well-known in the business. His aunt and mother are respected folk musicians as well. It was only inevitable that he would be a star.'

'Genes are not destiny,' N said bitterly.

'He sings about heartbreak and melancholy, often in French. In fact, if you'll just let me play some, I think you'll agree there's something Edith Piaf about him . . .' I said, heading for the stereo.

'No, really, thank you,' N said. 'I know who he is anyway. And Edith Piaf? Now that's a stretch if ever I heard one.'

'You may not like the music, but few would deny the man certainly *ne regrette rien*.'

'The drugs habit? The bad haircuts? Dressing as Judy Garland for his concerts, complete with fishnets and tap shoes? The friendship with Elton John, for fuck's sake. Elton John!'

'You sure know a lot for someone who doesn't listen to his music.'

'Oh, I never said I don't listen to it.' N wiggled his eyebrows over the steaming mug. 'I just don't like the talented bastard.'

vendredi, le 26 mai

If the first rule of *Fight Club* is don't talk about *Fight Club*, the second rule of *Fight Club* is don't talk about *Fight Club* and you should always follow the three-day rule with new potential lovers, where does that leave me at almost a week since I met SF for drinks and no contact? So I rang, right?

The phone trilled twice, then went to voicemail. Hm.

Guess he must be busy and will ring later. It was lunchtime at work after all.

Didn't leave a message – short of imparting urgent information (such as, say, hotel room, client's name and agreed fee) what's the point of voicemail? He'd see he had a missed call and ring back, obviously.

By the end of the day, nothing. Went home.

Did bod all, played around on the Internet all night. Did check the phone from time to time, I've a habit of leaving it on silent, so I can miss things. But there was nothing to miss.

Late evening: nothing.

As I didn't have to be at work tomorrow anyway, stayed up later than usual. And still nothing.

Argh. I hate boys.

samedi, le 27 mai

Who knows, maybe he's visiting his parents. Or out with his son. Or . . . I don't know, doing whatever it is men do when they're not doing, er, me.

Sunny day. Put on a string bikini top and went outside armed with the latest Thomas Pynchon, a bottle of lemonade and the phone. Sent a light, flirty text – careful not to mention the missed call. Put on sunglasses and waited.

And waited.

And waited.

Now, this waiting thing, it's a bit of a novelty to me. But I could already see that the charm of trying to chase a man down was going to wear off quickly. Yes, I liked him. Yes, I thought there might be possibilities. But I am also a firm believer in my own value as a person, especially as a sexual person. As a girl whose preference is to be serviced three times a day if at all possible, waiting over a week for even a kiss by text is a little much. There are, as they so often say, other fish in the sea.

And then I remembered toe-floss man, vomiting behind a rhododendron, and all the other fish I'd met lately. Truth be told, meeting people just isn't the same past our mid-twenties. It seems everyone comes with a laundry list of requirements and a tolerance of strangers somewhere short of twelve seconds.

Well, I won't be that person. He'll ring. I just know it.

dimanche, le 28 mai

So, not really knowing what else to do, I turned to L. Maybe it had been long enough since last burdening her with dating woes.

'I mean, you must have had . . . ah, shite . . . I didn't mean men don't call you back . . . I just mean, you know, all that magazine reading must have taught you something about what to do when a man's sending mixed signals.'

'His signals aren't mixed,' L harrumphed as she opened another bottle of wine. I tried to remember the last time I'd seen L not drinking, and frankly, couldn't. 'He's broadcasting a clear "I want to get laid with minimal effort and am unwilling to invest anything more than it takes to get into your pants – maybe not even that much." Do yourself a favour and don't get involved with this guy.'

'I guess,' I said. But while some part of me figured she was probably right, I didn't want to believe it. All the chemistry couldn't have been imaginary. So why the incognito act? One thing I learned as a call girl was how to approach a situation from a man's point of view. Not only sexually, but emotionally. There were a lot of clients, young, eligible chaps who seemed to be using prostitutes. It had eventually dawned on me that unless they're looking to get married, the prospect of getting involved with a woman beyond the physical must be pretty daunting. I could definitely sympathise. As sexually attracted as I've always been to women, I'd never want to date one.

'Trust me,' L said, downing half her glass in one glug. 'This is how men operate these days. They've had it on a plate since day one; why should they try? When there's Internet porn and – god, I hate to even use the word – prostitution.'

Hey, that stung. 'It can't all be that bad,' I frowned. Plenty of people manage to pair off somehow.'

'Sure,' L spat bitterly. 'And when was the last time you went to an actual wedding where the bride wasn't deluded or pregnant or both?'

She had a point, maybe. 'I don't know,' I said. 'I'd like to give this one the benefit of the doubt for now.'

She shook her head. 'Go ahead, I can't stop you, but you'll regret it,' she said. 'Much in the same way I'm going to regret opening the next bottle.'

mardi, le 30 mai

So it's nanoseconds until final dress rehearsals, and still no sign of SF, not to mention no texts or calls. His son Euan is still coming, but keeps turning up late – catching the bus, apparently. I can't go so far as to ask after his father, but it's a victory – however small – to know I'm not the only one SF is letting down.

The thing about these kids is, they're really amazing. Watching the leads transform, thanks to cheap charity shop costumes and too much eyeliner for both sexes, to a simulacrum of adult lovers really is remarkable. Such confidence.

When the girls strip off in the wings to prepare for the next scenes, I'm almost envious. Not of their as-yet-unblemished beauty, but of the complete guilelessness with which they do so. I've seen the boys and girls flirting with each other: it's artless fawning, successful because of equal parts ignorance and confidence. It's everything I am not. And yet I do wonder, at times, who if any of these might end up choosing the route I did? Will it be the obvious wild child, or the glowing-but-quiet late bloomer?

mercredi, le 31 mai

The phone rings. SF. Twice, three times. I briefly imagine letting it go to voicemail, but don't. I could leave it but then I'd be obliged to ring back. When it comes to playing the game, goodness knows I have a lot to learn. So I take the only sensible option and answer it.

'Hey.'

'Hello. I'm sorry I didn't ring you back.' Well, at least he gets straight to the matter at hand. 'Been busy, and things got away from me. Haven't even been able to drive Euan to rehearsals.'

If there's anything I'm a sucker for it's a straight dealer. 'Go on then.'

'My schedule should be clearing up next week, we should get together soon?' he says.

'Yeah, all right.' I look down at my feet, dear me, how long has it been exactly since the last pedicure? 'But you call me. I'm not chasing you down again.' I'm trying to sound glowering, but I'm glowing really; my faith in men was never really in any doubt at all. They're simple creatures, incapable of effective subterfuge. Feed and water them on time, switch on the telly and make cooing noises, and they're putty in your hands, at least, they should be. They're children.

'I like your style,' he says. 'But then that much is probably already clear.'

Ten steps to getting on in the world as an ex-sex worker:

1 Don't lose your eye for quality knickers, nor your nose for a good sale.

2 Defend legalised sex work where possible and necessary, but not too vehemently, lest others start to wonder.

3 Accept that someday you might find yourself on the wrong end of a relationship where the man enjoys certain services from certain types of ladies. It's up to you where to draw the line. But keep in mind that to forgive is divine and also sometimes unavoidable.

4 Be the initiator in the bedroom, so if no. 3 should ever happen, you can honestly say you did all you could.

5 Nothing succeeds like success: fuck the critics and defy the stereotypes.

6 Erase the old numbers from your phone for good. You won't need them, they won't ring you again anyway and you never know who might go through your numbers in the future and what sort of awkward questions that might cause.

7 Tip well when in restaurants, just in case that aspiring model on the wait staff is wrestling with the same decision you once had to make.

8 Never forget that no matter the love, no matter the relationship . . . we're all paying for sex. Not with cash money, perhaps, but we're all paying just the same.

9 All those hair and makeup tips and tricks you hoarded so carefully? If all else fails, they're probably hiring over at the editorial offices of *Cosmopolitan*.

10 Don't let having turned over a new leaf stop you from seeing the opportunities that abound in life: grab them, girl, grab them!

Juin

jeudi, le 01 juin

Am of two minds about L. The last time I saw her she was very aggressive about what she thought of SF – and of me. Maybe that was the frustration speaking; I don't know when the last time she went on a date was, much less the last time she had sex that didn't involve four AAA batteries.

On the one hand, if it had been one of my male friends – N, say, or A2 – I'd probably let it drop. Maybe slide in a snide comment here or there, but the matter would soon blow over. And if I consider L a friend, well, that's what friends do, isn't it? Irritate each other, but keep coming back for more?

On the other hand, she's a woman. I don't know much about other women, but I know myself, and I know I have a line. Her constant reliance on cheap magazine philosophy, her strange love/hate feelings for men as a species . . . not bad in and of themselves (I mean who doesn't do the same?) but when she turns it on me, I don't know how to respond. I don't know what women do. I'm used to being the only hen in the coop.

But I know if I do nothing, something will be done for me. Best case scenario, she drops out of my life – not great. Worst case, she continues to harangue me for my perceived faults – even worse. If she were a man, I'd be thinking breakup.

Guh. Who knew girly friendships would turn out to be like romantic relationships, only harder?

'What do you think,' Alex said, spreading the printouts across my desk. 'This one, or this one?'

We were meant to be going over a conference call for next month. It was a new experience for me. People halfway across the world would be not only listening to me rabbit on about business nonsense but also following along on their computer screens as I clicked through a presentation highlighting our results for the last two quarters. From what I understood – from what Giles had said – a substantial contract could be riding on what essentially came down to twenty minutes of Internet chat. No pressure then. But, apparently, this was taking second place to Alex furnishing a new office.

'I don't know. They both look nice. Listen, Alex—'

'Because you see, this one is ergonomic, but this one just whispers good taste, doesn't it?'

'I guess so. Now, about these pie charts you did, there's a small—'

'Say, where did you get your chair? I really like that.'

'It was here when I got the job,' I said. 'Could we just—'

'Really? Do you think I could swap it for one of these?' she said, thrusting the printouts in my direction. 'Go on, pick one.'

'Actually, I'm rather fond of this—'

'Pick one,' she said in a voice that was one part growling tigress to three parts petulant princess, and I could see this was the way things were going to be from now on.

'I don't need a chair,' I said, as one would when being firm with a screaming toddler. 'I need for us to have this presentation sorted.'

She rolled her eyes and crossed her arms across her chest. 'Fine. Whatever.'

Yes, I can see it's going to be a fun time to come.

dimanche, le 04 juin

SF was as good as his word and came back to the group nights. He even stayed late to help clean up after a dress rehearsal long after Euan had bunked off with mates, and offered me a lift home. I shrugged and smiled, but of course said yes. In the evening traffic, city lights sweeping across the two of us, we said nothing. I love the city at night, sleek and subdued, the tourists all passed out on their Novotel beds, the theatre mobs filing into cavernous rooms in the West End, the last few office workers of the day heading home, untucked and dishevelled. These are my people: uncertain, distracted, in between where they have been and where they want to be.

The car pulled up outside my house. He turned the engine off and we looked at each other. I smiled. 'Come in for a coffee?'

SF smirked. 'Is that a euphemism for . . . ?'

'You got me. I don't have any coffee. I meant would you like to come in for a tea?'

'I love tea. I'd love to.' We went inside. He shed his corduroy jacket on the sofa and sat down. 'Nice cat,' he said.

'Thank you,' I said from the kitchen. 'He was an unwanted gift.'

'Really? I like a cat about the house.'

'Mmm. I'm growing accustomed to this one. He's a good ambassador for the species. How do you have your tea?'

'Oh, there really is tea? Drop of milk, please.' I walked

through with the mugs. SF was giving the cat's chin a good scratch, and a loud purr emanated from the animal. He rarely, if ever, purred for me. 'Bit cold in here.'

'Is it? Do you want a blanket?'

'No, of course not, it's completely the wrong time of year,' he said, but I could see his hand was pale and shook slightly. I fetched a wool blanket out of the cupboard. 'Now you're going to make me feel like I'm mothering you,' I said, tucking the blanket round his thighs. 'I'll be dosing you with kaolin and morphine next.'

'Don't joke, at my age, loose bowels, et cetera,' he said, grinning.

'My, you do know how to charm the ladies. Would you like company under that blanket?'

'Actually,' SF said, pulling at the waistband of my work trousers, 'I'd like more than that.' I sunk onto the sofa, straddling his lap with my thighs, and we kissed.

It was a gentle kiss, not what I was expecting. He opened his mouth only slightly, his soft tongue, when it explored mine, was timid, almost boyish. The hand that had pulled me to him so confidently fluttered and eventually settled lightly on my waist. It was the kiss of a nervous teenager, a kiss from the back row of the cinema, a kiss that echoed in my hindbrain like a half-remembered fleeting crush. It was devastating.

'I can't do this,' I breathed into his neck. And at that moment I was aware of my hips, rubbing slowly against his. Oh, I might say I didn't want this, but in fact could not remember the last time I had wanted something more.

'No, of course, we don't have to do anything,' he whispered into my neck. 'We can sit and hold hands all night if that's what you want. I can leave if that's what you want.'

I pulled back and looked at him in the orange lamplight, his eyes soft and hopeful like a young man's, like he didn't know that I was all but his, a sure thing. 'That's not what I want. I just . . . I haven't been with anyone in a long time. I'm on my period. I haven't shaved. I . . . I wasn't expecting anyone to come back to mine. I'm sorry.'

'Don't be sorry, no,' he said, as if surprised I was apologising to him.

'Come to bed with me,' I said. 'I want to hold you.'

But of course, once there, me undressed to beige silk knickers, he in tight black boxers, that wasn't exactly what happened. Under the cream and blue Victorian quilt he sucked my nipples; I rubbed my face and cheeks on the thicket of his chest hair. Every bit of him was masculine – almost excessively so. He filled the bed with his height, his breadth. I ran my hands over his gorgeous body and could think only one thing – you amaze me, you amaze me – over and over. When I finally reached into his pants and touched the tip of his cock he arched and gasped. I wetted my fingers and rubbed the skin between his balls and anus. 'Show me how you touch yourself.'

He grabbed his cock tightly under the glans and masturbated furiously. The harder I rubbed him, the faster he pulled, his body wriggling, finally crying out when I slipped the end of my finger past the ring of his arse. I hovered over him, waited until he was very close, and when he came dived down to taste every drop of it. It seemed he was coming for ages, his muscle clamping my finger tight, tighter. Waves of salty come poured over my lips. He screamed like a woman and when it was done and I had rolled off him, kissed me open-mouthed.

'That was . . . amazing.' I smiled and murmured something about going to sleep. He kneaded my breasts and rubbed my hips, but I pushed his hands toward my waist instead. It wasn't that I didn't also want to come, but I savoured the moment, for a few seconds he had belonged completely to me, had been in my control. I'd wait until another time when I felt prepared for him to have his turn with me. He fell asleep, the cat curled on the quilt by his feet. I stared at the ceiling until long past midnight, thinking of the last time I felt this way about someone.

lundi, le 05 juin

I woke before the alarm and rolled over. SF's eyes were already open, he was watching me.

'Morning.'

'Morning.'

'You're welcome to a shower if you want it,' I said and sat up.

'No, thank you. I hate to shower then put the same clothes back on. I'll do it at home.'

'Cup of tea?'

'Do you have coffee?' I shook my head. 'Tea's perfect.'

'Cool.' I threw on a white towelling dressing gown I've had for a couple of years now. I can't remember where it had come from, a souvenir from some random hotel suite, most likely. 'How do you have it?'

'Julie Andrews,' he said. 'I mean . . .'

'Yeah, I know, white none,' I smiled. This was cool. I went downstairs and left him to get up and dressed in his own time.

He sat on the sofa; I was on the chair, cradling a mug in my hands. He absentmindedly patted the cat. 'Love having a little cat about the house,' he said.

'You said.' We both nodded and looked at each other. 'Well . . . you know what they say . . . an awkward morning beats a boring night . . .'

'Do they? I've never heard that,' he said. 'It's good. I don't feel awkward though.'

No, eh? I wondered how often he did this. 'Well. I . . .' I wound the tie ends of the dressing gown around my fingers tightly. It had been a good night, I wanted to see him again, so why could I not simply say so?

'You need to get ready for work. And you want me to go.'

Well, if I couldn't admit at least to enjoying the evening, he was giving me an easy out and I appreciated it. 'Yes. Um. Sorry. Shall I ring you a cab?'

He shook his head and extracted his mobile from the inner pocket of his coat. 'I'll do it,' he said. 'You just go do your thing.'

Little could he know that as far as 'my thing' was concerned, we'd already done that bit.

mardi, le 06 juin

Head-to-head comparison (fnar, fnar): Sex Work v. Office Work

Office Work: In spite of yourself you will end up hating the new girl, because she has a bigger desk and is getting more clients than you.

Sex Work: In spite of yourself you will end up hating the new girl, because she has bigger breasts and is getting more clients than you.

Office Work: Working through lunch generally involves having a ploughman's at your desk.

Sex Work: Working through lunch generally involves getting ploughed on someone's desk.

Office Work: You will meet loads of new people, they will fuck you and you will most likely never see them again.

Sex Work: You will meet loads of new people, they will fuck you and you will most likely never see them again. But they might tip.

Office Work: A-levels are so important, you'll study hard, stay up long hours and feature them prominently on your CV.

Sex Work: A-levels are so important, you'll get a guy hard, screw for an hour and feature them prominently on your website.

Office Work: No one ever lost a pay rise by sucking up to the boss.

Sex Work: I think you know where this is going . . .

mercredi, le 07 juin

Many a languorous afternoon in the office have I wondered how exactly people wasted time before the Internet. So you might be able to eat up a few minutes here and there by wandering to the common room to make a cup of tea, or by carefully restocking your stationery from the communal cupboard, or by chasing a leggy secretary round the desk (not that I have one, more's the pity). And maybe you will have made so many cups of tea that you need not even pretend to go to the loo every hour. But even so you're looking at, at best, ninety minutes of time wasted per day. That's child's play in the world of seeming busy. I bet this is why people used to smoke.

That said, smoking, while it leads to heart disease, lung cancer and emphysema is not remotely as dangerous to your health as Googling someone. That shit should come with a warning. Having something like a spare minute or five to stalk – I mean, research – SF, I found out three startling things:

- He's five years older than he said.
- He regularly posts to vintage radio websites. Not harrowing knowledge as such, but in trawling the archives of said online resources, I learned . . .
- He's married.

Checked the date of the post mentioning his wife – less than a month ago. Fuck's sake. Were there ever a time to take up smoking, this might be it.

jeudi, le 08 juin

At least there was an explanation for why he had been so erratic on the phone. Thing is, I'm not against married men as such. I did once hold that conceit – that of the few limits I did have sexually, married people were one of them. Alongside children, animals and the dead. But being a prostitute put paid to that and, while there were plenty of unattached clients, there were at least as many married ones. And it wasn't for me, someone who was taking money for sex, to pass judgment on someone else's private life. So I crossed that line and it stayed crossed.

I traced my finger along the window of the bus. Why is it no matter how I get home, walking, bus or Tube, it always takes the same amount of time? Sigh.

And I've slept with married people since then, recreationally. Except that to date they were all women. So did that mean deep down I really did believe in some sort of female solidarity, that if I had the choice not to be with a married man, I should choose that? Morality's a funny thing – if your motives are black and white, there will inevitably be a problem. When they're not, same. No choice was going to be a good one, as far as I could see.

Argh. Traffic again. I was on the upper deck so could see in front of us and not three vehicles away was another bus on the same route. That was the main problem with getting rid of Routemasters as far as I could see: you couldn't just hop off and walk like you used to. I loved that when I first moved to London, dropping into the middle of a crowded street like a giddy child, running in front of moving cars, dodging, laughing. Invincible.

Whatever happened, I had to make a decision one way or the other. Sure, I could turn off my phone, avoid people involved with the youth group and try to disappear. Life would go on, I knew that, even if someone I barely knew lost a bit of respect for me. But I couldn't have faced doing it that way – not like when I was younger. Doing so would be an evasion. I'd just have to tough it out like all the other grown-ups do. Whatever happened, I couldn't just get off and walk.

vendredi, le 09 juin

Went for some essential maintenance in the hair-removal department in advance of seeing Silver Fox this weekend. Shaving is irritating, not to mention of only limited effectiveness. But the last time my lady-parts saw the business end of a waxing strip was sometime in the Mesozoic era – I'm not so frightened of scaring anyone off as I am of actually losing them in the jungle. The appointment went smoothly, or so I thought, until this morning.

Looking down at myself in the shower, I spotted what

looked like purple ink along the remaining hairline. I rubbed, but it didn't come off – and in fact it hurt. I looked closer.

Bruising. A clear, neat line of bruising on my pussy. *Il faut souffrir pour être belle.*

samedi, le 10 juin

His lips brushed against my nipple, parted and his tongue darted out, pushing against the pink flesh. I felt suddenly faint, my eyes prickled: to my surprise, the image in my mind was not of what this beautiful man might be about to do to me, but of my ex. The last tongue to touch me there had been his. Hot tears welled up in my eyes and I was overwhelmed with the feeling that every movement of SF's hands on my body, his insistent hips thrusting towards mine, was obliterating the lingering remains of the Boy on my body.

Sure, I'd had sex with other people since meeting the Boy. But I'd reserved some part of myself from all of those men, to the point that memories of them now seemed more distant and less distinct than those of my last boyfriend from some six months ago. Somewhere in the reptilian part of my brain I was finally processing that it was all over, we would never be together again, and this man, whatever he turned out to be to me, was more than just a one-night stand.

I closed my eyes and gripped SF's hair. Was I ready to do this yet? Would this mean that every day would put more and more space between my body's memory of the Boy, until eventually he was just an abstract collection of impressions rather than a real, fully fleshed sensation?

SF looked up. 'Are you okay?' he asked. My body was rigid; I'd gone stiff with fear.

But fear of what? Of enjoying another man as much as I'd enjoyed my ex? Fear of moving on?

Eventually, every lover becomes a memory. The ones who had paid me became one very quickly: often, by the time I was in the taxi home, they were already becoming a story, a snapshot, not a real person. The process was slower but no less final with lovers I'd chosen. The one who'd broken my heart when we were students was now, as far as sexual memory was concerned, a single blowjob while I was blindfolded and he masturbated me with a finger vibe. A1 was my first anal sex, which I couldn't even remember whether I'd liked. A2 was a session with him tied to a chair and me putting a giant purple vibrator in his arse. They were still special to me, cherished men and memories, but they were the past. The Boy was becoming the past.

I kissed SF deeply, harshly, with teeth and tongue, eyes closed so neither of us could see I was on the edge of crying. He grew hard against my hip. I pushed his hands onto my upper thighs, where he grabbed me; I turned over, put my face into the pillow, and offered him my arse, sobbing silently into the white cotton sheets.

dimanche, le 11 juin

Sent a text to SF: V distracted at work. Fancy the cinema soon and a . . . chat? X

To which he replied: Extremely distracted myself . . . trying not to be as am on a train leaving London, but back in two days. Tempt me then?

I hadn't meant to sound quite so glib or saucy in the text. As it happened I was very distracted, almost obscenely so.

Without having told anyone about it, I was turning the situation over and over in my head. 'I can tell when you're worrying a thought in your head,' Mum used to say. 'You get those furrows.' By now I would have bet you could plant potatoes in them. He was so perfect, so . . . what was the catch? Because there must be one.

Looking forward to seeing you soon – maybe grab drinks when the play is over?

The phone beeped, so I knew he'd received the message. But no response for an hour, or two. Bit odd. I went to lunch and purposely left my phone on my desk so I wouldn't be tempted to check it every ten seconds for a reply.

When I got back, nothing. Full bars so it wasn't reception. I even rang the mobile from my office phone. And then worried maybe he'd been trying to phone at the same time.

Oh, for goodness' sake, of course he wasn't going to ring. You stupid woman – you only just slept together, now you're smothering him with calls and requests to meet up! This is breaking rules one through five thousand of how to be attractive to men. You know better than that. Be cool, damnit.

'You cool?' Giles leaned in as he passed my open door. 'Seem to have been keeping a low profile lately. Everything going well with Alex?'

I looked up from the desk. I'd been staring at the phone, willing it to ring, beep, anything. 'You know me, working hard,' I said.

'If you think I believe that, then woman, we really have no future together,' Giles laughed. He had seemed to bounce back so effortlessly from what happened with Alex. Had she hurt him? Embarrassed him? Threatened his career, maybe with a harassment suit? I wouldn't have put any of it past her, not now. But he was as ebullient as ever and gave nothing away. 'You're going to wing that conference call next week as you always do. And it's going to go brilliantly, as it always does. Make it look effortless.'

Yeah, brilliant. Effortless. Like so much else in life.

lundi, le 12 juin

On the night of the performance I was meant to be backstage, helping girls through costume changes and making sure props were . . . well, more or less where they should be. But I told the director that due to a family problem I'd be late, could I trade with one of the ushers instead and be backstage after the first scene? She was distracted with the planning and so agreed over the phone.

Family emergency, my sweet arse. I wanted to see whom SF was bringing to the musical.

I was on the opposite corner of the room when they came in. Probably just as well. So this was Euan's mum then. Yes, I could see the resemblance, in spite of the salon-blonded hair and liberal use of Botox. SF whispered in her ear as he guided them to the seats with a hand lightly in the small of her back. She arranged herself carefully, at an angle perfect for watching as well as being watched. Yes, this woman was every inch SF's opposite number from her Tods loafers to her buttery highlights.

I was rooted to the spot – how to get past them without being noticed? Thankfully, the house lights went down and I scuttled backstage to relieve the harried usher who'd been lumbered handing out plastic swords and Woolworths tiaras to the cast.

One of the benefits of being on the other side of the stage is being unable to see the audience. I didn't have a clear view out and even if I had, the stage lights obliterate any possibility of seeing into the depths of the room. And just as well, the kids were magical. With the right stage, the right props, the right makeup, all it takes is a little bit of work to hold the attention of a thousand eyes. Every boy was a hero, every girl a siren. It passed in a flash and I hardly remembered doing anything, only knowing that it all, somehow, was done.

When the house lights came back for the bows – Euan in particular seemed keen to drag me on stage, and the director and I stood awkwardly like leaden pilgrims among the colourful natives – I scanned quickly and noted the two empty seats near the front. Maybe SF had been called away suddenly on work. I bet for Euan that wouldn't have been the first time such a thing happened. Or maybe they were waiting outside, hoping to congratulate him personally. I didn't wait to see and slipped out the back.

mercredi, le 14 juin

'Got it,' Alex hissed as we passed in the corridor.

'What, the charts? Thank goodness, and not a moment too soon. I'm glad you found time to go back and correct them.'

'The . . . oh, no,' she said. 'I assumed you'd do that. Data manipulation isn't really in my remit anymore, is it? I meant the chair,' she said. 'Just like yours, only a newer one. Better.'

Newer. Better. And I thought I'd left behind a world where those words meant the same thing. 'Great,' I said, through gritted teeth.

jeudi, le 15 juin

Text from SF: Missed you on Sunday. Dinner tomorrow? X

Sigh. Text messages, the last resort of the coward.

You arrange it for tomorrow. You send on the details. I'll meet you there.

Takes one to know one.

vendredi, le 16 juin

I had to dress for either way: getting lucky or going home alone. Is this what it's like out there? How do other women deal with it? What outfit says, Come and get me, unless I tell you not to? What bra and knickers can most accurately convey, Gimme that hot, hot sex, which I totally and utterly wasn't expecting. As for the makeup I was stuck with minimal, because there is no fine line to be found between Natural Look and Come on My Face, is there? In the end I went with a black dress, black lacy bra and pant set and a newfound appreciation for why other women dress so damn boring all the time.

SF, to his credit, showed a socially acceptable amount of gentlemanly appreciation for the effort. I returned the favour: he'd managed to get rather a good table on little notice. This was certainly a level of competence equal, if not surpassing, some of my more favoured former clients.

We exchanged only the most superficial of pleasantries about the weather, the news and the play until he ordered dessert.

SF took my hands over the dark oiled wood table. 'There's something we need to talk about. I've not been completely honest with you.'

I nodded, expecting the words to come out in a flood. But they didn't, instead he stared at my hands distractedly.

'I know what you're going to say,' I said. My voice was hardly above a whisper; I didn't want to frighten him. Also, it being a popular restaurant and therefore possessed of about ten excess tables in far too little space, I didn't want anyone to overhear. 'I know you're married.'

His eyes met mine. What I was expecting was surprise followed swiftly by amazement, then apology. I expected for him to beg forgiveness, or make promises about leaving his wife that any sensible woman would know could never come to fruition. But he was steady as a rock. 'I know that you know,' he said. 'I could hear it in your voice when I came over to yours the last time.'

'Were you . . .'

'Upset? No. You're a smart woman. I would have been more surprised if you hadn't figured it out.'

'So this leaves us . . .'

And that, unexpectedly, is when I felt SF's hands grow clammy. He drew them back, under his side of the table. He looked suddenly vulnerable, almost adolescent. 'That's what I wanted to talk to you about. I like you. I more than like you. On a fundamental level I feel the two of us are very compatible, in bed as well as out of it.'

There had been plenty of men like him – clients – when I'd been a call girl. So focussed, so accustomed to achieving success in the world of reason, that everything outside of that, including human relationships, was anathema, as foreign as a franc. Their view of the world simply did not square with the notion of old-fashioned romance.

'Which is why I'd like to propose a mutually beneficial financial arrangement.'

And when, inevitably, they found straightforward business practices incompatible with getting the love lives they wanted, they turned to working-girls. I liked these men. I understood these men. They were my people.

SF's eyes bored into me. 'Hear me out. Before you run out of here screaming, hear me out. Please don't think I think of you as a . . . as a common whore. It's because you're not that kind of woman, that I need a woman like you in my life.'

That's when I knew we had officially come through the looking glass. I've been called many things in my life, but a woman of upstanding moral fibre has never been one of them.

'I'll cover your costs, and then some. You'll be looked after. I won't even come to your home if that's what you want . . . there is the pied-à-terre in Marylebone . . .'

I breathed in, held it, released.

'You've not said no,' he said, perhaps slightly incredulous.

'I've not said yes, either,' I hissed as the puddings were brought to the table (cheeses for me, rhubarb three ways for him). He hadn't said any particular sum of money, but I knew men like SF well enough to know he would have done his research and whatever amount he offered, it would be in line with the going rate . . . for courtesans.

'Tell me you'll think about it.'

'I don't know what else to say so, okay, I'll think about it.'

samedi, le 17 juin

There were a couple of missed calls in the last couple of days to my office phone that had probably been L, but she hadn't tried my mobile and hadn't left messages. I had thought of telling her what happened, asking her advice. But no matter what glossy magazine wisdom she might be guarding on the subject of affairs, I knew I could never tell her about the courtesan aspect of it. Even admitting to carrying on with a married man would be enough to tarnish me in her opinion forever.

My boys, N and the As, they most likely wouldn't care either way. Which was great as far as it went, but sometimes you really do want reasoned advice, not just endless cheerleading support. If my cousin J had been closer and not living the beach life in Yucatan, it would have been him I asked for help. I guess this is what people usually went to their sisters for – but me and my sister had never been close like that.

''Sup gorgeous,' Giles smiled at me. 'Looking good today.'

I tipped a wink at him and walked on. He never changed, that one. So . . . why not confide in Giles? Of anyone in my acquaintance I knew he had been in a similar situation, of sorts – with Alex. Except then, he'd been the aggressor and of course no money had changed hands. No, can't tell a colleague. Lovely though he is. No. Got to figure this one out on your own, girl.

lundi, le 19 juin

'I want to see you,' I said to SF, keeping my voice low. I was pacing back and forth on the landing of the stairwell. He refused to ring my office phone.

'Have you come to a decision?'

'Maybe. Maybe not. I need to know more.'

'Fair enough,' SF said. 'Let's talk. You ask me whatever you want to know.'

'I guess the first thing, and maybe it isn't a question with a short answer, but what about your wife?'

SF took a deep breath. 'The short answer is, our marriage in all qualitative ways, is over. But I can't afford to end it. On many, many levels.'

I could imagine. His wife, if he chose to divorce, could probably take more than half of his net worth, especially with a son still at school. I was no homebody but imagined losing not just money and a house, but a family – a child – yes, it would be more than a superficial loss.

I could only comprehend the very edges of what that meant to someone who had once chosen to spend his life with a single woman. Someone who had probably been madly in love and then, over years, watched his dream change into something unrecognisable. Only with a wife, a family, he was stuck. When I'd found the Boy was cheating on me again, I walked, and no one suffered anything more than the emotional fallout. But unlike what the romantic stories like to say, it's not the emotion that ruins people's lives. It's losing money. Losing face. If a relationship ends you might feel like you want to die – if you lose all money, all hope, you might actually follow through with that feeling.

'Let's go out soon,' I said. 'No agenda, no pressure.'

'You're a remarkable woman, you know that,' SF said. 'Not to mention a dangerously sexy one. I want to spoil you as you deserve.'

I smiled. 'Be careful or you'll be offering the moon on a stick next.'

He laughed. 'Maybe, but the courts would give my wife half,' he said.

'Hello.'

'Hi.'

'So, um.'

'You're the one who rang,' I said. I meant it much less frostily than it came out.

'Yes . . . yes I did,' L said. 'So, um. Do you want to meet for a drink sometime?'

I smiled to myself. 'Honey, I'd love to. Where and when?' The doorbell rang. 'Hold on, I have to get that,' I said, and put the phone down.

It was L, phone in one hand, bottle of Prosecco in the other. 'I'm an arse. Do you have two glasses?'

So, I learned there really is no trick after all when it comes to being friends with girls. They're just as awkward and sweet and silly as men.

jeudi, le 22 juin

So in the end it was N I asked for advice. Good old N, who always cuts right to the chase.

'So you want to fuck him and don't want a relationship.'

'Yes, in a nutshell.'

'And he's married, so he doesn't want a relationship either.'

'Correct.'

'And he's going to give you money.'

'That's right.'

'So, how is this different from what you used to do exactly?'

And when he put it that way, I really couldn't give an answer. Because he was right – it wasn't.

'Question you have to ask yourself is, is that still what you want to be?' he said. 'It doesn't matter to me, I've got your back whatever. But does it matter to you? Isn't that why you left the agency?'

It had been an age since I'd been to the cinema. It was perfect: you can stay close to home, but enter separately, sit in the dark. It's a perfect cover.

SF came back to mine after the film and I opened a bottle of wine he'd left several weeks previous. We were on my sofa snogging, deeply, and I reached for the growing hardness in his trousers.

SF drew back and put a finger across my lips. 'Have you decided yet?'

'I don't know, I don't know what to think,' I said. 'Maybe I think too much, I should just go with the moment . . .'

'No,' he said, shaking his head and repositioning his body so we were no longer touching. 'I can't have sex with you until we're agreed on where it's going.'

'I don't want to marry you,' I said. 'I don't want you to leave your wife unless that's what you want to do.'

'You say that now,' he said sadly. 'But in six months' time, what? I believe you are an honest person and not trying to fool me. I want an arrangement where we both understand that there are rules and they will not be broken.'

That's one thing I learned as call girl – that each person has a line, and that it's different for everyone, but always there. We all have boundaries. For some clients it's only cheating with sex workers; other men will cheat, but never with sex workers. For some working girls it's not kissing; I was happy to kiss but never came with a client – which left me wondering, if I said yes to SF's proposal, what about orgasms? 'Is that what the money represents to you?' I asked him, hugging a cushion. 'If so, why not . . . you know . . . use a call girl? There are plenty who would be happy to meet a man like you on a regular basis,' I said. 'Um. From what I hear.'

'As long as we're being honest, and because you should probably know before you decide,' he said, 'I've done that. I tried several call girls over several years. But deep down you always know she's watching the clock. And once she's gone, she'll be going on to who knows how many men? They're nice women, don't get me wrong, but you are only as special to them as the colour of your money. I want a deeper connection. I want someone who can not just give the sex I'm missing at home, but the mental stimulation. And I don't want to worry that she has a hired tough lurking outside, or that I might be set up.'

'And if it's found out, you don't want your wife and colleagues to know you were going to hookers,' I said.

'A bit of that too,' SF said. 'Is this too much information? Is this going to be a no?'

'No, no,' I said, leaning forward to kiss him on the nose. If anything, it made me think more of him. He had his reasons, reasons he'd carefully considered. And while I didn't relish the thought of being the Other Woman – never had – I respected the boundaries he was trying to set with the emotional constraints he had to deal with. 'It's not a yes. I still have to think about things. But thank you for being honest with me.'

vendredi, le 23 juin

I was coming up the stairs after lunch and happened across Giles, standing on the landing looking at his phone.

'Hey. You all right?'

He looked at me and blinked slowly. 'No, no I'm not actually.'

His answer surprised me. For one thing, no one ever answers that question honestly. For another, especially not Giles. 'Is there anything I can do?'

He shook his head. 'No. Not really. I just want you to know . . . I want you know, I really pushed for you.'

'Cheers, fella. But you don't have to say that. I guess the person who really wanted the job got it in the end.'

'Yeah,' he sighed. 'She really wanted it. You didn't, or at least you weren't sure, and that to me shows you at least thought it through. She . . . I don't know what she is. Some sort of monster. She'd going to destroy everything I worked for in this position.'

'So?' I shrugged. 'Bigger and better things, G. Get out and move on while you can. It will be fine. I'll be fine too.'

He nodded, but I wasn't convinced. There was something my father said once – back when the Boy was treating me badly early on, sitting around his flat with nothing to do all day, unemployed – that a woman has all kinds of things in her life, but if a man doesn't have his work, he has nothing. And in spite of the reductionist flavour of that particular conversation (daddies do just want to make you smile after all), I knew what he meant.

I put my hand on Giles's shoulder. 'It's going to be okay,' I said. 'I know I haven't seen the last of you.'

dimanche, le 25 juin

N shook his head. 'You know what I'm going to say, so I don't know why you even ask . . .'

'Always be honest and let the chips fall where they may?'

He winked. 'Got it in one. It's the only way to be. I know

you like to keep things close to your chest, but seriously – something like this, you have to be honest with him. And yourself.'

I remembered when I had first told N I was considering becoming a call girl. We'd been in the gym and were sitting in a steam room, relaxing. It all came out in one, how I hated what I was doing, where I was living; how the endless loop of find job, apply for job, get a rejection letter at best – if you're lucky – was wearing me to a sliver. And all he'd said then, apart from asking how much it was, exactly, per hour, was to thank me for telling him. That he'd been honoured to be the first to know. We'd stayed close after the breakup, but if there were a single moment I knew he was a forever friend, that was the one.

'What do I do about my job though, if I say yes?'

'Stay with it if you like it. Leave it if you don't. It's not as if it sounds like this guy's asking for a lot of your time.'

'No, but the maintenance . . . the planning . . . the time investment alone . . .'

'Hey, remember when we were together? You used to like that sort of thing, the shaving and waxing. You know, before it was a professional obligation.'

He had a point there. It had been so long since I'd been sexy for its own sake.

lundi, le 26 juin

My closet has three parts behind three sliding doors. On the very left, clothes and shoes I wear regularly; in the middle, those I don't; on the right, deep storage. Once upon a time the middle closet would have been where I kept all of my work gear, but much of that has gone into deep storage now

– along with boxes of photographs, trinkets and other mementoes of the Boy.

I start with the deep storage. But it's not the Boy I'm after. I can leave it now. Someday, maybe someday soon, I'll be able to chuck it all away without so much as opening the boxes. Or maybe time will dull the pain and I'll be able to see it with fresh eyes, see the fun times and laughs we must have had once. Not today. Today, it's a land mine. I'm only after the old work clothes.

A few dresses, a silver jersey one with cut-outs that has been drawing compliments for almost a full decade. I try it on, still hot. A few suits a little too fitted and low-cut for the office. The giant shopping bag packed with a tangle of suspenders in almost unimaginable colours. I wonder for a moment whether it would be possible to calculate how much I spent over the years on all of this – what's the bag worth? And then I decide that's not something I want to spend my time thinking about. There's so much else to do . . .

mardi, le 27 juin

'You gorgeous, gorgeous girl. I can't believe it!'

'Uh, Mum, did you ring the wrong daughter?'

Peals of laughter. 'You silly thing. Your sister was the one who told me! I'm so bowled over, really, this is far too much.'

'We went halves on it, as she will surely have mentioned. And it was her idea to be honest.' As she will surely have mentioned. Repeatedly.

'Yes, but this is the first time . . . you know, dear, I always knew about your father covering for you on my birthday.'

'In his defence, I usually returned the favour on your anniversary.' The date of which I only knew, incidentally, because it was engraved on the silver cake slice in the Welsh dresser.

'Doesn't matter. Oh, and Artie doesn't know yet, so don't let's tell him.'

'Sure, for all the times I ring him up for just a chat. Artie, the guy who replaced affection for my father in my mother's heart. Let's get down and rap about issues, man.'

'Joke if you must,' Mum said sternly, though still sounding thrilled and warm. 'You are your father's daughter after all. But whatever you say I know your secret.' Did she? Did she really? What's that then? 'Under all that brittle exterior, you do care.'

mercredi, le 28 juin

'Something wrong?' Giles asks.

'Uh?' I hadn't noticed he'd been standing there, was just staring at a fifty-pence piece in my hand. Remember when a coin flip could make your decisions for you? Which meant either that you were so superstitious that you'd believe an inanimate object embodied fate, or that the decisions were so unimportant that it genuinely didn't matter what happened either way.

'It genuinely doesn't matter,' I said.

'What?'

'Sorry . . . I, uh, Giles, what did you say?'

His eyebrows twitched. 'Nothing, you're clearly thinking something over. I'll get back to you after the Japanese conference call, okay?'

Conference call? I'd completely forgotten. Had he mentioned something about it last week, or . . . ? 'Yeah, of course . . . after the call. Sorry, just trying to plan how it's going to go.'

He tapped the door frame twice and smiled. 'Good girl.'

vendredi, le 30 juin

Sometimes it feels as if I've been seeing this man forever, but really it's only been a couple of weeks. My preparation is down to a well-timed art: the shaving is done in under ten minutes, the plucking in under five; the last hair in place well in advance of the taxi's arrival. Makeup still needs a certain amount of time but it's a reliable result now I have the look down. Because we have only a handful of nights together every month and rarely go out in public as a couple, the capsule wardrobe is well established. This doesn't eliminate the expense entirely; the last shoes I bought were a pair of Louboutins identical to a pair I'd claimed as a business expense this time last year.

Half seven and a knock at the door. Of course he has the key; it's his flat. I've kept my own, but am looking for a boarder now. Anyway it will be lovely to have a little place to get away to when I need to be alone. And because SF so likes a little cat about the place, the cat will stay here too.

I smile widely as the door swings open. 'Darling,' I say, sliding his coat off his shoulders. 'Wine?' It's already poured. So many rooms I walked into as the visitor; now I'm the hostess. It's relaxing.

The laid-back moment lasts only so long, though, because SF is a demon in the sack. Truly, I've not met a man so keen to do the things he does with me. As for what he does? Absolutely everything. Making up for lost time, perhaps. In preparation for tonight I've left the needles in the bathroom next to the spirit alcohol and the wipes. He loves the teasing, the intensity of sensation, the wicked sense of getting away with something as I take him from howling pain to ecstasy and back. Just as I love it when he does the same to me. The needles are only a suggestion, not a requirement – he was sufficiently impressed with a previous display of my self-fisting that he's having a fad for putting things up his backside. We're on to four fingers at the moment and every time I suck him to orgasm while doing it, I feel the ripple of a muscle that's readying itself to accept even more so who knows, tonight might be the night we go all the way. Considering what various parts of him will look like in the morning, it's probably just as well his wife doesn't see him naked anymore.

I wonder how long our little bubble can last – Giles has mentioned that I seem to be taking off from work earlier and earlier these days, and when SF mentioned that if Euan chooses a university in London, it would only make sense if he gets this flat – but for the most part, it's me, him, all the time in the world, and his remarkable proclivity for anal play.

My search for the perfect man and the perfect job? They are, for the record, officially on hold.